MOTIVE FOR MURDER

June smiled and patted her husband's hand. "My husband is going to do everything he can to keep Mystical Feather going."

"Thank you for being so candid with me. I have one last question. There are rumors that Royal killed certain members in order to make room for new people who could replenish the money he bled from the Mystical Feather Trust. Do either of you know anyone who disappeared?"

June looked at the table and sighed. "Well, of course there was Natasha's mysterious death."

Claytie squeezed his eyes shut and rubbed them with his fingers. Then he looked up with fatigue written in the crevices around his mouth. "We heard rumors. The first one we know of was Royal's twin sister, Eugenie. She disappeared right after their mother's death."

"Do you think Royal killed her, too?" I asked.

"I asked, but Natasha's spirit was never specific," June said. "At first, everyone thought Eugenie had gone away to grieve for her mother. But she never returned, and nobody knows, to this day, where she went. Between you and me, I'm sure Royal killed her, too, and buried her body somewhere in these mountains."

After the Tollivers told me their story, I said, "That brings us right back to my original question. Who do you think killed Royal St. Germain?"

Books by Mary Marks

Published by Kensington Publishing Corporation

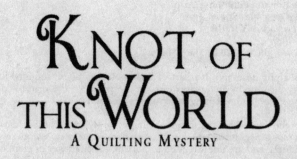

KNOT OF THIS WORLD

A QUILTING MYSTERY

MARY MARKS

KENSINGTON BOOKS

www.kensingtonbooks.com

This book is dedicated to all the earnest seekers who wish for a better world.

ACKNOWLEDGMENTS

I can't believe this is my eighth book. None of them would've seen the light of day without my writing group and their valuable feedback—Jerrilyn Farmer, Cyndra Gernet, and Roger Cannon. I couldn't write a decent story without them. Thanks also to my reader Nancy Jane Isenhart Holmes for her comments and ideas.

I did a lot of research for this book. The best experience came from an interview with Captain Eric Buschow, Public Information Officer for the Ventura County Sheriff's Office. Captain Buschow was very generous with his time. By the end of our conversation I knew a lot more about police procedure.

And what would I do without John Scognamiglio, Editor in Chief at Kensington Books? He always gives positive feedback and support. Also, Lou Malcangi is the super cool artist at Kensington who does all those fantastic book covers.

In this digital age, business transactions can take place over the internet without the people involved actually meeting each other in person. That's the kind of relationship I had for over seven years with Dawn Dowdle, my agent from Blue Ridge Literary Agency in Lynchburg, Virginia. This spring we met face to face for the first time at a conference, and I could tell her in person how grateful I was for her faith in me.

Finally, I want to acknowledge all my readers who take time to post reviews and/or send emails. Thank you!

CHAPTER 1

"**B**irdie!" I rushed forward to embrace my old friend.

My seventy-something friend had dyed a turquoise streak in her long, white hair, which undulated through the weave of the braid hanging over her shoulder. "We wanted to escape before the hot season began, dear. Those summers in Arizona are too extreme for us."

Birdie Watson, one of the original members of the Tuesday morning quilters, had been wintering in Arizona with her new husband, Denver. Now they were back in the San Fernando Valley, and she was ready, it seemed, to rejoin our group today.

She wore her signature denim overalls and white T-shirt. As she limped into my living room, I noticed she no longer wore white socks with her Birkenstock sandals. Instead, her toenails were painted turquoise and silver rings circled three of her toes.

Marriage apparently agreed with her, because she also seemed to be a little broader across the rear.

Birdie sat in the middle of my cream-colored sofa and rubbed her knee. "My arthritis is getting worse. The doctor says I'm ready for a knee replacement. But I've got another solution in mind."

Before I could ask what she meant, Lucy Mondello walked into my house and shoved a plate of oatmeal cookies into my hands and grinned. "Do you like my surprise, Martha? I looked out my window yesterday and saw the Winnebago parked in Birdie's driveway." The tall, orange-haired grandmother lived across the street from the Watsons. "So, we hatched a plot to surprise everyone this morning."

"What surprise?" Jazz Fletcher breezed through my front door, impeccably groomed and wearing a pink polo shirt. Although he was the same age as me, he had well-toned muscles and a flat stomach. A small sneeze and a little *yip* came from inside the pink tote bag he carried, a signal from his petite dog, Zsa Zsa, that she wanted to be released. Jazz reached inside and tenderly lifted out the little white Maltese. Today she wore a pink pinafore and rhinestone barrette in her topknot. As soon as her paws touched the floor, she immediately sprinted to the sofa.

When Jazz realized why the little dog was unusually excited, he made his way to the living room. The six-foot-tall man sat next to Birdie and enveloped the small woman in a hug. I returned to the kitchen to pour five cups of coffee. Birdie's voice was so soft I had a difficult time understanding their conversation as I filled the little pitcher with half-and-half. But I did hear her mention "a mystical white feather."

Last to cross my threshold was Giselle Cole. In her early forties, she was easily the youngest member of our group. As usual, my red-headed half-sister wore one of her many designer ensembles. This morning it was a blue silk tank top and a white linen suit with the jacket lined in the same blue silk. Rather large diamond studs sparked on her ears. She handed me a pink cardboard box tied with white twine. "Eclairs." When she noticed the older woman sitting on the sofa between Jazz and Lucy, she turned to me and raised her eyebrows. "Who . . . ?"

When I told her, she smiled broadly and marched to the living room. "So you're the famous Birdie Watson everyone talks about! I'm Martha's little sister, Giselle." She thrust her hand toward the older woman.

"Hello." Birdie smiled, wincing a little as Giselle grasped her arthritic fingers.

Giselle plowed ahead, apparently unaware of the brief pain she'd just caused. "You're the one who used to be a hippie flower child. You must be disappointed the Age of Aquarius never happened. Or maybe it did happen but died in infancy. Either way, I'll bet it was tough letting go of the fantasy and adjusting to the real world."

I brought in a tray with steaming cups and placed it on the coffee table next to a platter of sweets. Then I glanced at Birdie to see how she was reacting to my sister's tactless comments.

Just for an instant, confusion flitted across

Birdie's face. "You mentioned the Age of Aquarius. Are you interested in spiritual matters, dear?"

Giselle sat in one of the two easy chairs I had recently reupholstered in velvet in the color of a Creamsicle. She paused for a moment and shrugged. "Sometimes, I suppose." She reached in her Gucci tote bag and extricated a Grandmother's Flower Garden quilt she'd been working on. "Martha's teaching me a little bit about Judaism. There's a lot of spiritual reasons for stuff Jews do. I'm learning it's not always about money."

I rolled my eyes. Giselle had been raised in the Catholic faith and had little or no knowledge of Judaism until she met me. "I can't wait for the day when you learn enough to stop making such asinine comments, G."

"What?" Giselle feigned an innocent stare. Her green eyes were one of the few things we had in common, inherited from our Irish father.

Birdie reached for a cup of coffee. "I believe everyone has their own spiritual journey in this lifetime. What we don't learn now, we'll have a chance to learn next time around. That's why Denny and I are going to live in the Mystical Feather commune."

"What's that?" Lucy put her sewing in her lap and sat at attention. Lucy claimed she had ESP and was deeply interested in metaphysics.

"It's a spiritual discipline started in the nineteen thirties by Madam Natasha St. Germain. She was a famous medium who encountered her true spirit guide while fasting and meditating. He revealed many secrets of the spirit world and instructed her to bring those truths to the material world. When she came out of her trance, she discovered her guide left plumage—three white feathers, to be exact—on the table as a sign. So, she established the Mystical Feather Society."

"Fascinating." Jazz moved a little closer to Birdie. "What is a spirit guide?"

Birdie sat up a little straighter. "It's a spiritual entity that's assigned to each individual before birth. It manifests itself as a person, an animal, or a being of light. Its mission is to protect the individual and help them fulfill their life's purpose."

"You mean like a guardian angel?" Giselle snorted. "I don't believe in angels."

Lucy frowned at my sister. "Don't be so sure of yourself. There are many famous people who've been guided by these entities. James Van Praagh. Alison Dubois." She turned back to Birdie. "Who was Madam St. Germain's spirit guide?"

Birdie smiled softly. "An albino raven."

Giselle laughed out loud. "Hence the white feathers? Oh, come on. How can you believe all that nonsense?"

"To you it may be nonsense, dear. But not to us. Denny and I received our own sign when we went walking in the hills around Sedona at the vernal equinox in March. We spotted three white feathers on the path in front of us."

The more she spoke, the more my gut clenched. "Where is the commune? What, exactly, is involved in joining?"

"The actual commune is not far from here, in

the mountains of Ojai, California. Denny and I aren't getting any younger, dear, and neither one of us has any heirs. So, we'll be selling the ranch in Oregon, our house here in Encino, and the one in Arizona. The money will go into the Mystical Feather Society Trust, which runs the commune. We'll be well taken care of until our spirits leave our bodies."

When my sister glanced at me, I could tell she was as disturbed as I was. Jazz also looked alarmed.

Even Lucy's smile faded. "Oh, hon, I sure hope you know what you're doing. That's a big commitment to make."

Giselle murmured, "Especially on the word of an albino raven."

Birdie seemed unflappable. Either she didn't hear the comment or she chose to ignore it. She pointed to a photo in a silver frame of me holding my new baby granddaughter wrapped in the pink quilt I made for her. "Oh, Martha dear, Quincy's baby is precious. What's her name?"

"Daisy. She's five months old and bright as a button. I practically have to pay my daughter to let me babysit."

Birdie sighed. "I hope to see her before we move to Ojai. Once we arrive in the community, we'll be pretty much incommunicado."

An alarm started clanging in my head. "What do you mean? You can't have visitors? You can't use a phone?"

"Well, there will be an orientation period in which we'll learn the secrets of the Mystical Feather.

Then we'll receive instruction on the techniques of meditation in order to contact our own personal spirit guides." She smiled. "During that time, we must have no distractions from the outside world. I hope you understand."

"When do you plan to go there?" Jazz scooped up Zsa Zsa and held her protectively against his body.

"As soon as our properties are sold. Then there will be a formal welcoming ceremony in which we turn over to the community all our earthly goods and they will embrace us as full members. We already have a buyer interested in the ranch, and our real estate agent thinks she can sell the other places within the month."

Giselle frowned. "But, Birdie, aren't you in your seventies? At this time of life, why is it important to meet your spirit guide? Let's face it. Isn't his work pretty much over?"

For once, I was grateful for my sister's ability to shoot right at the heart of the matter. Everyone else must've felt the same way because all motion had stopped and all ears were focused on what our friend might say.

Birdie laughed. "Ask me that question again when you've reached my age, my dear. Where there's life, there's always a thirst for knowledge and enlightenment. Take my arthritis, for instance. It's merely a symptom of a stressful existence. Once I've become an *Adept*, my guide will help me completely reverse the disease."

For the rest of the day, I scarcely heard the conversations. My stomach churned and my heart sat heavy in my chest. Hadn't Birdie just described typical cult tactics? Make outlandish promises, isolate the individuals from their normal support network until they've been thoroughly indoctrinated, and keep them dependent by seizing all their resources. How could I prevent Birdie and Denver from making such a terrible mistake?

By three that afternoon, everyone had gone home but Giselle. "Martha, I hate to say this, but I think your friend Birdie has gone off the deep end. I mean, really. She's about to give all her money away?"

The thought of being without any independent resources must've been impossible for my half-sister to comprehend. She'd inherited her family's business, a very prosperous oil company. Giselle owned her own private jet and five houses and shopped at stores I'd never been inside of. And despite the fact she could really piss off people with her lack of tact, she had a keen mind.

"Another thing bothers me, Sissy. Where is Birdie's husband in all this? Doesn't he have a say? Is it possible that both of them can be that stupid?"

I sighed. "I know what you mean, G. That ranch in Oregon they've put up for sale has been in Denver's family for generations. Why would he just give it up? I'd really like to find out what's going on in his head."

"I hope it's not the same mumbo jumbo that's going on in your friend's head. If it is, I'm afraid there's nothing you can do. They're both adults with no family to hold them back from the precipice."

Giselle was right. I had no legal recourse. But maybe I could find another way. And I knew just where to start. I reached for my phone and sent a text message.

Emergency. Contact me ASAP.

CHAPTER 2

I spent an hour on the computer trying to find information on the Mystical Feather Society. Wikipedia confirmed the facts Birdie had given me about the beginnings of the society, but I could find no further details about the present-day commune.

At five on Tuesday evening, I got a phone call in response to my emergency text. "Hey, Martha. Long time no see." Paulina Polinskaya's hard, East Coast accent drilled through the phone line. "Sorry I didn't get back to you sooner. I was with a very difficult client who wanted to speak to her deceased husband. As soon as I contacted his spirit, she started shouting at him for dying and leaving her with a dozen unpaid bills. He said if she hadn't spent like a drunken sailor while he was alive, maybe she wouldn't be facing all that debt. I had to play peacemaker for over an hour until he broke the connection. What's the emergency?"

"Do you remember a friend of mine, Birdie Watson? In her late seventies, long white braid?"

"Yeah. It's been a couple a years, but I think I remember."

"I want to stop her from making a dangerous mistake."

"Do you want to bring her in for a reading?" Paulina was a psychic I met while trying to solve the murder of my friend Harriet Gordon. I encountered Paulina again when my friend Jazz was a suspect in another murder. Both times she was helpful. Sort of.

"I need information on a group called the Mystical Feather Society." I told her about Birdie and Denver's plan to sell everything they owned and turn the money over to the trust and live on the society's commune in Ojai.

"Yeah. I heard about them. Madam St. Germain's books are still popular today. She was a gifted medium. If this is a cult, like you said, it makes sense they're in Ojai."

A chill traveled down my spine. Paulina was confirming what my gut had told me earlier. Ojai, California, was located about eighty miles north of Los Angeles, nestled in a valley just south of the Los Padres National Forest. It was well known as a very liberal artsy community and a magnet for all kinds of philosophical disciplines. The headquarters of the Theosophical Society sat on several tranquil acres to the north of downtown Ojai on Route 33, while St. Thomas Catholic College stood just south of Ojai on Route 150. Every religious retreat imaginable could be found in between.

"I've got to find a way to keep my friends from going through with their plans."

"I'll find out more, if you want. I'm going to a meeting of COW tonight. Someone there will know."

"COW?"

"Contacting Other Worlds. LA chapter. It's a professional organization with members from all over the globe."

"There's an association for mediums?"

"Are you surprised? We have a president and board of directors. Mediums are thoroughly vetted before they're allowed to join. Members are called *Adepts*."

"Just out of curiosity, what do you call the president of COW?"

"The Supreme Bull."

We ended the call as Crusher walked in the doorway.

He hung up his leather jacket, removed his shoulder holster and ATF badge, and put them on the table in the hallway. Then he walked over and gave me a kiss. "Hey, babe. How was your day?"

"Awful." I told him about Birdie and Denver. "I've got to find a way to talk some sense into them before it's too late. Do you think you can reach out to your FBI contacts for a little research on the Mystical Feather Society?"

"Mystical Feather? That's a new one to me.

Yeah, I'll call my guy tomorrow and see what he can dig up. What's for dinner?"

I'd been so busy trying to research the group, I'd forgotten about eating. I did a quick mental scan of the contents of the refrigerator. "You have a choice: tuna sandwiches and potato chips here or going out to a restaurant."

He chuckled. Crusher was used to my laissez-faire attitude toward cooking. "Let's go grab a steak."

That night I dreamt Birdie and Denver had tossed their phones on the ground and jumped into a deep, dark hole. I called the police and the fire department, but nobody could reach them. Wednesday morning I woke up with a headache and my jaw hurt, a sign I'd been grinding my teeth all night.

Crusher had already gone to work and left behind a half-empty carafe of coffee. I poured myself a cup and shuffled into my sewing room. I'd already made a crib quilt for my granddaughter, Daisy, but I wanted to sew a larger quilt for when she transitioned to a real bed.

I chose the Sunbonnet Sue pattern, which featured a side view of figures in long dresses and oversized bonnets that covered their faces. The appliqué pattern was fairly simple. The beauty of the quilt would be in my choice of fabrics. And heaven knew, I had a whole wall of shelves filled with folded pieces of fabric. I'd use plain colors for the bonnets and for the dresses I'd choose conversation prints—those fabrics with a wide range of themes depicting everyday objects. They first appeared in the early 1900s and were geared toward juvenile topics like toys, animals, and children playing. Nowadays, these prints had come to reflect every sphere of life, including different foods, sports logos, vegetables, holiday items, and tools for activities like sewing or gardening, to name just a few. I began sorting through my collection of juvenile fabrics, setting aside the small prints most suitable for the dresses. One fabric had little white lambs on a turquoise background. Another had petite sailboats in red, white, and blue.

Around noon Paulina called. "Last night at the COW meeting I talked to a seer named Mansoor the Magnificent. He knows about the Mystical Feather Society, but he was unwilling to share any information with me. He's insisting on talking directly to you. But only if he likes your aura. He's willing to see you at my house today because I told him it's an emergency. Can you be here at two?"

"Yes. Of course. And thanks for setting it up."

Paulina cleared her throat. "There's one more thing, Martha. Last night I had a dream about your friends. I saw them dead on an altar surrounded by white feathers."

"Good Lord!" I gasped.

"Oh, dreams don't have to be literal, they can be metaphors. But the message was clear. Your friends are in danger. Oh. And before I forget, bring cash. Mansoor charges a fee for his time. A hundred fifty. That's the standard for professional consults in our industry. As a favor to you I'm waiving my finder's fee."

Industry? I didn't know whether to laugh or be irritated. "Thanks for the favor. I'll see you soon."

Paulina's house stood on Venice Boulevard in West LA. The lavender bungalow prevailed stubbornly as the last vestige of a bygone neighborhood. The pre-WWII cottage was squeezed between a strip mall and an auto body shop. Purple morning glories bloomed profusely on a trellis near the front door. A large wooden sign stood in the cracked concrete of what used to be a front yard.

PSYCHIC
TAROT, PAST LIVES
SPIRITUALIST
(SEE MY RATINGS ON YELP)
(FOLLOW ME ON TWITTER, #PAULINAPREDICTS)

I climbed the steps and knocked.

Paulina answered the door, wearing a silk muu-muu printed with purple hibiscus, lavish green leaves, and orange birds of paradise. Her long black hair formed a tidy bun at the nape of her neck. Black kohl rimmed her eyes in generous strokes, and her fuchsia mouth grinned. "Martha! It's good to see you." She surprised me by springing forward and wrapping me in a strong hug.

She stepped aside as I entered the dim living room, with walls painted the color of terra-cotta.

Flames on the white candles nearest the door flickered briefly with the in-rushing air. A little chihuahua with a round belly and spindly legs waddled toward me and barked a wheezy hello.

I stooped to pet the well-fed animal. "Is this Hathor?"

Paulina had adopted the pet of a murder victim over a year ago. The dog was unrecognizable with her increased girth.

"Yeah. She still suffers with PTSD from witnessing that murder. The only thing that seems to comfort her is a scoop of vanilla ice cream."

I could relate. "Well, she seems happy right now."

"Come and meet Mansoor."

I stood and looked toward the dining room and saw the man for the first time. I couldn't be sure of his exact age, but I guessed he was somewhere between his early twenties and his early thirties. A red turban was wrapped around his head in expert folds. Not a speck of lint marred the perfect fit of his black suit. He sat with a straight back and clasped delicate hands on the purple velvet cloth of the table, ebony eyes studying me with liquid curiosity. One of his slender fingers displayed a large gold ring with a blue crystal.

He didn't get up from the table as I approached. "I am Mansoor the Magnificent." He spoke with an accent I couldn't place.

"I'm Martha Rose." I offered my hand, but he kept his folded together in front of him.

His tight little smile revealed perfect white teeth. "You can place my fee on zee table, pleess."

I sat and rooted around in my purse for my wallet. I counted seven twenty-dollar bills and two fives and plunked them down on the table between us.

He eyed the money as he spoke but didn't touch it. "Tell Mansoor what you weesh to know about Mystical Feather Society. Eef your aurrra eez good, I speak. If not, I no speak."

I covered the bills with a protective hand. "You don't get a penny of this money without telling me everything. By the way, what kind of phony accent is that, anyway? Where are you from?"

He rolled his eyes. "Okay. Okay. Jeez. Don't get excited. I'll tell you everything I know." All of a sudden, the accent went away, and I placed his country of origin somewhere between Brooklyn and Jersey City.

Paulina picked up the pile of cash and handed it to Mansoor. He touched it only with his fingertips and stuffed it inside his wallet. Then he pulled out a moist towelette from his pocket, tore open the foil, and began scrubbing his fingers.

Paulina whispered, "Mansoor has a thing about germs."

I took a deep breath and told him about Birdie and Denver. "Is Mystical Feather a cult? How can I prevent my friends from joining?"

He nodded with a sober expression. "It won't be easy."

"Why not? Talk to me."

"The Mystical Feather Society started out legit.

As a matter of fact, Madam Natasha St. Germain's books are still read today. She had a real gift for helping people. But she died suddenly in nineteen seventy-five, and everything changed when her son, Royal St. Germain, took over. The dude's a real piece of work."

"How do you mean?"

Paulina leaned forward. "Mansoor's right. I saw Royal once. He's got shifty eyes and a very muddy aura. Right, Mansoor?"

The turbaned man nodded. "First of all, the guy's got no talent for the spirit world. He couldn't read a simple aura if it whacked him in the face. And contact the dead?" he scoffed. "Forget it. I heard rumors his only relationship with the dead was when he dispatched someone to the afterlife."

I needed more than speculation if I was going to convince Birdie not to join. "Is there any reason to believe those rumors might be true?"

Mansoor shrugged. "I heard rumors people complained they could never reach their relatives once they joined the commune. . . ."

Mansoor was right. Almost by definition, a cult kept power over its members by keeping them isolated from outside influences.

"Go on," I said.

"Madam Natasha made a lot of money from the sale of her books and classes she held all over the world. She used that money to set up the Mystical Feather Society and eventually the retreat in the mountains of Ojai. She endowed a trust that would perpetually fund the retreat. The idea was that people could sign up for a week or two of classes to connect with their spirit guides and find spiritual enlightenment."

"But my friend Birdie intends to live there for the rest of her life. When did things change?"

When Madam Natasha died, she left a will naming her son, Royal, as her successor and sole trustee."

"Why would she do that if he had no talent for the spiritual world, as you said?"

"I wasn't there. But they say that as talented and spiritually adept as she was, she had one blind spot. Her son. He was a real charmer."

Again with the "they say." I wonder how much real evidence he has. "So, how, exactly, did the part-time retreat turn into a live-in commune?"

"Royal did that. He liked having groupies. Lots of free sex. He spent money lavishly until the trust fund ran low. That's when he expanded the retreat to include permanent residents. People could still come for classes and a temporary stay in the dormitories. But he built little houses for those who chose to live there permanently. That group formed the core community, with an elite membership requirement. Members had to be people with money— people willing to give everything they owned to the trust in exchange for spiritual enlightenment and a lifetime home on the commune."

Just like Birdie and Denver said. "How can usually smart people be duped into something so, so . . ."

Paulina, who had remained silent while Mansoor spoke, said, "I know it's hard for someone like you to understand, Martha, but people who are spiritual seekers, especially those who practice Madam St. Germain's writings and teachings, are thrilled to find a group who think and believe like they do. And what better place to live than the society practicing her vision at a retreat under the leadership of her son? How old did you say your friends are?"

"In their late seventies."

"Ah." Paulina closed her eyes and nodded. "People in that age bracket have concerns about their health failing. Maybe Royal promised to look after them when they became too old or too sick."

My pulse began to race. Mansoor mentioned rumors that Royal dispatched people to the afterlife. What had Birdie said? *We'll be well taken care of until our spirits leave our bodies.*

Mansoor sat back and turned up the palms of his delicate hands. "Royal is very charismatic when he wants to be. Especially with the elderly. You're right to fear for your friends."

I shuddered. "So far, you've only mentioned rumors."

Paulina held up a finger. "Where there's smoke, there's fire."

"I need concrete proof to show Birdie and Denver they're making a huge mistake. How sure are you about what you've just told me?"

Mansoor the Magnificent sat up straight, closed his eyelids halfway, and sniffed. "I am a seer. With the help of my spirit guides, I see things. I hear things."

Oh great! With no hard evidence except the visions of a seer, how was I going to convince Birdie and Denver of the danger they were about to confront?

CHAPTER 3

I left Paulina and Mansoor and drove back to Encino, my mind racing. If the rumors about the Mystical Feather commune were true, Birdie and Denver were in grave danger. But if Royal was suspected of "dispatching his members to the afterlife," wouldn't he be on law enforcement radar? I was eager to see what Crusher found out from his FBI contact today.

Once I got home, I went straight to the place where I did my best thinking. My sewing room. I combed through dozens of fabrics until I found just the right conversation prints for all the dresses in my granddaughter's Sunbonnet Sue quilt. Then I searched for complementary solid colors for the bonnets. Each block would be a twelve-inch background square with one Sue appliquéed in the middle. I figured, with sashing and borders, I needed twenty blocks for a twin-sized bed quilt. I assembled twenty combinations of fabric. For the turquoise fabric with the little white lambs, I found a soft yellow for the bonnet. Using a plastic template, I proceeded to trace the pattern pieces onto the fabrics and then cut them each by hand.

I let my mind wander as I worked. Where was Denver in all this mess? Was he merely going along with Birdie because he wanted her to be happy, or did he genuinely buy into the insidious hype about the society? If he was just going along, if he didn't really believe in the society's message, maybe I could convince him to stop Birdie. I resolved to talk to Denver alone.

Crusher came home at five thirty and found me in my sewing room. "Hey, babe. What's that delicious smell coming from the kitchen?"

Oh crap. I forgot all about dinner again. I finished cutting the last piece of appliqué, put the sharp Gingher scissors on the cutting table, and stood to give him a welcome-home hug. "Gosh, Yossi. When did preparing dinner become my exclusive job?"

In the beginning of our living together, we both had agreed to share the domestic chores. If one cooked, the other cleaned up after the meal.

He threw back his head and laughed. "About the same time breakfast became my job, I think." He had a point. Since he almost always got up earlier than me, he usually cooked a substantial breakfast. And since I almost always got home earlier in the day than he did, I usually prepared our evening meal.

"You must have a great sense of smell because I'm going to make those tuna sandwiches we didn't have last night. You'll even have a choice between barbeque chips or plain."

Fifteen minutes later I placed plates of tuna on rye with a side of kosher pickles and an open bag of plain potato chips on the kitchen table. I plunked down a bottle of Heineken in front of Crusher and cracked open a can of Coke Zero for me as I sat. "See? Gourmet fish salad on bread seasoned with caraway seeds, a side of cucumber spears preserved in a garlic vinaigrette, and paperthin petals of fried potato. *B'tei avon.*" Good appetite.

While he chewed, I told him about my visit with Paulina and Mansoor. "Did you have a chance to ask your FBI contact today about Mystical Feather?"

He nodded and swallowed. "Yeah. The FBI keeps track of all known cults in the US. But when I asked about what constituted a cult, my guy was vague. The reason Mystical Feather is on their radar is they received a couple of complaints from concerned families who couldn't contact their loved ones after they joined the group."

Wow! What Mansoor told me might be true. People *did* disappear. "And? Did the FBI investigate?"

"They questioned Royal St. Germain, who maintained that, in both cases, the missing persons decided to leave the group. He didn't know where either of them had gone to. He claimed his members were free to come and go as they wished."

"And the Feds just accepted his word for it?"

He shrugged. "Well, according to the notes on file, St. Germain invited them to search the place, even though they hadn't brought a warrant. The agents found nothing suspicious, although one of them wrote that some of the members avoided eye contact."

"So that was it? The whole FBI investigation?"

He pulled a handful of chips out of the bag and dumped them on his empty sandwich plate. "Apparently so."

"Well, that's no help. They could've at least deployed cadaver dogs or used ground-penetrating radar to see where St. Germain might've buried the bodies of those missing people."

"Babe. There was no probable cause to conduct a further search, especially after the agents interviewed the dude. Besides, what evidence do you have that St. Germain killed people besides rumors you heard from a psychic?"

Crusher was right. I had no evidence beyond my gut feeling something was terribly wrong and my gut was seldom wrong.

The next morning, I called my best friend, Lucy, and told her what I'd learned from my visit to Paulina and Mansoor and added what Crusher's FBI contact told him.

When I was finished, she gasped. "I knew it! I got one of my bad feelings, right down to my bones, the moment Birdie started speaking. She and Denver are making a horrible mistake."

I used to ignore Lucy's bad feelings and her claim to have ESP. However, despite my doubts, I came to respect her sharp intuition about things because she was frequently right. "I've got to find a way to speak to Denver alone. He's more likely to be honest if Birdie's not around. Are they home now?"

"Just a minute, hon. I'll look out the front window." There was a brief pause. "Yep. They're home. I see Denver in the driveway fiddling with the Winnebago. Since Birdie can't drive, if Denver's home, that means she is, too."

"Let's pay a surprise visit. You keep Birdie occupied in the house, and I'll talk to Denver outside. I'll be over in ten minutes." I ended the call and threw on my size sixteen stretch denim jeans, a white T-shirt, and a pair of navy blue Crocs. Then I grabbed my purse and car keys and drove to Lucy's house, just a couple miles south of me.

As I parked in front of Lucy's, I was relieved to see Denver still in the driveway across the street working under the hood of their Winnebago. Lucy had the front door open before I had a chance to knock. She grabbed my arm and pulled me inside.

Lucy always looked perfectly put together. Unlike me, she woke up early, along with her husband, made his breakfast, and packed his lunch. Also, unlike me, she put on makeup and dressed carefully in an outfit she'd selected the night before. Today she wore a grass green cotton sweater over a white shirt with matching green pants and yellow flat shoes. Her orange hair was carefully curled, and her brown eyebrows were expertly drawn. "Come on in, girlfriend, and let's work this out before we go over there."

"Good idea. Let's tell Denver we decided on the

spur of the moment to say hi. Then you'll go inside to talk to Birdie and keep her distracted."

"What'll I talk about?"

"Anything. Just don't bring up the subject of Mystical Feather. We don't want to be obvious about the purpose of our visit. Then, while you're keeping Birdie busy, I'll stay outside and strike up a conversation with Denver."

Lucy nodded. "Okay. Got it. Let's go." She walked quickly to the front door.

"Wait, Lucy. We'll look suspiciously like we're on a mission if you walk that fast. Just be casual. Let's saunter across the street and talk to each other as if we don't have a care in the world."

We left the house and moseyed across the street, arm in arm, wearing big smiles. "Hi, Denver." Lucy and I spoke at the same time."

The white-haired retired rancher sat on the steps of the RV with what looked like a greasy engine part in his hands. He looked up and a broad smile creased his weathered face. "Mornin', ladies." He stood to greet us.

I poked Lucy with my elbow. "I came to visit Lucy today, but when I saw you across the street, I just had to come over and say hello. It's wonderful to see you again." I stepped forward and gave him a big hug. Then I looked at Lucy and inclined my head toward the house.

She took the hint. "Is Birdie inside?"

When Denver nodded, she turned and made her way up the porch and inside their Craftsman-style home.

Once we were alone, I forced myself to smile.

"Birdie told us Tuesday of your plans to sell your properties."

"Uh, yeah. Twink's got a plan." Denver's pet name for his wife was short for Twinkle. *Don't ask.*

"Yes, I think she may have told us a little about it. You're going to live on a commune?"

He sat on the steps again, picked up a screwdriver with an oily blade, and began cleaning it with a red cotton rag. "Yeah. That's right. It's called the Mystical Feather Society. Up in Ojai. Very peaceful place to end our lives."

I shuddered at the possible double meaning. "End your lives? Is there something we should know? Are you ill?"

Denver barked out a laugh. "Hah. Poor choice of words. It's a peaceful place to live out the remainder of our lives, however long that may be."

He gestured toward the interior of the RV. "I feel a coffee break coming on. Why don't you come on inside where we can sit comfortably and talk? Twink and I were up at six, and you know her. She just had to bake something. Today it's cranberry scones."

I followed him into the interior of a surprisingly comfortable space, even though the walls were beige fiberglass and the furniture was permanently bolted to the floor. I sat on the sage green upholstered banquette, which wrapped around two sides of the dining table. Denver washed the grease from his work-worn hands. Then he placed a teaspoon of instant coffee in each of two mugs he pulled from an overhead cupboard and turned the flame on the propane stove under a stainless-steel kettle.

"Just give it a few minutes, and we'll have some nice fresh coffee. Meanwhile, help yourself." He pointed to six scones sitting on a plastic plate in the middle of the table and handed me a paper napkin.

I chose a round scone about the size of a dinner biscuit and placed it on my napkin. "Why did you choose that particular place in Ojai?"

He rooted his hand under his shoulder-length white hair and scratched his neck. "I didn't choose it, really. Twink did. We went to Sedona for the spring equinox because Birdie said she felt a calling. People up there were eating mushrooms and talking about their spirit guides. Birdie wanted to try it and asked me to take care of her while she went on her 'journey.' "

"Did you eat mushrooms, too?"

"Naw. I wanted to make sure she came out of it okay. Anyway, the next day I woke up and found her talking to this Mystical Feather dude. That's when he told us he was the son of Madam Natasha St. Germain. Twink knew all about her. Even had some of her books. The dude claimed his mother came to him in a vision and told him to talk to us."

"What did he want to talk about?"

The kettle whistled, and Denver got up to prepare the coffee with cream. "He basically asked us a bunch of questions about how long we've been together, how we met, you know. That kind of stuff."

My BS radar started pinging. I was sure St. Germain wanted to suss out whether Birdie and Denver had money. "Did he talk about himself?"

"Yeah, some. Mostly he talked about the commune. Asked us if we might be interested in starting a new chapter in our lives. Like joining the commune."

"So you said yes? Just like that?"

"No, I said we needed time to think on it. Later that day, me and Twink hiked up this hill to watch the sun set. We walked slowly because of her bum knees. Twink told me about the amazing healing powers of Madam St. Germain. She supposedly could cure arthritis. When Twink spotted three white feathers on the path, she took it as a sign. After dark, we went back to our RV and found St. Germain waiting for us inside."

"He broke into your RV?"

"Naw. We never lock it. Anyway, he said he could tell from our Winnebago we were exceptional people."

He probably snooped around to discover whatever he could about their finances.

Denver continued. "He said his mother came to him in a new vision. She told Royal we were the ones he was looking for. We were the 'Elect.' "

"So it was then you agreed to sell everything just like that? Without seeing the commune?"

"Not at first. He asked us some more questions, like did we anticipate any resistance from friends or families and were we willing to go all in. You know, give everything up in exchange for being welcomed into a loving community of like-minded people who would care for us even if we became ill or incapacitated. Become part of a spiritual family, like."

"Did you ask him anything, or did he do all the talking?"

"He talked. We mostly listened. Twink and I discussed it that night after he left. She made up her mind. St. Germain assured her that her spirit guide would show her how to heal her arthritis. She said it would be a dream come true if we became members of Madam St. Germain's Society."

More like a nightmare. "Since you've come back, have you visited the commune? Seen the people there? Talked to anyone else involved?"

"Nope. I'm just going along for the ride. The only place I want to be is with her. Wherever she goes, I go."

"Denver, what if I told you Madam St. Germain's son, Royal, has been investigated by the FBI? Would you still go?"

He swallowed a mouthful of scone. "Investigated? I'm not surprised. Back in the sixties when we lived on that commune in Oregon, the Feds hassled everyone. Accused us of being subversive. Called us Commies. I'm not concerned about what the FBI thinks. It's just the way the government treats people who prefer to live an alternate lifestyle."

"What if I told you there are rumors he killed some members of the society?"

"Who said? The Feds, again? What evidence do they have?"

What could I say? Mansoor the Magnificent heard rumors? Had visions? "I just want you to check out the place thoroughly. Go take a look before you commit yourselves. Talk to the people there. Selling everything you have and giving it away is nonreversible. If you change your minds, you'll have nothing to come back to. You'd be virtual captives up there."

"Martha, I think you're letting your imagination run away with you. But thanks for your concern. Like I said, whatever Twink wants. That's what we'll do."

Dear God. How can I stop this train wreck?

CHAPTER 4

Denver clomped over to the sink in his old brown cowboy boots, rinsed out our coffee mugs, and put them on the drainboard. Then we left the Winnebago and went inside their house. With the exception of the turquoise streak in her snow-white hair and silver rings on her toes, Birdie looked exactly as she always had: denim overalls made soft and faded over years of washing, a white T-shirt, and Birkenstock sandals.

Birdie and Lucy sat on the sofa in the same places they had occupied over many years, countless Tuesday mornings, and dozens of quilts. I sat in my favorite easy chair, while Denver disappeared down the hallway toward the bedroom.

I brushed my fingers over the fuzzy nap of the green chenille upholstery, remembering how I used to lay out my scissors, thread, thimble, and packet of needles on the broad arm in preparation

for a few hours quilting. I missed those times together with my two friends Lucy and Birdie. Our
lives were less complicated then. More intimate.
Now things were different. Birdie had married
Denver and Crusher and I were engaged and living together. Jazz Fletcher and Giselle Cole had
joined our group, bringing the number from
three to five. But if I couldn't think of a way to stop
her, Birdie would soon be gone again—maybe forever.

"Martha, dear, what were you and Denny talking
about for such a long time?" Birdie knew me well
enough to know I wasn't likely involved in mere
idle chatter with her husband. "I saw the two of
you going into the Winnebago."

"Yeah! He made me an offer I couldn't refuse.
Fresh coffee and cranberry scones. Which were, by
the way, delicious. How I've missed your morning
baking, Birdie. Especially your applesauce cake
with raisins and your ginger cookies."

"Yes, I thought about that." She reached into
the pocket on the bib of her overalls and handed
me two three by five cards with writing on them.
"Since Denny and I are about to give away everything, I thought you'd be pleased to have my secret recipes for your two favorites. And, of course,
you and Lucy have first pick of all my fabric and
sewing supplies.

Lucy gasped. "Not your fabric!"

Birdie shrugged. "I'll have no use for them
where we're going."

My heart sank. With every word she spoke, she
seemed to slip farther and farther away. A quilter's

personal stash of fabric was like art, stamps, or coins to a passionate collector. She would never give away her fabric unless she lost her sight, the use of her hands, or had just heard the doctor give her a fatal diagnosis. "Are you sure you want to give up quilting?"

"Quite sure, Martha."

"Well, thank you. Of course. But I wish you wouldn't go. At least not before visiting the cult and seeing for yourselves how people live there and if they're as happy as Royal St. Germain paints them to be."

My dear friend frowned. "*Cult?*" Her back stiffened. "Is that what you think we're doing? Joining a cult?"

I hesitated for a moment, wishing I hadn't put that particular four-letter word out there. But I had, and now she knew exactly what I was thinking. How should I respond? I decided to be direct. There was little time for finesse. "Actually, Birdie, I'm not the only one who thinks Mystical Feather is a cult. The FBI put Royal St. Germain on their watch list."

Lucy spoke up. "Listen, hon. They suspect he may have, you know, *gotten rid* of some of his members." She used her fingers to make air quotes.

Birdie laughed. "Lucy, dear, all you have to do is meet him. If you did, you'd know he couldn't possibly do anything like that. He's very warm and spiritual."

"What a great idea!" I jumped on the suggestion. "Why don't we all take a trip to Ojai? We could meet Mr. St. Germain and talk to him. We could also look around the commune and talk to the other members there. If you're right, a visit could ease our minds and help us feel better about letting you go. We just want the very best for you."

Birdie studied our faces for a moment and shrugged. "Why not? If it'll set your minds at ease, I guess we could go this weekend. We could easily fit in the Winnebago. That is, if Denny can fix that motor."

Lucy and I looked at each other. I could tell she was up for the challenge. "Great. How about we meet you here at nine on Saturday morning? We should reach Ojai in an hour and a half. Maybe Mr. St. Germain will invite us to join him for lunch. If not, we could eat in one of the many good restaurants in town."

Lucy stood to leave. "Great idea." She embraced Birdie. "See you on Saturday, hon."

We didn't speak on the short walk back to her house, but once inside, Lucy couldn't hold back. "Martha! You and Denver were in the RV a long time. I thought I'd die being all alone with Birdie. She asked what you wanted with him. It was hard not to spill the beans. I'm not as good a liar as you are. Tell me what the two of you talked about for that long a time."

"Basically, he's determined to go through with their plans to join the commune. Even after I told him about the FBI."

"Oh, my bad feeling is coming back." She rubbed both of her arms and shivered. "What are we going to do once we get to the commune on Saturday?"

"You're right. We need to come up with a plan."

For the next hour we went over every scenario we could think of. Finally, we came up with a strategy we hoped was foolproof. Step number one was to call Paulina.

"Hi, Paulina. It's Martha, and I've got you on speaker so Lucy can hear as well."

Lucy leaned toward the phone and said in a loud voice, "Hi, hon."

"It's lucky you found me between clients," the psychic said. "What's the deal with your friends. Have you warned them?"

I sighed. "Yes, but they're determined to go through with it. They're starting the process of giving stuff away." I told her about our planned trip to Ojai on Saturday. "The reason I called is we kind of need your expertise on, uh, spirit guides, auras, contacting the dead, and stuff like that. I mean, neither Lucy nor I have the knowledge to challenge anything St. Germain claims about the spirit world."

Paulina said, "I actually knew you were going to call on me."

Sure, sure. What else would a psychic say? "If that's the case, do you also know what I'm about to ask?"

"Yeah. Me and Mansoor will go to Ojai with you on Saturday."

Lucy poked my arm and whispered, "She's amazing!"

I rolled my eyes. "No, not Mansoor. He's too obvious. Royal might feel defensive and refuse to talk to us."

Paulina said, "What if I tell Mansoor to lose the turban and wear jeans? We could pose as a couple who are followers of Madam St. Germain. Which isn't far from the truth."

"I don't know . . ."

"Listen. Mansoor is genuinely gifted. Plus, he knows more about the Mystical Feather Society than all of us. This is a golden opportunity, Martha."

As much as I hated to admit it, Paulina was right. The two of them could prove to be very helpful. "How much is it going to cost me this time?"

"You're such a pessimist! When did you become so cynical?"

"Since the age of seven when I was determined to meet the tooth fairy."

She laughed. "What happened?"

"I went to bed, put out a thimble full of chocolate chips for her, and pretended to sleep. I can't tell you how much willpower it took for me not to eat that chocolate. Anyway, after about a half hour, someone came into my bedroom. I could tell it was my Bubbie because I got a whiff of her Bengay. She crept up to my bed, took my baby tooth. Then she poured out the chocolate chips into her hand, and swapped them for a quarter."

"That was the going rate? I got a dollar for every one of my baby teeth."

"Anyway, that was the night the magic in my life was replaced by a healthy skepticism. Which, by the way, has served me well."

Paulina said, "Well, this one's a freebie. St. Germain gives all us genuine psychics a bad name. COW refuses to admit him as a member. Mansoor will jump at the chance to expose him. Just like me."

I looked at Lucy, who nodded in agreement. I turned back to the phone and gave Paulina directions to Lucy's house. "We'll meet here at eight thirty. I've been inside the Winnebago. It's quite spacious. There'll be plenty of room for all of us to travel in comfort."

"I'll make a believer out of you yet," Paulina said.

Lucy leaned toward the phone again. "I already believe in you, hon."

CHAPTER 5

The first thing I did when I woke up Friday morning was to reach over to Crusher's side of the bed. When I found it empty, I opened my eyes and looked at the clock. *Darn!* Tonight was Shabbat and I had the whole family coming over for dinner. I had every intention of getting an early start on my long to-do list, but the clock didn't lie. It was already nine.

I sat up and swung my legs over the side of the bed. Every movement of my muscles burned with the pain of fibromyalgia. My back was so stiff I couldn't stand straight. I shuffled to the bathroom and even the bottoms of my feet hurt. How was I going to get everything done feeling this way?

I swallowed a Soma and an over-the-counter pain reliever. Then I dragged myself into the kitchen and poured a cup of tepid coffee from the carafe

Crusher had brewed three hours earlier. A minute in the microwave and the coffee steamed again. I added some cream and sat at the kitchen table, sipped French roast, and waited for the meds to kick in. I'd been living with fibro for so long, I no longer remembered what it felt like to be pain free for a whole day.

By nine thirty, I could stand straight again and begin my day. I rinsed out the empty coffee cup and placed it in the dishwasher. As I turned to go back to the bedroom, I spotted a note from Crusher on the kitchen counter that I'd missed. A few brief words were penned on a yellow sticky note.

> *Babe.*
> *Surprise guest for dinner tonight. Set an extra place.*
> *Love you. Yossi.*

I stopped and counted. Nine people would be coming for Shabbat dinner. Giselle and her fiancé, Harold Zimmerman, were bringing Uncle Isaac. My daughter, Quincy, and Noah were bringing the baby, and Crusher was bringing a surprise guest. That was eight adults altogether. Not a problem. I'd made holiday dinners for at least twice that many in the past. I just needed to hustle if I was going to cook and clean in preparation for tonight.

If only I hadn't postponed the food shopping from yesterday to today. And who is this mystery guest, anyway?

I ran to Ventura Kosher Meats and bought a

large brisket already soaked and salted. Kosher meat not only had to come from a clean animal that had been ritually slaughtered, it also had to be brined to remove the blood, according to the Jewish laws of *kashrut.*

Thank goodness the butcher was only a short distance across the shopping center from Bea's Bakery, my next stop. As usual, the bakery was crowded with shoppers. I took a number and waited in the crowded space. Loaves of freshly baked challah, rye, and pumpernickel bread sat in overhead wooden bins, while pastries and desserts were displayed inside the glass cases. Time seemed to drag by as I tapped my impatience with my fingertips and shuffled from foot to foot.

Darn. Why do I always wait until the last minute?

Finally my number was called, and I had to elbow my way through the crowd. I bought two raisin challahs, the last large slab of apple strudel in the glass case, a cinnamon babka, and two dozen *mandel broit* (almond cookies) for dessert. The bread and dessert were *pareve,* or dairy free, because, according to Jewish law, meat and dairy may not be eaten at the same meal. Another stop at the supermarket and I was ready to begin preparations for the evening ahead.

I got home at eleven, unloaded the groceries. The next three hours were spent cleaning house and doing laundry. By two, I began to prepare dinner. I added plenty of onions, potatoes, and carrots to the brisket in the roasting pan. Crusher was definitely a meat and potatoes kind of guy. I peeled and trimmed two bunches of fresh, tender asparagus spears, and grilled two large eggplants for *baba ganouj*, a chilled puree of eggplant, garlic, lemon, parsley, and salt.

While the brisket and potatoes were roasting, I set the table with the white cloth my grandmother crocheted when she was a new bride. I also arranged my good silver and the good white plates with the blue rims. I was the fourth generation of women in my family to own the antique china. My great-grandmother brought them to this country on the ship from Poland packed in wooden barrels and nestled in excelsior to prevent breakage. What began as a service for thirty-six had been reduced over the decades. Only eight coffee cups remained now, but twenty dinner plates still survived.

At four, the house was filled with the warm smells of Shabbat dinner. I folded the last load of towels from the dryer and headed toward the bedroom to get ready for company at six. The shower soothed my muscles, and I soaked in the heated downpour for ten minutes. As I toweled off, my legs felt rubbery and weak. I hadn't stopped moving since nine thirty that morning. I wrapped up in my fuzzy blue bathrobe and lay down on the bed for ten minutes with my feet propped up on a pillow.

The next thing I knew, Crusher was gently shaking my shoulder. "Wake up, babe. It's five thirty."

"Oh my gosh, the brisket is still in the oven." I swung my legs over the side of the bed, preparing to head for the kitchen.

Crusher put a restraining hand on my shoulder. "Relax. I'll take it out. Our mystery guest is also here."

"Who?"

He grinned and headed for the kitchen. "I don't want to spoil the surprise."

I burned with curiosity as I quickly dressed in a long, black skirt, a pink blouse, and my grandmother's pearls. I fluffed out my shoulder-length gray curls, slipped on my expensive black heels, and headed down the hallway. I stopped in my tracks when I saw the mysterious guest. Wearing a dark pin-striped suit and wire-rimmed glasses, he was the last person I ever expected to say yes to a dinner invitation—let alone one on the Sabbath.

John Smith was the only name he acknowledged, although I was sure it was an alias. We met a few months ago when he investigated the attempted murder of my neighbor and her foster daughter. He was high enough in the FBI counterterrorism branch that Crusher addressed him as "Sir."

He rose to greet me and extended a bouquet of pink roses in his hand. "Good evening, Ms. Rose. So kind of you to offer me dinner. I'm told flowers are especially welcomed on the Sabbath."

I took the roses and thanked him. "Since we'll be breaking bread together, John, let's use first names. Mine's Martha. What brings you all the way from Washington, D.C.? Surely you're not here just to sample my brisket." He followed me into the kitchen, where I filled a vase with water and placed the roses in it.

"You're right about that, although I anticipate

tonight's meal with great pleasure. I'm here on a case, which I can't discuss. I'm sure you understand."

Crusher cleared his throat. "Uh, I ran into Director Smith at a joint FBI/ATF briefing yesterday and told him a little about your friend Birdie. It turns out he is somewhat familiar with the Mystical Feather group." Crusher briefly glanced at the FBI agent. "So, I asked him to join us for dinner tonight."

That was another reason I loved Crusher. Instead of trying to control my curiosity, he often thought of ways to help me and my friends find answers. "How do you know about Mystical Feather?" I asked Smith.

"I used to be assigned to Criminal Investigations. St. Germain was on our radar back then."

"I heard a terrible rumor that some of the members of the society have disappeared, maybe forever."

Smith nodded. "Without evidence, we couldn't prove anything. When I transferred to Counterterrorism, my focus shifted to more global threats. But you're right to be concerned about your friend and her husband."

I led him into the living room, and we sat on the sofa. "I already told them Royal had been investigated by the FBI, and they didn't care."

He nodded solemnly. "Unfortunately, once someone is committed to a particular philosophy, it becomes difficult to persuade them otherwise. People become involved because they perceive a group can satisfy certain emotional needs. No doubt you've observed something similar: when the topic is religion or politics, people's minds seldom change."

"But Mystical Feather has nothing to do with either politics or religion, does it? I thought they practiced metaphysics, like contacting their spirit guides."

He shrugged. "That may be how Mystical Feather started out, but, after the death of Natasha St. Germain, it morphed into something more sinister. If your friends have been seduced by Royal's promises, I'm afraid you might not be able to persuade them to abandon their decision to join."

"Do you think Mystical Feather is a cult, then?"

"Maybe to some extent. Cults are like a religion, with a godlike dictator at the head who demands complete loyalty and surrender to whatever vision he's promoting."

Smith was a font of information sitting right next to me, and I wasn't going to let the opportunity pass. "A bunch of us, including my friends Birdie and Denver, are going to pay St. Germain a surprise visit at the commune tomorrow. Can you give me any advice as to what to ask or say or do that will demonstrate to Birdie she's making a mistake?"

At that moment, the front door opened, and my daughter, Quincy, and her husband, Noah Kaplan, arrived with my five-month-old granddaughter, Daisy. The baby slept in her mother's arms, peacefully bundled up in the pink basket quilt I'd made for her. I forgot all about Mystical Feather, rose from the sofa, and reached for Daisy. I could tell by the occasional movement of her tiny lips she must have been dreaming about eating. Soft brown fuzz covered her head. But one day it would be covered in curls; either copper-colored like her mother's or black like her father's. Crusher introduced Smith as a "colleague," while I crooned to the sleeping Daisy.

Next to arrive was my half-sister, Giselle, with her fiancé, Harold Zimmerman, and my uncle Isaac. Uncle Isaac shuffled in wearing leather slippers, dark slacks, a white shirt open at the neck. His embroidered Bukharin skull cap sat on his white curls like a square box. The early stage of Parkinson's made him kind of wobbly. Giselle escorted him to an easy chair.

"Good Shabbos," he said to everyone as he sat. As soon as he saw the sleeping baby, he said, "Ah. Give the *bubeleh* to me."

I placed Daisy carefully in his arms, where he cradled her tenderly and seemed oblivious to anyone else in the room.

Giselle's fiancé, Harold, also wore a black pinstriped suit. With his bald head and glasses framed in black plastic, he and John Smith could have been bookends. He shook hands with Crusher and his "colleague" Smith.

Giselle wore a little black dress and stiletto heels that made her seem as tall as Harold. "Happy Sabbath, Sissy." She kissed me on the cheek and handed me a bottle of pinot grigio. "You know, I've seen you wear that same outfit every Friday night. You really ought to do something more creative about your wardrobe. Come shopping with me tomorrow. Saks is having a sale on their spring collections.

Maybe you'll get lucky and find something nice in the plus sizes."

I don't know what irritated me more: the criticism of my wardrobe or the reminder I had to shop for plus sizes and she didn't.

"Sorry, G. I've already made plans." I kept tomorrow's visit to Ojai a secret because I didn't want my sister to be included. All she had to do was make one tactless remark, like the one she'd just made, and our chances of finding anything incriminating would be ruined. Before she could quiz me on my plans, I said, "Excuse me," and busied myself in the kitchen steaming the asparagus and transferring the roast and potatoes to a serving platter.

Ten minutes later, I called everyone to the table while I recited the same blessing over the candles that Jewish women all over the world recited on the eve of the Sabbath. "Blessed art thou, oh Lord our God, King of the universe, who sanctifies us by Thy commandments and commands us to kindle the Sabbath lights."

Everyone repeated the Amen, and, in the chorus of voices, I distinctly heard the one belonging to John Smith.

My eighty-something uncle Isaac usually had the honor of reciting the prayers at the beginning of the Sabbath meal, but tonight he asked Crusher to do it. Uncle Isaac seemed frailer than I'd ever seen him, and I was alarmed by the weakness of his voice.

Even though John Smith sat next to me, I was

reluctant to continue our earlier conversation during dinner. Giselle would surely overhear us and demand to be included on the trip to the commune.

I was glad when my sister and Harold had to leave early with a very tired Uncle Isaac. I could hardly wait until Quincy and Noah took the baby home. I intended to question John Smith once more. As soon as my daughter left, I heaved a sigh of relief and turned to the director. "We didn't really have a chance to finish our conversation earlier."

"I don't know how much more I can tell you."

"I just want to know what to ask or say or do once we reach the commune. You know, anything that might prove to Birdie she's making a mistake."

"St. Germain is too smart to fall for any trick questions. Your best chance would be to look for someone who seems unhappy or nervous. Try to get them alone. They might be willing to talk. If you do learn anything, call me personally." He wrote down his private cell phone number and handed me his business card. "The bureau would love to nail this guy."

Isn't that what Paulina and Mansoor said?

Smith smiled and made a subtle bow. "And thank you for a delightful evening. It makes for a nice change to have a home-cooked meal."

He looked at Crusher and gestured toward the door. "Levy? A word?"

The two of them stepped outside and talked briefly.

When Crusher returned, he said, "Babe. You need to be very careful tomorrow."

His warning caught me off guard. "Why? What did you two talk about?"

"People have gone missing from Mystical Feather. The FBI has never been able to prove anything, but Royal St. Germain is now on their watch list.

CHAPTER 6

Saturday morning I dressed in my jeans and a pink pullover sweater. I arrived at Lucy's house at eight, an hour before we were scheduled to leave. Her husband, Ray Mondello, answered the door. For a man in his sixties, he looked remarkably young, with a firm physique and jet-black hair that betrayed only a few white strands.

"Good morning!" He kissed my cheek. "What kind of trouble are you and my wife getting up to today?" The sarcasm in his voice came through loud and clear. He'd never forgotten I'd been responsible in the past for dragging the mother of his five sons into some dangerous situations.

Lucy gestured wildly behind his back, with a cutting motion across her throat that broadcast: *Under no circumstances tell him about the commune.*

I lifted one shoulder, raised my eyebrows, and turned my palms up. "Not much."

Lucy rolled her eyes in relief and joined the two of us in the doorway. "Come on in, Martha, and have a cup of coffee. We have plenty of time before that *new fabric store* opens." She poked me with her elbow when she said those last words. Still in a white terrycloth bathrobe, she turned to her husband and handed him a sack lunch. "Here you go, hon. Meatloaf sandwich, a banana, and Oreos. Just like you wanted." Since Ray was two inches shorter than his wife, Lucy had to bend slightly to give him a kiss before pushing him gently toward the door. "Have a great day."

He paused, looked at both of us, and shook his head. "Stay out of trouble, you two."

Lucy's laugh sounded somewhat brittle. "There's no trouble to get into." My best friend was right. She wasn't as good a liar as I was. She poured a cup of coffee for me and excused herself for ten minutes. When she returned, she wore an all-yellow outfit.

At eight thirty on the dot, Paulina Polinskaya and Mansoor the Magnificent knocked on her door. As promised, Mansoor had transformed himself into a seeker of truth. I never would've guessed that hiding under his red turban had been shoulder-length black hair. The top was pulled back in a man bun, and the back hung loose. He slouched through the door in a pair of jeans ripped at the knee and an old and faded Rolling Stones T-shirt.

I nodded my approval. "I would've passed you on the street without recognizing you."

He smiled out of the corner of his mouth. "I'm looking forward to the chance to take this guy down."

Paulina looked nearly like herself. On the one hand, she wore a white blouse over a long skirt printed with bright flowers. However, instead of pulling her dark hair back in a bun as she usually did, she let it hang loose. She'd also declined to paint her customary extravagant eye liner and bright fuchsia lips. Devoid of makeup, her face reflected classic beauty with high cheekbones and smooth, natural skin. I also noticed, with some curiosity, that even though she was short and round, she bore a strong resemblance to the taller, more daintily boned Mansoor.

After Lucy greeted Paulina, she introduced herself to the younger man. When she offered her hand, he shoved his fists into the pockets of his jeans and pretended not to notice.

Instead, he mumbled, "Nice to meet you." Then he raised an eyebrow. "Do we have a plan?"

"Yes. Sit down while I tell you what I learned last night from our contact in the FBI." Mansoor shuffled across the floor in his brown leather sandals. I waited until everyone had settled on the plush blue furniture in Lucy's living room and repeated my conversation with John Smith. "He doesn't think we can trip up St. Germain with any clever questions but suggested instead to try to find someone within the commune who might be willing to talk."

"You mean like a dissident?" Even though he hadn't touched Lucy, Mansoor tore open a moist towelette and began scrubbing his hands. I could smell the rubbing alcohol from where I sat and briefly wondered what he'd do if someone tried to hug him.

Paulina rearranged the folds of her skirt. "That'll be so easy."

"Really?" I leaned back. "Enlighten us."

"Have I taught you nothing, Martha?" Paulina clucked. "For starters, the color of someone's aura will tell me if they're troubled."

Mansoor added, "She's right. It's pretty basic stuff. Psychic one oh one."

Lucy's gaze bounced back and forth between the two of them. "What do we do if we find someone like that?"

"Step aside and let the pros handle it," Mansoor pointed at Paulina and himself.

Like I'll ever let that happen. "The thing to remember is St. Germain can't know what we're doing. As far as he's concerned, you're just two seekers who are avid fans of his late mother's teachings."

Once we agreed on the story we'd tell, the four of us headed across the street to the Watsons' house. Denver stood in the driveway carrying what I recognized as an old Longaberger market basket made of woven maple splints. At one time, those baskets were prized as a status symbol by quilters who wanted to carry around their sewing in style. Since the company went out of business, those distinctive baskets had become valuable collectors' items. And from the heavenly aromas emanating from inside it, I guessed the basket brimmed with a variety of home-baked goods.

I pointed to the red-and-white-checked kitchen

towel covering everything and inhaled deeply. "Sure smells good. Is that for us?"

Denver chuckled and spoke with a drawl. "You know Twink. She was up before dawn baking enough bread, cakes, and I-don't-know-what-all to feed a regimental army." He stopped speaking when he noticed Paulina and Mansoor.

I jumped in and made the introductions. "This is Paulina and her friend Mansoor. They are avid followers of Madam Natasha St. Germain and asked to come with us this morning. I figured there was enough room in the Winnebago to accommodate two more. I took the liberty of saying they could join us."

When Denver offered his hand to Mansoor, Paulina stepped between them with an otherworldly smile spread on her face and sandwiched Denver's hand in both of hers. "I've already met your wife, Birdie. You have a calm aura. Blue. Very rare, but powerful." She held onto his hand and turned it palm upward, tracing the deep lines with her finger. "I see you'll have a long life. Many more years ahead of you." She glanced at him, but Denver's face never changed.

She continued to study his palm. "I also see you're a man who's not easily fooled."

Denver shifted his weight and withdrew his hand from her grasp. "Thanks." He opened the door of the Winnebago and gestured for us to enter. "Twink's already inside, rarin' to go. Ladies first."

Mansoor hung back as Birdie hugged Paulina.

"So nice to see you again, dear. I had no idea you were a follower of Madam Natasha St. Germain. How nice you and your friend could come with us. In your line of work, you must have a spirit guide, right? Did you find your guide through Madam's teachings?"

"Oh, definitely!" said Paulina. "That's why we asked to join you."

"You must tell me all about it," said Birdie.

Lucy kept staring at the Longaberger basket. "Um, Birdie, as long as you're giving away everything, what plans do you have for this basket?"

Denver started the engine. "Take your seats, everyone."

Birdie sat up front with Denver. The passenger seat looked more like a comfy armchair. The four of us arrayed ourselves around the table on the upholstered banquette. Once we were on the 101 freeway heading north, Birdie swiveled her chair around, allowing her to face backward toward the interior of the Winnebago. She smiled and gestured toward the middle of the table. A white kitchen towel covered a pan of freshly baked chocolate chip zucchini muffins. "Help yourselves. We'll be on the road for at least an hour and a half."

Mansoor needed no more encouragement. He reached for the food, peeled the pleated paper from the outside of the muffin, took a large bite, and chewed. He smiled at Birdie and said with a mouthful of food, "You remind me of my *bunica*, my grandmother. She baked fresh bread every day for our family." He glanced briefly at Paulina then looked at Birdie once again.

Paulina helped herself to a muffin but said nothing, and studiously avoided looking at Mansoor. They were hiding something.

"What can you tell me about Madam St. Germain?" asked Birdie.

Paulina pointed at Mansoor. "He's more of the expert, you might say."

He washed down the last bite of muffin with water from one of the sealed plastic bottles on the table. "Natasha was born in Eastern Europe after the First World War. She learned early on that she had special gifts. So, at the tender age of eighteen, she traveled alone to Paris to study with Zohar, the greatest medium of the time. Under his teaching, she found her spirit guide, an albino raven named Pierre, who instructed her to immigrate to the United States, where she was to establish the Mystical Feather Society."

Lucy nibbled on the crisp edge of a muffin top. "When was that?"

"She left France right after the Second World War broke out and settled in Bridgeport, Connecticut. She became a highly sought-after medium and healer. She married Alexander St. Germain in nineteen fifty. He died nine years later. They had a set of twins—a son, Royal, and a daughter, Eugenie. When Natasha died suddenly in nineteen seventy-five, her entire personal estate and the Mystical Feather Trust went to her son."

"Wait. What about Eugenie?" Lucy asked.

"She pretty much disappeared when her mother died. The rest of the story you already know—how Royal turned the society into a cult of personality."

Birdie listened intently and frowned. "If you think so little of Royal St. Germain, why are you coming with us to the commune?"

Darn! I wished Mansoor hadn't used the word cult.

Mansoor was only momentarily ambushed by his slip and recovered quickly. "I don't listen to those nasty rumors. I want to meet Royal and judge for myself." He patted his hand on the air just above Paulina's shoulder. "We might even decide to join the commune. Being part of the Mystical Feather Society would be a dream come true for us, wouldn't it?" He smiled at Paulina. Then he reached for a napkin and wiped the air off his hands.

"Oh, yeah. A real privilege." She nodded vigorously.

Birdie seemed mollified for the moment. I, however, was bothered by the news that Madam St. Germain's daughter, Eugenie, had disappeared. Why didn't she inherit half of her mother's estate?

CHAPTER 7

We continued north for forty minutes on the 101 until we reached the town of Ventura and turned east on the 126 Freeway. Citrus orchards flanked the highway for the next ten miles in a part of Southern California where farms managed to hold their own against the tsunami of urban sprawl.

Denver downshifted the vehicle as we left the highway in Santa Paula. We headed north on Route 150 and drove past a Mexican restaurant, the historic Union Oil Company building, an old railroad depot, Victorian-era homes, and onto a two-lane roadway that wound through the mountains toward our destination.

After twenty minutes of driving, Denver slowed down and made a left-hand turn on Sulphur Mountain Road. "We're almost there."

We drove past a ranch with horses on our left

and a row of green Dumpsters on our right. Mountain residents had to bring their garbage down the hill for easy collection in the metal bins below. The letters "MFS" were painted on the outside of one of them.

Almost immediately, we began a slow ascent up the narrow road past oak trees clinging to the slope on our right and rocky hillside on our left. Because of the particular geology of the area, the road cut had opened an occasional seepage of tar that oozed slowly from the mountainside like blood from a wound.

Lucy also noticed the tar. "You know, that oil could provide a brushfire with enough fuel to light up this mountain like a torch." With the prolonged draught in California, it seemed like brushfires were on everyone's minds.

After another ten minutes of slow climbing and an occasional grinding of gears, we reached the top. A beautiful view of the narrow Ojai Valley spread below. A metal mailbox sat on top of a wooden post at the beginning of a poorly paved driveway on our left. A wooden sign underneath announced MYSTICAL FEATHER SOCIETY.

Birdie beamed. "I'm really excited to finally be here. I can't wait to see Royal again."

We turned into the driveway and drove slowly past an adobe building with round Spanish tiles on the roof and a sign that read:

MYSTICAL FEATHER SOCIETY
BOOKSTORE AND TEAHOUSE
PUBLIC WELCOMED

Several vehicles were parked next to the building. A white-robed man with a dark beard appeared in the doorway, apparently drawn by the sound of our vehicle turning into the driveway. Curiosity satisfied, he waved briefly and disappeared back inside the store.

We bounced for about two hundred feet until we came to a chain-link fence with another sign:

MYSTICAL FEATHER SOCIETY
PRIVATE RETREAT
CLOTHING OPTIONAL
INFORMATION IN THE BOOKSTORE

Lucy looked confused. "Why does the sign say 'Retreat'? I thought this was a commune."

Mansoor said, "Technically it's both. Programs are available for people to spend a limited time here taking classes and meditating. Other people have chosen to live here permanently."

The gate was closed, but the padlock hung open by a careless hook, as if someone forgot to lock up. Denver slowed to a stop.

Mansoor jumped up from his seat at the table. "I'll get the gate." He reached in the pocket of his torn jeans and extracted a pair of latex gloves. He blew each one up like a balloon before slipping them easily over his hands. He pushed open the door of the Winnebago and dropped to the uncertain terrain of the driveway.

We watched as he unhooked the padlock and swung the gate wide open, beckoning with his arm for us to enter.

Birdie looked at her husband. "Do you remember Royal ever mentioning anything about 'clothing optional?'"

Denver grunted. "Nope."

Lucy poked me in the side with her elbow and whispered, "Does 'clothing optional' mean what I think it means?"

I whispered, "I hope not."

Lucy shivered slightly and rubbed her arms. "I hate to say this, but I'm getting a very bad feeling." She looked at Paulina as if waiting for confirmation from the psychic. She didn't have to wait long.

Paulina squinted her eyes and peered out the window. "You're very astute, Lucy. There are some unhappy spirits here." She closed her eyes. "But I don't get the sense they're a threat. I think they want to tell us something."

I glanced at Birdie to see how she reacted. But she appeared to be lost in thought.

Denver drove the Winnebago onto the property and stopped just beyond the fence to give Mansoor a chance to close the gate and climb back into the vehicle. The younger man looked at Paulina. "Do you feel it? This is a very active space. I sense more than one spirit."

Birdie didn't seem to be listening. She sat transfixed, scanning the native xeriscape of spreading oak trees and low-growing shrubs, like buckwheat, purple salvia, and white matilija poppies. She'd been an avid horticulturist, both in her own yard and with fabric. Her appliquéd quilts featured the colorful blossoms she cultivated in her garden.

"Oh, I hope they let me work the soil here." She turned to her husband. "Remember when we used to grow our own food at Aquarius?" Birdie referred to the time in the 1960s when she first met Denver in a commune near Ashland, Oregon.

A slow smile spread across Denver's face. "I sure do, Twink. And if they're smart, they'll let you loose in the kitchen, too."

She pointed to the Longaberger basket. "That's why I'm bringing all these baked goods. I want Royal to sample what I can contribute."

He chuckled. "'At's my girl!"

I grew increasingly uneasy. Even after the declaration that "unhappy spirits" lurked about, neither Birdie nor Denver seemed to hear the warnings from Paulina and Mansoor. Not that I believed in that stuff, but I knew Birdie did. Yet, she seemed unfazed.

We jostled slowly over potholes as we made our way up the road. About fifty yards ahead, a dozen small adobe buildings sat next to a large wooden and glass structure shaped like a giant yurt. Birdie tugged on her braid and pointed to the circular building. "Oh, look, Denny! I'll bet that's the Lloyd Wright meditation center Royal was telling us about."

Two old white vans were parked next to a new red Mercedes under the shade of an oak tree and behind some bushes. Denver maneuvered the Winnebago next to the Mercedes and cut the engine. He stood and stretched. "Let's go." He picked up the basket, opened the door, and helped Birdie down the steps. "Come on, ladies." He reached up and helped steady Lucy, Paulina, and me down the steps.

Mansoor was the last to leave. "Do you want me to lock up?"

"Naw," said Denver. "We never bother. If someone needs something we got, let 'em have it."

Although the sign at the driveway entrance read PRIVATE RETREAT, our arrival didn't seem to cause concern or trigger an alarm. We couldn't detect a soul on the property. Nobody came out of the buildings to greet us. The only movement came from two angry crows chasing a hawk away from their nest in the top of a sycamore tree.

Lucy checked the wristwatch she always wore. The bezel of the tiny gold timepiece was surrounded by diamonds and attached to a diamond bracelet, a fiftieth-anniversary present from her husband, Ray. "It's nearly eleven. Where is everyone?"

"Perhaps they're all meditating, dear. Let's try that big wooden building." Birdie had to hang onto Denver's arm while she navigated the fifty yards of uneven terrain leading from the parking area.

I picked my way slowly across the dirt, kicking an occasional stone and stirring up dust with the toe of my navy blue Crocs. I strained to hear what Paulina and Mansoor were discussing in low voices behind me. The only words I heard were "Not now!"

I guessed the diameter of the large circular structure to be about forty feet. The walls were nearly all glass, affording a 360-degree view of the surrounding mountains and valley. Peering through the glass, I could see the roof inside was constructed with polished wooden beams meeting in the center, like the ribs of an umbrella. In between the beams were tongue-and-groove planks made of the same polished wood.

Birdie sighed. "Isn't it lovely?" She turned to face Lucy and me. "Royal said Madam Natasha commissioned Lloyd Wright, the son of the famous architect, to design a building conducive to meditation and communing with nature. It was completed in nineteen seventy-three, two years before her death."

In addition to the dozen small adobe structures scattered across the property to the right, three long, low wooden buildings and a two-story whitewashed house sat slightly down the hill on our left.

By the time we'd covered the distance from the parking lot, I was out of breath. I briefly stopped walking. "This place is bigger than it seems from back there."

Through a closed glass door, we observed about thirty people sitting on the floor. Some wore white robes, others sat naked on top of white cloths. They held hands in a circle with their eyes closed, seemingly in a trance. Some were young, some old, but they all seemed to be fairly fit. I toyed with the idea of joining the retreat myself, just not until I lost about fifty pounds. But the thought of parading my naked body persuaded me otherwise.

Lucy quickly looked away from all the exposed

flesh and made the sign of the cross. "Holy mother of God. Thank the Lord Ray isn't here."

A man with white hair spoke, but we couldn't hear him through the closed doors. Paulina leaned in close. "Looks like we arrived during a séance, Martha. If we go inside and interrupt, the spirits might get angry and decide not to cooperate with us. We should wait until they're through." She clucked her tongue. "All of those people's auras. The different colors are tinged with brown. Something's way off."

"But I want to hear what they're saying." I moved toward the entrance until a pair of hands wearing latex gloves landed on my shoulders and held me back.

"Don't," Mansoor hissed. "You'll ruin everything."

"What's *everything*?" I whispered back. "Do you know something the rest of us don't?"

Mansoor took a breath, drew himself up to his full height of around five feet ten, and wrinkled an offended forehead. "I am a Seer." As if that explained everything.

A moan escaped from Paulina's lips, and her eyes rolled back. She began to sway as if she were about to faint. Still holding the basket of goodies in one hand, Denver reached to grab her shoulders with his free arm. She stopped swaying and opened her eyes. "There are dark powers at work here."

I pointed to the white-haired man leading the séance. "Is that Royal St. Germain?"

Birdie peered through the glass and shook her head. "No. Even though he's in his sixties, Royal's hair hasn't turned gray. It's still mostly black. But there's something about that man that seems familiar. . . ."

Mansoor scowled at us. "Wait here and under no circumstances go inside. Paulina and I will look for Royal. He must be around here some place because I'm guessing the red Mercedes we parked next to belongs to him." He pointed to a white-washed house with a blue front door and lemon trees in front. "I'm also guessing the larger house belongs to him."

He leaned toward me and whispered, "Trust me on this." Then he and Paulina walked away, heads bent together in deep conversation.

"He's right about waiting outside," said Lucy. "We can't just barge in on their naked church service. It's not the polite thing to do."

Birdie patted Lucy's shoulder. "It's not really a church, dear."

Denver crooked his free arm at the elbow and offered it to Birdie. "Come on, then. We'd best wait over there. Don't want to piss off the spirits." He steered us toward a long bench under the shade of a nearby oak tree.

Paulina had said the auras of the group revealed something was seriously wrong. Her observations certainly confirmed what John Smith of the FBI hinted about Mystical Feather. No wonder the auras were "tinged with brown." Not that I believed in that stuff.

The bench was made from a tree trunk split down the middle and polished smooth. Lucy brushed the dry, spiky oak leaves off the surface with her fingertips before sitting down. "Did you notice what was painted in the center of the wooden floor? A five-pointed star with an eye inside. And the whole thing was surrounded by a circle."

"Yes, I saw it. That's a pentagram. It's used for magic." Birdie grabbed Denver's hand. "Did you get a look at that man with the white hair? Do we know him?"

"I wasn't paying much attention, Twink."

Ten minutes later we heard three loud pops. The crows in the sycamore tree flew out of their nest, scolding and complaining.

I sat straight up. "What . . . ?"

"Probably some off-season hunter." Denver removed his cowboy hat, combed his hair with his fingers, and put the hat back on. "Huntin' season's in the fall. But there's always gonna be some bozo who refuses to follow the rules."

Lucy jerked her thumb toward the yurt and muttered in my ear, "Don't they get cold sitting like that?"

We waited another twenty minutes for Paulina and Mansoor. Finally, they emerged from behind the bushes that obscured the parking area.

By the time they covered the distance, Paulina panted heavily. "We made a full circle. Knocked on every door, but nobody answered."

"Did you hear the gunshots?" I asked.

Lucy's head bobbed up and down and she consulted her watch. "Twenty minutes ago. Three of them."

Paulina glanced at Mansoor. "Is that what they were? It was hard to tell for sure."

Mansoor removed a tissue from his shirt pocket and wiped the moisture from his forehead. When he raised his arm, I could see sweat staining the armpits of his T-shirt. "We even checked out those vans, but they were empty."

Paulina gestured toward the glass-and-wooden yurt. "They're still at it?"

Birdie nodded. "Yes. We've been watching. Nobody has entered or left the place."

"I sense they're engaged in a powerful battle," Paulina said.

Mansoor nodded. "Yeah. There's some serious, ah . . . stuff going on, all right."

"Oh, sure," I said. "Invisible auras. Invisible spirits. Invisible combat. Good versus evil. That's the trouble with trusting psychics. How can a regular person like me verify such a claim?"

Denver stood and once again assumed the leadership of our little group. "We obviously came on the wrong day. No use waitin' around any longer. For all we know, those folks could be meditating for hours." He hefted the Longaberger basket once again.

Birdie sighed. "Denny's right. Let's go have lunch in town and come back later. Maybe they'll be finished by then."

"I sure could use some water to drink," Mansoor said.

We retraced our steps back to the RV, more than thirty minutes after we'd arrived. The door of the Winnebago stood slightly ajar.

Mansoor said, "I'm almost certain I latched up this door when we left."

Denver shrugged, "Don't worry, son. It sometimes does that. Let's take our places inside. We'll drive back down the mountain and on into town. Come on, Twink. Age before beauty." He winked at Birdie and steadied her as she climbed the stair step to the door.

A girlish giggle escaped from my seventy-something friend until she stepped inside the Winnebago. "Denny! Oh my god! Denny!"

At the sound of her distress, Denver dropped the basket on the ground and hurried inside. The rest of us pushed all at once to be first inside the RV.

"What's wrong?" I said.

Birdie pointed to the bed in the back of the Winnebago. Sprawled on top of it was a dark-haired man. His eyes stared blindly at the ceiling and his mouth hung open in silent protest. Clearly, he'd never see another birthday. Three closely spaced bullets had burned small holes through his white shirt around the region of his heart. I guessed he'd died instantly because very little blood oozed from the places where the shots had penetrated his body.

Birdie's face became ashen and drawn. "It can't be. I don't believe it."

Denver made her sit in the passenger seat and handed her a plastic bottle of water from the table.

"Do you know him?" Lucy's eyes were wide with disbelief.

Mansoor twisted the cap off another fresh bottle of water. "Now it all makes sense." He closed his eyes and took a long drink.

"What makes sense?" I demanded. "Who is he?"

Mansoor spoke quietly. "Meet Royal St. Germain."

CHAPTER 8

Before I called 911, I advised everyone to remove their valuables from the RV because once
the police took possession of it, they wouldn't let us
back inside.

Mansoor screwed the cap back on his bottle of
water. "Sounds like you have some experience with
this kind of thing."

"A little," I lied. Truth was, I'd learned a lot
about police procedure not only from Crusher,
who was a federal agent, but from my own investigations of no less than ten homicides over the last
few years.

We grabbed our purses and sweaters. Then I
made the call and waited for the police with our little
group outside the Winnebago. Denver picked up the
basket again and kept his other arm around Birdie's
shoulder. Lucy and I huddled into one another for

support and gripped each other's hands. Paulina stood alone while Mansoor paced back and forth. We were far enough from the parking area to have a clear view of the yurt some fifty yards away. The racket from the crows had fallen silent. I looked up and spotted the reason why. Five dark birds circled in the bright blue sky overhead. From their size and the beige feathers underneath their dark wings, I guessed they must be turkey vultures, nature's cleanup crew.

I bit my lip. "I suppose one of us should go tell those people their leader has been killed."

Everyone just stared at me.

"Fine," I said. "I'll go."

"Wait! Interrupting a séance can have deadly consequences," Paulina declared.

"Well, someone has to tell them."

Paulina grabbed Mansoor's arm and drew him toward her. "This is a job for the pros. The rest of you should stay here and wait for the police."

None of us were about to argue the point as she and Mansoor headed toward the yurt.

Less than ten minutes after I phoned, we heard several vehicles approach. They kicked up a cloud of dust as they tore up the private road, stopped briefly at the gate, and continued onto the Mystical Feather commune. Four black and white SUVs pulled to a stop where we stood near the parking area and the urgent blare of their sirens ended with a final *whoop whoop*. Big letters on the side of the vehicles spelled SHERIFF, VENTURA COUNTY.

A small flock of frightened faces began to assemble just outside the yurt and crowd behind the white-haired leader of the séance. Birdie peered at the man as he spoke to Paulina and Mansoor, waving his arms in our direction. My friend narrowed her eyes. "I'm sure we know him from somewhere, Denny."

"Beats me, Twink." Denver shook his head and watched as one deputy stepped out of each vehicle.

They wore the distinctive tan shirt and green trouser uniform of the Ventura County Sheriff's office. Apparently, Ojai wasn't a large enough town to support its own police force, so, like other small towns in the area, they contracted with the county to provide law enforcement.

A tall sheriff in his forties, with closely cropped brown hair, stepped in front of the others and approached the four of us standing about twenty feet from the Winnebago. From the three stripes sewn on his sleeves and the way the other deputies deferred to him, I guessed he was the man in charge.

He scanned our faces with intelligent eyes. "I'm Sergeant Diaz, Ventura County Sheriff's office. Someone reported finding a body?"

"I did. I'm Martha Rose." I pointed to the Winnebago.

The sergeant gestured with his head, and a deputy whose name tag read Willard entered the RV. A female deputy took out a notepad and pen and began to take notes the old-fashioned way.

I turned back to the sergeant. "He was shot to death. Maybe a half hour ago by now."

Diaz asked, "You saw it happen?"

"No, we were sitting over there, outside the meditation center." I pointed in the direction of where nearly thirty people stood with Paulina and Mansoor facing our direction. "That's when we heard three loud pops in a row."

"Definitely gunshots." Lucy spoke up.

Deputy Willard emerged from the RV and nodded. "Affirmative, Sarge. We've got a DB."

Denver handed the Longaberger basket to Birdie, who had to grip it with both hands. He took off his hat, stepped forward, and offered his hand. "Name's Denver Watson, your honor. This is my wife, Birdie. That's our Winnebago. The body in the back belongs to Royal St. Germain. Plugged three times in the heart by a dang good shot."

"I think the shooter's long gone by now," I added.

Diaz pointed to the crowd, some of whom had not yet opted for clothing. "Where were they when you heard the shots?"

"Inside, sitting on the floor and holding hands. All except those two dark-haired people wearing regular clothes. They're with us." I would hardly describe Paulina's flamboyant purple velvet cape as "regular," but compared to the older woman standing next to her with the sagging tattoo on her bare breast, it was normal.

"Did you see anybody enter or leave the building?"

I shook my head. "Nobody went in or came out."

Diaz spoke to an eager young deputy. "Go to that round building and secure the area. Keep everyone inside. No one leaves until we've had a chance to get statements from them." He wagged his head. "And, for piss sake, tell them to put on some clothes." The deputy turned on his heel and trotted toward the assembled crowd.

Then Diaz turned back to us. "Did you see anyone running from the area?"

We all shook our heads.

"Did you see or hear any vehicle leaving the property?"

"No. Nothing like that," I said.

"I suppose you'll be needing statements from each of us?" Birdie, who had been silent since discovering St. Germain's body, spoke for the first time. "I imagine your forensic team will be checking everyone for GSR as well?" Birdie was a fan of every police show on TV and was familiar with cop speak.

Diaz stopped and considered our white-haired friend for a long moment. "That's right, ma'am. Whoever fired the weapon will have gunshot residue on his hands."

She continued as if lecturing a student on the finer points of criminal investigation. "Unless, of course, they wore protective gloves and clothing, which they quickly disposed of after the shooting. Presumably along with the weapon."

To his credit, Diaz showed no sign he was annoyed by the elderly lady lecturing him. "Right. But let's not get ahead of ourselves. What's in that basket?"

Birdie smiled. "Food, Sergeant. I baked this morning especially for Royal and his followers."

"May I look inside?"

Without a word, she handed over the basket. The sergeant carefully removed the kitchen towel to discover the delicious bread and pastries inside. "Would you mind removing these items one by one?"

Both Birdie and Denver reached over and began to remove the loaves of bread, cookies, and pastries, all packed into transparent plastic Ziploc bags.

When the basket was empty, Diaz handed the basket back to Denver. "Thank you."

He next spoke to Deputy Willard. "Call Major Crimes at HQ and get more uniforms up here." He made a wide sweep with his arm toward the compound. "We've got a lot of people to interview."

Willard nodded and spoke into the radio unit on his shoulder.

"How long has the Winnebago been parked there?" Diaz asked Denver.

He looked at Birdie. "When did we arrive? About eleven?"

She nodded.

"What is your business here?"

I talked fast. "Six of us drove up from Encino

this morning to visit Royal St. Germain and tour the commune. My friends here," I indicated Birdie and Denver, "are thinking of becoming members of Mr. St. Germain's group. Anyway, when we arrived, those people were sitting on the floor of the yurt."

"The floor of the what?" a female deputy asked as she took notes.

"That big round building, where all those other people are standing. They were conducting a séance and we didn't want to interfere. So, Birdie, Denver, Lucy, and I waited on that bench just outside the yurt while our two psychic friends went looking for Mr. St. Germain."

"Your two *what?*" the female deputy interrupted with a snort.

I glared at her. "Psychics. Paulina Polinskaya and Mansoor the Magnificent. As soon as we arrived, they sensed something was terribly wrong from the brown edges on everybody's auras." The deputy snickered behind her hand but I chose to ignore her. "So, while the four of us sat waiting, they searched for Mr. St. Germain everywhere, but they couldn't find him."

"Can we sit down?" Birdie asked. "I've got bad knees."

The sergeant pointed to the bench next to the yurt. "Yes ma'am. We'll go over to the bench where you sat before. I want to view the scene from there, anyway."

Denver and Lucy walked on either side of Birdie, helping her navigate the distance.

The sergeant walked beside me, reaching once to support my arm when I stumbled over some pebbles. "Steady."

Deputy Willard and his female colleague followed behind as we slowly trekked to the bench of polished wood.

My breathing had become labored with the effort of walking fifty yards. *I definitely have to start exercising more.* Who was I kidding? I never exercised.

I sat down and steadied my breath. "After Paulina and Mansoor returned, we decided to drive down the mountain and into town. Our plan was to have lunch in one of your unique restaurants and come back to the commune later. We hoped the séance would've ended by then and we'd get to meet with some of the members of the group, as well as with Mr. St. Germain."

Twenty feet away at the entrance of the yurt, the young deputy was doing a good job of detaining the Mystical Feather group. Several of them had already slipped white robes over their heads. I guessed those were the white cloths they sat on. The séance leader approached the deputy standing in the doorway and spoke in a trembling voice, "You must tell us what's happening."

"This is just for your protection," the deputy soothed. "We're waiting for the detectives to arrive to take your statements. As soon you're interviewed, you'll be free to leave."

The older man's voice took on an edge of ... what? Authority? Anger? "How long will it take for the detectives to show up?"

"This is a weekend," said the deputy. "Most of the officers are off duty, which means we have to call them at home. But don't worry, they'll come as soon as they're contacted."

Now the anger in the white-haired man's voice was clear. "Are you saying we could be waiting for hours?"

The deputy's voice softened and became almost conciliatory. "That's right, sir. Unfortunately, we can't let you leave this building." He proceeded to herd the older man back inside the building with the others.

Birdie grasped Denver's arm. "Did you think that man's voice sounded familiar?"

"Hard to say, Twink."

While the door was still open, I got another glimpse of the interior of the yurt. The soaring space under the umbrella of the wooden ceiling created a cathedral-like feeling. I spotted the pentagram painted in the exact center of the floor, just the way Lucy had described it: a circle containing a five-pointed star with an eye in the center. Four brass censers hung from the ceiling in what I guessed to be the cardinal points on a compass. Smoke curled up from them, filling the air with incense.

Sergeant Diaz looked toward the parking area and shaded his eyes with his hand. "You're right. You can't really see the vehicles from there through all that vegetation." He looked at each of us in turn. "Think back. Could you have seen someone whose movements looked so normal you forgot about them?"

I closed my eyes and thought hard. What had I seen? The only image that popped into my head was Paulina and Mansoor hurrying back to us from the direction of the parking lot. My eyes shot open. Surely they couldn't have been involved in the murder. What could possibly be their motive?

CHAPTER 9

Lucy frowned and shook her head slowly as if to dislodge some obscure data. Finally, she looked at Sergeant Diaz. "Nope. We didn't see another soul. Nobody entered or left this building. But Paulina and Mansoor might've seen something in the parking area. They said they searched not only all the buildings for Mister St. Germain but also those parked vehicles while we waited here."

The sergeant looked at deputy Willard and gestured toward the two dark-haired people in regular clothes. We watched as he escorted Paulina and Mansoor out of the yurt and back to our group. "This is them, Sarge."

"Names?" asked Diaz.

The female note-taker had her pen ready.

The short, round Paulina pulled herself up to her full height of under five feet. "Paulina Polinskaya." She looked at the deputy taking notes. "That's spelled P-O-L-I-N-S-K-A-Y-A."

Diaz then turned to Mansoor. "You?"

Mansoor lowered his eyelids halfway and bowed with a flourish. "Mansoor the Magnificent. That's spelled . . ."

Diaz rolled his eyes and cut him short. "Your real name."

The two psychics glanced at each other and Mansoor spoke quietly. "Mike."

"Full name?"

"Michael Polinskaya."

"What?" I burst out. "You're related?" I examined their faces and saw a resemblance in their dark hair, high cheekbones, full lips, and large almond-shaped eyes.

Paulina patted the air in front of her as if trying to calm everyone. "Mikey's my younger brother. Our relationship's not commonly known because we try to keep our careers separate."

Mansoor raised one eyebrow and removed his latex gloves. "We each have unique gifts inherited from a long line of psychics."

"Just a minute. I'll take that." The female deputy reached into her pocket and withdrew a small plastic evidence bag.

Mansoor handled the gloves with his fingertips and dropped them in the open sack. "Did you know there are literally millions of species of microscopic pathogens? You'll find nothing on those gloves except a lot of germs."

"Don't be so sure, *Magnificent*. Even if you were

wearing these when you shot St. Germain, there'd still be traces of GSR."

"Me? Shoot St. Germain?" Mansoor scoffed. "What possible reason could I have?"

Paulina stepped between the deputy and her brother. She drew a circle in front of the woman with her open hand. "Your aura's fluctuating between dark red and clear red. You might think about ways to curb your anger and competitiveness. I also see an underlay of unfulfilled sexual passion. Perhaps if you had a partner in bed, you'd be a lot happier."

With every pronouncement, the deputy's face burned. One glance at her boss, however, told her to keep her mouth shut.

Paulina turned to Sergeant Diaz and smiled. "Your aura, on the other hand, is an orangey yellow. You're a detail-oriented perfectionist. Unlike your passionate deputy here, you rely heavily on science for answers."

Sergeant Diaz sighed and addressed Paulina and Mansoor. "Back to planet earth, please. Did either of you encounter anyone else on your search through the compound? On the grounds or in the buildings?"

Paulina said, "No. As far as we could tell, the buildings were empty."

He pressed further. "Did you actually enter any of the buildings?"

"No way." Paulina held up the palms of her hands. "That would be trespassing. We just knocked on doors, and when nobody answered, we moved on to the next building."

"How about in the vicinity of the parking lot? Did you see anyone in or around the vehicles?"

"We were only there long enough to look inside the two white vans and the red Mercedes. The car doors were unlocked, by the way. Anyway, when we didn't find anyone, we walked back to report to our friends here."

Just then we heard the engines of more vehicles making their way up the driveway in a cloud of dust. The first to appear was a black-and-white van bearing letters reading, "Ventura County Crime Scene Investigation." That would be the forensic team examining Birdie's Winnebago. Three people emerged in plainclothes and donned white protective overalls, booties, head coverings, and latex gloves.

"You'd better make other arrangements for transportation," said Diaz. "That RV belongs to the forensics people now."

"I'll call Yossi." I pulled out my cell phone, and I was immediately directed to voice mail. "Hi, honey. We've hit a teensy little snag here in Ojai. The six of us need a ride home. The sheriff just seized Birdie's Winnebago because Royal St. Germain was murdered on the bed inside. Please call me back as soon as you get this message."

Lucy tugged on my sleeve to get my attention and made that slicing motion across her throat again.

I ended the message with, "Oh. And please don't mention the dead body to Ray Mondello in case he asks where his wife is."

While I left my message, more black-and-whites

arrived and parked. One of the deputies began the task of stringing yellow tape around the parking area. An unmarked blue Ford sedan pulled in next to the forensic van. A man and a woman in civilian suits got out and started walking toward us.

"The detectives have arrived. They'll be taking your statements. Wait here." The sergeant turned away and walked toward the newcomers, presumably to brief them on what he knew.

We looked at one another, sighed, and waited for the second time that day.

Lucy's cell phone chimed with an incoming call. She took one look at the screen and paled. "It's Ray! What shall I tell him?"

Birdie grabbed the end of her braid. "It's always best to go with the truth, dear."

Lucy momentarily closed her eyes, took a deep breath, and slid the icon on the screen of her smart phone. "Hello, hon . . . Well, shopping for fabric took longer than expected. . . . Didn't I mention the fabric store was in Ojai?" She cringed as he spoke on the other end. "I don't know how much longer we'll be. How about I call you when we're leaving? . . . It takes about an hour and a half to drive back to the Valley from here."

She slumped as she listened to his response. "There's a good reason Birdie's RV's not in the driveway right now, hon. There was a bunch of us who wanted to go shopping. Denver offered to transport everyone in the Winnebago. Unfortunately, we now have to leave the RV in Ojai and find another way home. . . . No, I'm fine. Nobody's hurt. . . .

What's wrong with Denver's RV?" She looked at me, eyes wide with panic. I gestured for her to hand me the phone.

"Hello, Ray? This is Martha. The funniest thing happened to us today. . . ."

CHAPTER 10

After conferring with Sergeant Diaz, the two plainclothes officers headed for the Winnebago. Diaz walked to the door of the yurt and cleared his throat. All conversation stopped as he spoke loudly enough for us to hear him from the bench twenty feet away. "You folks'll be escorted to the dining hall, where you can sit more comfortably. Once you've given the detectives your statement, you'll be free to go."

The white-haired leader stared at our group and whispered something to a gray-haired woman next to him. She looked in our direction. Her eyes widened in recognition and her hands flew to cover her mouth. She took a few steps toward us but was stopped by one of the six deputy escorts. She had to join the other members as they walked in meek single file to one of the long, low buildings to the left of the yurt.

We rose to join them, but Diaz motioned for us to stay seated on the bench and walked back to our group of six. "Since you discovered the bodies, the detectives will probably speak to each of you first."

"But we just told you everything we know," said Lucy. "As it is, Ray is going to kill me!"

Diaz frowned. "Are you saying someone has threatened your life?"

I jumped to her defense. "It's just a metaphor, Sergeant. Ray is Lucy's husband, and he's really a nice man. He's just concerned because Lucy and I have been involved in several murder cases together. Ray gave us both an ultimatum to stop. Which was kind of unnecessary, I might add, since we don't exactly go trolling for dead bodies on purpose."

Lucy showed the sergeant her cell phone screen. "Ray thinks I went shopping today. But when he phoned just now, I had to tell the truth. See? That's his number."

The sergeant aimed his very deep frown toward me. "*Several* murder cases?"

My mouth had gone dry, and I licked my lips. "Well, including Royal St. Germain, this is only my eleventh homicide."

"*Only* your eleventh? How exactly were you involved in eleven homicides?"

I winced. *Why did I say that?* I knew my little confession would probably mean an even longer delay while they looked us up in CLETS, California's statewide criminal identification data base, or in NCIC, the national criminal data base. I already knew my name would come up in a local search as having once been arrested for obstructing justice. Even though I had never been arraigned, I knew from experience that my name and fingerprints remained permanently in the system.

"Actually," I tried to smile at Diaz, but my face felt like all the elastic had disappeared, "I seem to keep stumbling across corpses."

"Not always, hon," said Lucy. "Remember your friend who was dead in her closet for ten months before anyone found her? You never saw her corpse. You also solved a thirty-two-year-old cold case involving your father's murder. You never saw his corpse, either."

Birdie played with the loose end of her long white braid, teasing out the turquoise-dyed streak with her fingers. "Lucy's correct, dear. And don't forget the recent double homicide you solved. You didn't actually see the corpses of that poor little girl's parents."

"Right." I relaxed, and this time my smile felt more at home on my face. "So, technically, Royal St. Germain's is only the seventh dead body for me."

Both Lucy and Birdie spoke at the same time.

"Yes."

"Exactly."

Diaz's mouth gaped open in disbelief as his gaze kept shifting among the three of us. "I hope you're not planning on meddling in this investigation." He made a point of impaling each of us with his pointed stare. "Until and unless you're cleared, you are all potential suspects."

Denver Watson had remained silent until now. He stood and took a step closer to Diaz. "Can we talk man to man? I can vouch for these ladies, sheriff. My wife, Birdie, and her two friends here—there's not a one of them that's got a mean streak or murderous bone in their body. And besides, we're not getting any younger. Know what I mean?"

"No, I don't know. What do you mean?"

"We're a little older than you, Sheriff. We got kids your age. Believe me, when you get to be as advanced in years as we are, you just don't give a crap about things like you used to. Killin' someone just ain't worth the effort."

"So why aren't you vouching for these other two?" He thrust his chin toward Paulina and Mansoor.

"Don't mistake me, Sheriff. I ain't saying they're guilty. It's just I only met them this morning, so I couldn't say one way or t'other. Know what I mean?"

"Birdie, it looks like that elderly couple recognized you and Denver. Do you know them?" I whispered.

"I think so, but I'm having a hard time placing them."

Five more marked and unmarked vehicles arrived. I noticed as the two plainclothes officers emerged from the Winnebago, spoke briefly to the newcomers, and pointed them in the direction of the dining hall. Then the two plainclothes officers walked toward us.

The woman wore a bright blue pantsuit with a mustard yellow tank top under her jacket. She appeared to be somewhere in her forties. Her tightly curled bleached blonde hair was cut short like a man's and contrasted dramatically with her milk chocolate skin. She stopped when she reached the bench and pulled back her jacket just enough to reveal a sheriff's badge clipped to her slim waistband. "I'm Detective Della Washington." She pointed to the man next to her. "This is my partner, Detective Oliver Heymann."

Heymann smiled briefly and flipped open his jacket to reveal a badge clipped to his belt. He stood a head taller than Washington and appeared to be about ten years younger. His huge biceps strained the sleeves of his gray suit jacket, and his trousers barely disguised thick, muscular thighs—unmistakable signs of a serious body builder. The sandy-haired blue-eyed Heymann would be a formidable adversary if a suspect were foolish enough to take him on.

I briefly thought about applying to the sheriff's academy to see if I could lose some weight and tone my body while I was at it. But who was I kidding? I'd never survive the first five minutes of physical training.

They asked for our names. "You are the group who found the victim?"

"Yes," we all said at once.

"Which of you owns the Winnebago?"

Birdie and Denver raised their hands as if they were in a classroom.

"We are, ma'am." Denver pointed to Birdie and back at himself.

"We'll interview the two of you first." While she spoke, several deputies lugged four chairs and two tables from one of the other buildings and set up two interview areas inside the empty yurt.

Through the glass we watched Washington escort Birdie to one of the tables inside the round building and Heymann escort Denver to the other table. There was no way we could hear what they said, but they took at least a half hour to say it. While we waited, Paulina and Mansoor quietly moved about fifteen feet away until a watchful deputy said, "Far enough." The brother and sister stopped and huddled together in hushed conference.

Lucy leaned toward me and whispered, "You know Paulina better than anybody here. Why would she and Mansoor keep their relationship secret from us?"

"First of all, I wouldn't exactly call us friends. She'd have no reason to confide in me. But I'd been wondering the same thing. And something else is bothering me. Paulina told me, 'Mansoor will jump at the chance to take Royal down. Just like me.'"

Lucy gasped so loudly, the deputy guarding us turned his face our way. She lowered her voice. "Are you saying what I think you are?"

Before I could respond, Birdie and Denver emerged from the yurt. Denver stopped in the doorway and asked Detective Heymann, "When do we get the Winnebago back?"

Heymann screwed up his face. "Only after the killer is caught, tried, and convicted. Maybe not even then. Maybe not ever."

I was glad I warned everyone to remove their personal items before the sheriff arrived.

"Dang." Denver spat on the ground. "Who'll compensate us for the loss of our RV?"

Good! Denver was now thinking like a man who cared about his property. I hoped it meant he'd given up the idea of offering all their earthly goods to the Mystical Feather Society.

Heymann put a sympathetic hand on Denver's shoulder. "All I can do is advise you to check with your insurance company, sir. There's also a state fund to help victims of violent crimes."

"How do we know we'll qualify?"

"Oh, you'll qualify all right. There's nothing more violent than murder."

"Much obliged." Denver shook Heymann's hand and escorted Birdie to the bench.

Washington consulted her iPhone. "Martha Rose? Lucy Mondello?"

We stood.

"That's us," I said.

"Ms. Rose, you'll come with me, and Mrs. Mondello, you'll go with Detective Heymann."

Lucy and I followed the detectives inside the yurt. I carefully avoided stepping on the pentagram painted on the floor as the detective led me to the far table. The fire had gone out in the four brass censers, but the smell of frankincense sat heavily in the air like a holy fog, reminding me of the inside of a church.

Washington motioned for me to sit while she read something on the screen of her smart phone.

As she settled in her seat across the table from me, she turned on a small voice recording device, noted the time of day, and made eye contact. "Your name is Martha Rose, correct?"

I confirmed my birth date, address, and phone number. I found myself speaking in hushed tones.

"It says here you have a history with the LAPD. Arrested for obstruction of justice."

"That was a huge misunderstanding. The charges were dropped, and I was never even arraigned. It happened on my first murder."

She looked up from her phone and scowled at me. "Your first murder?"

Oh no, I wasn't going to go through that whole story again. Once a day was enough. "Believe me, I certainly don't go looking for trouble. Take today, for instance. Nobody at Mystical Feather knew we were coming for a visit. We just showed up in hopes of meeting Royal St. Germain and interviewing his followers. Completely innocent. Right? Yet somebody here—someone we never saw— lured Mr. St. Germain into our Winnebago and shot him. You could hardly call that predictable. I mean, how were we to know what would happen?"

"Easy. You could've set up this whole scenario before you arrived. . . ."

"Yeah, and my bubbie could've secretly eaten pigs-in-a-blanket on Passover."

She narrowed her eyes. "Why did you want to interview the people here?"

"Truthfully? My friends and I wanted to prevent Birdie and Denver from making a foolish mistake. Royal was a dangerous fraud."

"So, you did have a reason to stop St. Germain. Maybe permanently?"

"That man talked my friends into selling everything they own and handing it over to the Mystical Feather Trust. The money would've been a huge windfall for Royal and his lavish lifestyle. In exchange, my friends would join the group and live here in Naked Town."

A flash of amusement crossed Washington's face. "That's not illegal."

"In and of itself, maybe not. But Royal is suspected by the FBI because some of his followers seem to have disappeared."

"How do you know what the FBI suspects?"

I panicked momentarily. What if the information I got from John Smith was classified? I gave her a look that said, *You're going to have to rip my fingernails out before I tell you anymore.* "People in the Bureau I've worked with on other murder cases told me so."

"Names?"

"Respectfully, you'll have to query the FBI yourself."

She leaned over the table and jabbed her finger toward me. "You're refusing to give me pertinent information? Do you know I can arrest you for obstruction of justice and impeding a criminal investigation?"

I shrugged and pointed to my rap sheet on her iPhone. "Been there, done that. If you arrest me, the only thing I ask is that I be able to take my fibromyalgia medication with me. As I recall, the hard benches in the pokey were *murder* on my back and hips."

"Are you for real?" Washington scowled.

I smiled. "Come on, Detective. I have no doubt whatsoever that one simple phone call from you to the Bureau will confirm everything I've told you."

She paused and tapped her fingertips on the table. "We'll set that aside for now. Tell me about when you first arrived. Did someone from inside open the gate for you?"

"Didn't have to. When we drove up, we noticed the padlock was hanging open. At the time we thought that was kind of weird because of the sign on the driveway below said this was a private retreat. Anyway, Mansoor jumped out and opened the gate. We drove through and he closed the gate and got back in the RV."

"Did he close the padlock afterward?"

"I didn't see, but I doubt it. That would've prevented us from leaving if he had."

"Could anyone else see what he was doing?"

"Maybe Denver saw him in the rearview mirror. But that's pure speculation on my part. You'd have to ask him."

"Did you see anyone in the vicinity of the gate after you arrived? Maybe hear a vehicle in that area?"

"That gate is hard to see from here. But no, I don't recall anything like that."

While she scrolled down the screen on her iPhone, I looked through the glass walls out onto the mountainside and the Ojai Valley below. Thick scrub brush and oak trees provided a barrier around the compound, creating almost complete privacy. Using the vegetation as cover, anyone could easily come and go without being seen.

Detective Washington's voice jarred me out of my reverie. "Your friend Mrs. Watson said only four of you were sitting together when you heard the gunshots."

"That's correct. Birdie, Denver, Lucy, and me."

"Where were the other two? Paulina and Michael Polinskaya?"

I had to stop for a minute before I realized she was using Mansoor's real name of Michael. "They were off somewhere looking for Royal."

"So, at the time of the shooting, they weren't with you and not within your eyesight?"

"No."

"How soon after the shooting did you see them?"

"I don't know exactly. Maybe twenty minutes?"

"When they finally reappeared, what direction did they come from?"

I didn't like where this seemed to be going. "The parking area."

"How long have you known the Polinskayas? What is the nature of your relationship?"

"I met Paulina a couple years ago. We collaborated on a couple of investigations."

"And her brother?"

"I just met him two days ago. I didn't even know until a few minutes ago they were related to each other."

"Do you know anything else about their family or their background?"

"No. Why would I?"

Detective Della Washington gave me a half-smile out of the corner of her mouth. "I get to be the one asking questions right now."

I ignored her. "Why were you so interested in the gate, anyhow?"

"Sergeant Diaz had to use bolt cutters on the padlock to get in."

A chill ran up my spine. "Someone deliberately locked us in?"

Washington shrugged. "What do you think?"

CHAPTER 11

After giving our statements, Lucy and I joined Birdie and Denver on the bench once more and waited while the detectives interviewed Paulina and Mansoor inside the yurt. I lowered my voice and leaned toward the others, trying to keep the detectives watching us from overhearing our conversation. "Denver, when Mansoor opened and closed the gate for us, did you happen to see him shut the padlock?"

Denver pushed his brows together and scratched behind his ear. "No." He wagged his head slowly. "I wasn't looking. Why?"

I told them about the closed padlock.

Birdie seemed to sink into Denver's side, as if seeking safety under the protection of his arm. Was that a sign she finally realized how dangerous it was to be in the Mystical Feather commune? She reached for Denver's free hand. "For pity's sake, Martha. Why would anyone want to keep us here?"

"I think the killer saw our arrival as an unexpected gift from heaven. Maybe he wanted to make sure we remained at the commune long enough to lure Royal to his death inside the RV. That way we'd become the focus of the homicide investigation."

"Don't make sense," Denver said. "First of all, how could the killer know we'd be waiting on the bench rather than inside the Winnebago? The only people who knew we decided to wait were the six of us. Second of all, how did the killer lure Royal to the RV without being seen?"

"While we were being interrogated inside the yurt, I realized there is enough brush and trees on the mountainside surrounding the compound to provide cover. The killer could've been crouching in the brush nearby, listening in on our conversation."

Lucy consulted her watch and looked at the female deputy. "We've been here for more than three hours, and I have to use the ladies' room badly."

"Me, too," Birdie and I said together.

Regardless of how many Kegels we did, women of a certain age had to cope with the occasional failure of our pelvic muscles to keep us dry. We formed the Sisterhood of the Weak Bladder.

A sympathetic female deputy escorted us into the nearest small adobe house. The floor was paved with red Mexican tiles, which made the three-hundred-square-foot space feel chilly. On the whitewashed wall opposite the doorway, a lone window framed in dark wood faced east to welcome the morning sun. A double bed covered with a cheerful red-and-white Ohio Star quilt was pushed against the wall to our right. Two rolled-up yoga mats stood against the front wall next to the door. A tiny bathroom and closet finished the wall to our left.

"Sorry, Luce. I'm about to lose it." I ran ahead of my friend and barely made it to the bathroom in time. When I was finished, Lucy took a turn. While she was occupied, I looked at the wooden table with two ladder-back chairs arranged precisely in the middle of the window. I said, "Birdie, look at how dismal this place is. It looks like a monk's cell. Are you sure you want to give up everything and move here?"

"Not anymore. This place doesn't feel spiritual at all. It feels oppressive. Thank goodness Denny insisted on bringing me here first to see for ourselves."

Wait. What am I, chopped liver? It was my idea to check out the compound.

Next to use the facilities was Birdie. While we waited, Lucy gazed around the room, as if seeing it for the first time. She pointed to a framed photo on the wall above the head of the bed. A white-robed Royal St. Germain stood with a beatific smile and his arms outspread.

Lucy frowned. "What does that picture remind you of?"

I'd noticed one of these pictures also hung on a wall stud inside the yurt. Was it in every building?

"It reminds me of the huge Christ the Redeemer statue on top of Corcovado Mountain in Rio de Janeiro. And hundreds of other statues and paintings over the last two thousand years."

"Exactly!" My Catholic friend Lucy fumed. "How dare he compare himself to Jesus!"

"It takes a lot of chutzpah, I know, Luce. But it's not uncommon for a cult leader to present himself as the Messiah."

When Birdie emerged from the bathroom, the detective winked. "Wait here. I'll be right out." Another member of the weak bladder sisterhood.

Birdie gazed around the room and spotted a small framed photo sitting on the table under the windowsill. She moved to get a closer look, picked up the picture, and gasped. "I thought they looked familiar!"

Lucy and I joined her at the table and looked at the snapshot. A young blonde woman wearing a blue halter top and bell-bottom jeans held hands with a long-haired young man.

"Who are they?" I asked.

"Claytie and June Tolliver. I haven't seen them since I left Aquarius all those years ago." Birdie referred to the commune in Ashland, Oregon, where she and Denver lived in the 1960s. "They obviously recognized Denny and me. June looked like she really wanted to talk. I'm going to leave them a note. Do you have paper and a pen?"

I rummaged around in my purse until I found a small notepad and pen. She scribbled a quick message, folded the paper, and placed it on the table underneath the old photo.

Personal crises resolved, the deputy emerged from the bathroom, waved us outside, and closed the wooden door to the little house. Lucy and I helped Birdie slowly manage the uneven path back to the yurt, where Denver waited.

Birdie grabbed his hand. "We do know them, Denny."

"Who?"

"That couple." She told him about the Tollivers.

"Dang! It's been a long time, Twink. I'd never've recognized them."

"Well, I left a note. In case they need a place to stay."

Denver merely nodded his approval.

Deputy Willard approached us and pointed toward the driveway below the parking area. "Your rides have arrived. They're waiting at the gate below. The four of you are free to leave."

"Thanks," I said. "But we can't leave our friends Paulina and Mansoor. Do you know how much longer they'll be in there?"

He glanced inside the yurt. "Not a clue."

As we spoke, I noticed six of the white-robed cult members leaving the dining hall. I guessed they'd finished giving their statements. Two couples headed in our direction, including Birdie's old friends. Claytie Tolliver nodded toward Denver but said nothing. He and June disappeared into their adobe house. The second couple entered another adobe. The other two members trickled in the opposite direction toward another long, low building. What had Mansoor said? The small houses accommodated couples living here permanently, while the single members and temporary visitors slept in dormitories.

My cell phone chirped inside my purse. I pulled it out and read the text.

Waiting at gate with Ray. R U done?

I responded: **Waiting for Paulina and Mansoor. How pissed is Ray?**

Less than ten seconds later, Crusher wrote: **Very. Followed in his car.**

Poor Lucy. None of this mess was her fault, but she did lie to him about where she was going and why. Ray wasn't a control freak, but he was very protective of his wife. And once again, I'd dragged her to a murder scene. Would he try to end our friendship? Would she let him?

I looked at my three friends. "Yossi and Ray are waiting for us at the bottom of the driveway with two vehicles. I took the liberty of saying we were waiting for Paulina and Mansoor, but I don't think Ray is happy. What do you want to do?"

Lucy looked up from her cell phone. "Yeah, I just got a text from Ray. I can't leave him down below by himself. I need to go. She turned to Birdie and Denver. "Want to come with me?"

Denver pushed his cowboy hat up his forehead. "I reckon all this has been hard on Twink. She needs to get home where she can rest her poor knees." He looked at Detective Willard. "Can you give us a lift down the driveway?"

Willard reached for my arm to help me off the bench, "If you're done here, you need to leave, too, ma'am."

"I'm waiting for my friends to finish their statements. Then we'll leave together. I'm the only ride they have."

Willard nodded once and led my three friends to one of the black-and-whites. They disappeared down the hill toward the gate.

Five minutes later, the tires of Willard's car crunched slowly back up the driveway and parked near the other official vehicles. An unmarked SUV followed closely behind. The driver got out and shook hands with Willard before walking in my direction.

Crusher.

He closed the distance between us with a few huge strides of his long legs, sat on the bench next to me, and kissed my forehead. "You okay, babe?"

"Yeah. I just didn't want to leave Paulina and Mansoor stranded without a ride. How'd you get past the guards?"

He flashed his ATF badge and grinned. "Professional courtesy. Tell me what you know."

For the umpteenth time that day, I repeated everything that had happened since we arrived at eleven that morning.

When I finished, he said, "So, Paulina and Mansoor are brother and sister?"

"Yes, and I suspect there's more information they're keeping back."

He pushed his brows together. "The circumstantial evidence so far seems to point their way."

Crusher was right. None of us could vouch for their whereabouts at the exact time of the shooting. "But what would be their motive?"

We waited on the bench, and I told him about

Birdie's old friends. "She left a note inviting them to come and stay with her and Denny."

"Yeah." He ran his fingers through his beard. "If their old friends gave everything they owned to the Mystical Feather Trust, they won't have anything to go back to if they leave. They'll need all the help they can get."

At four thirty, Paulina and Mansoor finally emerged from the yurt. He reached in his pocket and, without looking, tore open a foil packet. Instead of extracting an alcohol wipe, he unfolded a single long piece of latex. He quickly stuffed it back in his pocket and looked around to see if anyone had observed his mistake. Our gazes met. His face reddened as I smiled and gave him a thumbs-up.

The pair approached us, and I made the introductions. "This is my fiancé, Yossi Levy. He's going to drive us back to the Valley."

Paulina studied Crusher's face. "I've met you before. At a funeral a couple of years ago. I never forget an aura. Yours is pure purple, the sign of a very evolved human being. That's my brother Mikey."

Crusher stretched his hand toward Mansoor, but Paulina patted his arm. "Don't bother. He doesn't like physical contact of any kind."

I winked at Mansoor and mumbled, "Well, that's not entirely true, is it?"

Mansoor had extracted another alcohol wipe and scrubbed the webbing between his fingers, acting like the last several seconds never happened. "They swabbed our hands with a chemical to test for gunshot residue."

"Yeah," Crusher nodded. "It's called a GSR detection kit. It's used at crime scenes to immediately exclude people as suspects." He grinned. "How'd you do?"

Mansoor meticulously scraped the skin under his fingernails. "We both passed, of course."

What had Birdie told Sergeant Diaz? That the shooter could've worn protective gloves and clothing and ditched them, along with the weapon. But I still had a hard time imagining either of these two killing Royal St. Germain. There was the problem of motive.

CHAPTER 12

I sat in front of the SUV with Crusher, and the two Polinskayas sat in the back seat. As soon as we drove off the mountain and turned onto Highway 150, I swiveled around to face them as much as my seatbelt would allow. "Mansoor, after we drove past the gate, did you close the padlock?"

"No. Why? The detective asked me that question at least a hundred times."

"Because someone locked us in."

Paulina gasped.

Mansoor said, "Well, that would've been stupid on my part. How would we have gotten out again?"

"Good question. While we're at it, since you're the expert on the Mystical Feather Society and Madam St. Germain, do you have any idea who wanted Royal dead?"

He glanced at his sister. "You saw those people. One of them probably did it."

"Or," Paulina piped up, "maybe the relative of a missing member decided to take revenge."

"Yeah," said Mansoor. "That's probably what happened."

Or, maybe one or both of you killed him. You certainly had the opportunity.

Crusher looked at him in the rearview mirror. "I thought you were a Seer."

Mansoor picked off a piece of lint from his knee. "Some evil is too dark to penetrate."

Crusher smiled out of the corner of his mouth. "Glad we cleared that up."

Emotional exhaustion weighed on me like a heavy blanket. I sank back in my seat and closed my eyes. We mostly rode in silence for the next hour and a half. Finally, we pulled up in front of Lucy's house in the gloaming just as the sun slipped under the horizon. Across the street, warm lights glowed in Birdie's house, but Lucy's place was dark. It was probably just as well. Now wasn't the time to show my face. I'd give Ray a day or two to cool off.

Mansoor exited the vehicle and pushed the door shut with his elbow. Paulina opened the passenger door on her side of the SUV, slid off the seat, and planted her feet on the cement curb. "Thanks for the ride."

I heard a faint chirp coming from her black BMW parked behind us, indicating she'd unlocked the doors with a remote key.

My gut told me the brother and sister knew much more than they had told us. "Thanks for coming with us today, Paulina. I'll be in touch in the next couple of days."

She winked and smiled. "I knew you were going to say that."

Almost as soon as we arrived home, Crusher asked, "Have you had anything to eat today?"

I became acutely aware of the hollow feeling gnawing at my stomach. "Now that you mention it, no. I'm starved."

"Do you want me to get some takeout or order a pizza delivery?"

"Can't wait that long." I opened the refrigerator and took a survey. I removed a loaf of farm-style bread, jars of mayo and Dijon mustard, a package of Hebrew National beef salami, and a head of romaine lettuce. Five minutes later, I wolfed down my sandwich in between gulps of Coke Zero.

Crusher ate his sandwich more slowly. "Do you have any more ideas about who killed St. Germain?"

"Mfff." I swallowed a large bite before speaking. "Not really. I was totally blindsided by Paulina and Mansoor's relationship. I always thought she was weird but trustworthy. Now I'm not so sure. Why would she keep something like that a secret? Is there any way you can do a background check on those two?"

"Babe. I'm a federal agent. You know I can." He gave a loud sigh. "Sometimes I think you love me just for my connections."

Oh brother. "Well, how can I convince you otherwise?"

His eyes twinkled, and he grinned in response. I knew I was going to sleep well that night.

The shrill of the phone woke us up early on Sunday morning. Annoyed at the intrusion, I poked Crusher in the back. "Answer it."

He mumbled and reached for the phone on his side of the bed. "Levy here." The phone kept ringing. "Not my phone." He grunted and laid back down.

The ringing stopped. "Probably a wrong number," I croaked in a morning voice. Less than a minute later, the ringing started again. *Oh crap. Who's calling this early on the weekend?* Eyes still bleary from sleep, I grabbed my phone from my side of the bed and slid the icon on the screen. "Hello?"

I instantly recognized my best friend's voice. "Martha? Something big is happening at Birdie's."

I sat straight up, suddenly wide awake. "What's wrong?"

"I don't know, but Ray doesn't want me to get involved. You'd better come fast."

"Can you give me a hint?"

"Two white vans and at least a dozen people, some in street clothes, some in white robes."

"Jeez." I looked at the clock. The big hand was on the three and the little hand was on the seven. "On my way." I ended the call and told Crusher why I was leaving.

"Do you want me to come with you?"

"I don't think so. If there's a problem, I'll text

you. Meanwhile, can you do that background check for me?"

He propped himself up on his elbow and reached for his phone. I sprinted out of bed (okay, maybe the word *sprint* is too athletic) and headed for a quick shower. By 7:30 I was out the front door, hair still wet.

Five minutes after that, I climbed the steps of Birdie's front porch and knocked on her door. Denver appeared and stepped back to allow me to enter. The normally quiet house buzzed with chatter. I surveyed the room and counted no fewer than eleven people ranging in age from their early twenties to AARP and beyond. Three of the older ones sat on the green sofa, and two occupied the easy chairs upholstered in a soft green chenille. Six more sat at the dining room table. All of them were eating scrambled eggs, buttered toast, and sweet pastries. Gobbling might be a better word for what they were doing.

I found Birdie in the kitchen, humming "Stairway to Heaven" and smiling as she poured cups of coffee. She arrayed the last of the baked goods from the Longaberger basket onto a stoneware platter and placed it in the middle of the kitchen table. I recognized the two white-haired people sitting there: Claytie and June Tolliver.

Yesterday I'd examined an early snapshot of the Tollivers taken at the Aquarius commune in Oregon, where Birdie first met Denver. June had been a blonde beauty with high cheekbones and laughing eyes. Now those cheekbones saved her face from total collapse, and her eyes looked as if they had forgotten how to laugh. She focused on the small plate in front of her and ate her breakfast with dainty bites.

In contrast, Claytie Tolliver's blue eyes homed in on me like a laser as soon as I entered the kitchen. His straight back and downturned mouth broadcasted a warning. He'd led the séance. Clearly, he enjoyed some kind of authority.

Denver introduced us and Birdie handed me a cup of hot coffee with cream. Then she gestured toward one of the two empty chairs. "Sit down, Martha dear, and have some breakfast."

I didn't need to be asked twice. I already had my eye on a sticky bun, a huge cinnamon roll topped with chopped pecans in a gooey brown sugar glaze. With a nod to proper decorum, I tackled the pastry with a knife and fork. "I'm happy to meet you both," I said between bites. "I'm sorry for the tragedy that struck your group yesterday."

June Tolliver glanced up and briefly met my gaze. "It was no tragedy. He had it coming."

"June!" One bark from Claytie and she pressed her lips together.

What a jerk. I decided to tackle him head on. "Who do you think killed Royal?"

He flinched. "Why ask me?"

I ignored his question and gestured toward the living and dining rooms, where eleven people sat scarfing down Birdie's delicious breakfast. "Didn't you bring all those people here?"

Again, he appeared off balance. "The Watsons left a note offering to help. We called last night."

"Then you have access to a cell phone?"

"Of course. Everyone does. Mystical Feather isn't a prison!"

"I'm asking you about Royal because you seem to be the one in control now. Am I right?"

He didn't reply right away, as if deciding how to answer.

June leaned toward him and murmured, "We're both in charge, remember?"

"Relax, Claytie," I said. "We saw you leading a prayer group when the shooting happened. So, I'm guessing you were able to convince your flock to leave the compound with you this morning."

"First of all," he sniffed, "we were not praying. We were communing with our spirit guides."

"My mistake."

"Second of all, these people are not my *flock*, they're my spiritual brothers and sisters. They joined June and me voluntarily."

"Why would all these people be eager to leave their home and follow you?" I stabbed the last bite of pastry with my fork, pushed it through the sugary goop on my plate, and popped it in my mouth. I enjoyed watching him shift in his seat.

"Not all of them live at Mystical Feather. Seven of them were there on a retreat. But all of them trust us because we have a history with Madam Natasha."

I glanced at Birdie. "A history?"

June Tolliver took a deep breath. "Claytie and I stayed at Mystical Feather for a year shortly after we left the Aquarius commune at the end of the sixties. When Natasha was still alive. It was a wonderful place back then. Peaceful, spiritual, affirming. We were her favorites, right, Claytie?"

"June . . ." He put his hand on her arm, but she shook it off.

So she does have some spunk. Good for her. "Did Royal live on the commune back then?"

"Oh yes." Her voice took on the authority of an eyewitness. "He and his twin sister, Eugenie, both lived there with Natasha in that big white house. Eugenie had the gift, just like her mother. But her brother, Royal, seemed lazy and not interested. He was distracted by his hormones, if you catch my meaning. Even though Natasha never said anything, I sensed he was a great disappointment to her."

"Junie . . ." Claytie's voice singsonged a warning, which she ignored.

"At any rate, Claytie and I left the retreat to start a business but returned to Mystical Feather for a month of classes and meditation every summer. After Natasha died, things began to change, but we continued our annual visits."

By this time, Denver had dragged a fifth chair to the table and he and Birdie sat listening quietly.

I reached for the pot in the middle of the table and poured myself another cup of coffee. "How did her death change things?"

June also helped herself to a refill. With each satisfying sip, she seemed to grow bolder. "We were here in nineteen seventy-five when Natasha died suddenly. We never even knew she was ill."

"How did she die?"

"They said her heart failed."

"*They* said? Was there an autopsy?"

June finally made brief eye contact with Claytie. He wagged his head once and muttered softly, "Don't . . ."

CHAPTER 13

June Tolliver seemed only too glad to talk about her suspicions. "They said Natasha had a weak heart. But she was a lifelong vegan in her early sixties with no prior heart trouble. Besides, she and I were like sisters. She would've told me if she were ill. No. Claytie and I became convinced she was helped to the grave."

There it was. The FBI had also suspected foul play. But where was the proof if the autopsy didn't find anything amiss? "Did you or Claytie ever discuss your suspicions with anyone?"

"No. Besides, Royal had her body cremated the day the coroner released it. Hard to prove foul play from a pile of ashes."

"Did you ever ask Natasha's spirit what happened to her?"

June sniffed. "She wouldn't say."

So much for being close as sisters. "Please clarify

something for me. I've heard Mystical Feather called both a commune and a retreat. How does that work?"

June sounded like she'd repeated her answer many times before. "Not everyone on the mountain lives there permanently. Aside from the members of the commune, we have various programs for visitors who are searching for spiritual enlightenment. In our bookstore we have brochures outlining classes lasting anywhere from one weekend to one month."

"What prompted you to live at Mystical Feather full time?"

Claytie placed his elbows on the table, closed his eyes, and rested his forehead in his hands. His voice came softly this time. "Seven years ago, we ran into Royal at a summer solstice celebration in Sedona, Arizona."

Just like Birdie and Denver. Sedona must've been Royal's preferred hunting ground.

Claytie continued. "He was very friendly. Said his mother's spirit often came to him when he needed advice. He claimed that while meditating the night before, her spirit told him to invite us to return to Ojai as full-time members of the commune. He called us 'the elect,' and we fell for it."

"Oh my goodness." Birdie gasped. "That's the same thing he told us."

Claytie squirmed and sighed. "Unfortunately, we weren't as smart as you. We should've checked him out beforehand. Instead, we sold our house and our business and turned over everything we had to the trust."

"What was your business?" I asked.

"We manufactured earth-friendly sandals made out of recycled tires and plastic bottles."

How much money can there be in old tire sandals?

Claytie seemed to read my thoughts. He puffed out his chest. "Zero Footprint Sandals are sold in seven different countries. We were very successful."

June reached over and stroked Claytie's neck. "Be careful, Papa. Remember your blood pressure."

Claytie ignored her. "As soon as Royal got hold of our assets, he started a spending spree. That red Mercedes is just the latest in a string of cars he bought over the years. I tried to talk some sense into him, but he ignored me.

"And that's when the visions started," said June.

Oh, oh, here we go. . . . "Visions?"

"Oh, yes!" she nodded vigorously. "Natasha's spirit returned to me again and again during my private meditations and in my dreams. She said I was the only one she could confide in. Just like the old days. She begged us to stay and protect her legacy of the Mystical Feather Society and all the people in the commune."

"The only one she confided in?" *That was pretty grandiose.* "She was your spirit guide, then?"

June looked at the table and chuckled. "More like best friend on the earthly plane! Royal was jealous of me because I was her favorite. Natasha urged me to stop him from depleting the trust. Since Claytie had business experience, she said he should take over the whole shebang."

Claytie took up his wife's narrative. "I cornered

Royal one day and convinced him that he needed some day-to-day help running the commune and the bookstore, as well as scheduling classes and retreats. And since I had business experience, I persuaded him to let me help."

"That's right," June said. "Royal was only too happy to leave the paperwork to someone else. We scheduled him for 'speaking tours,' often sending him away for weeks at a time. Of course, we never did anything without Natasha's approval."

"Junie and I took take care of the commune while he was gone."

"During his absence, how did you buy food and pay the bills if Royal controlled the finances?"

Claytie traced little figure eights on the tabletop with his finger. "He set me up as a second signatory on what he called the household account. It was a little pot of money we used to buy food and maintenance supplies. Royal transferred money from the trust to the household account on the first of every month. My task was to stretch those funds to cover the expenses for the next thirty days."

"It sounds like you took on a lot of responsibility," I said.

"Keeping the commune going was one thing, but, in other matters, we weren't as successful."

"How do you mean?" I asked.

June took an angry breath. "Royal liked only young women. He took advantage of them. Someone told us that, in the past, if one got pregnant, he'd force her to get an abortion. If she refused, he'd kick her off the mountain."

I put my cup on the table. "So, who will run the place now he's gone?"

The Tollivers looked at one another and Claytie said, "We certainly didn't plan on it, but I guess it's got to be me."

"Why do you say that?" I asked.

Claytie sighed. "I'm the one who's most familiar with the day-to-day operation of the commune. And nobody else wants to do it."

"You mentioned a small household account. What happens when that money runs out? How will you pay the bills?"

"Every time Royal went on tour, he signed a temporary power of attorney for me to use only in the case of emergency. I guess I'll be using that now."

June smiled and patted her husband's hand. "My husband is going to do everything he can to keep Mystical Feather going."

"Thank you for being so candid with me. I have one last question. There are rumors that Royal killed certain members in order to make room for new people who could replenish the money he bled from the Mystical Feather Trust. Do either of you know anyone who disappeared?"

June looked at the table and sighed. "Well, of course there was Natasha's mysterious death."

Claytie squeezed his eyes shut and rubbed them with his fingers. Then he looked up with fatigue written in the crevices around his mouth. "We heard rumors. The first one we know of was Royal's twin sister, Eugenie. She disappeared right after their mother's death."

"Do you think Royal killed her, too?" I asked.

"I asked, but Natasha's spirit was never specific," June said. "At first, everyone thought Eugenie had gone away to grieve for her mother. But she never returned, and nobody knows, to this day, where she went. Between you and me, I'm sure Royal killed her, too, and buried her body somewhere in these mountains."

After the Tollivers told me their story, I said, "That brings us right back to my original question. Who do you think killed Royal St. Germain?"

"It had to be someone outside our group," said Claytie. "You saw for yourself. We were in the middle of a séance when he was shot."

"Were there any members who didn't attend the séance?" I asked.

"The police asked us the same question. To my recollection, everyone was there."

Birdie grabbed the end of her braid. "Claytie, dear, is it possible someone left the séance without being noticed?"

"Everyone holds hands during a séance. They'd have to break the circle to leave, and that didn't happen."

Birdie persisted. "When we first looked in on you, everyone in the circle had their eyes closed. Isn't it possible someone took advantage of that and left without being seen?"

"No." Claytie shook his head. "Like I said, if the sacred circle is broken, the connection to the spirit world dies. It's like pulling the plug on the TV. No electric current, no picture."

When I'd been present at a séance led by Paulina,

she'd said the same thing. *Keep holding hands. Under no circumstances break the connection until I tell you it's safe to do so.* Always the Jewish mother, I had to ask. "You were sitting on the floor for hours. What would happen if someone urgently needed a potty break?"

June half-smiled.

Another member of the weak bladder sisterhood.

"We usually take care of personal needs before we begin."

"What's your next move?" I asked. "Does your power of attorney allow you to control the remaining trust funds? What about the property in Ojai?"

"Royal said the balance in the trust account was running dangerously low, but he said not to worry. He'd just recruited rich new blood."

"That means us." Birdie scowled. "How could we have been that gullible? After you discovered what was really going on, why in the world didn't you leave, Claytie?"

"Those who could leave, did," he said. "But like us, many of the members had given everything to the trust and had nowhere to go. Junie said we couldn't just abandon them."

"Especially when Natasha's spirit begged me to stay," June added. "We're going back up there today. There's a lawyer in Ojai. A former member. She'll help us figure that out."

"What will happen to the people who chose to stay on the mountain? For that matter, what will happen with the people in the other room who chose to leave? Do you have a plan?"

June smoothed back a loose strand of gray hair that had fallen over her eye. "Six of them are retreat visitors. Obviously, they had to cut their session short. The other five are commune members who are leaving Mystical Feather for good."

"That's right," said Birdie. "Denny and I have offered to help them reconnect with their families. Meantime, they'll stay with us until that happens."

"And the rest?" I gestured vaguely toward the north. "The ones who want to stay on the mountain?"

Claytie reached for the last of his coffee. "Like Junie said before, we're headed back there today. We'll continue to take care of everyone until this whole mess is resolved."

I pushed my chair back and stood. "Thanks for talking to me." I removed the small notepad I always carried in my purse and wrote down their phone number. Then I handed them a slip of paper with my number. "If you can think of anything else that might help, please give me a call."

Claytie took the paper but June plucked it out of his hand. "Why exactly are you investigating Royal's murder? You're not the law."

How should I answer? No, but I'm engaged to a federal agent and my son-in-law is an LAPD detective who once arrested me? "I feel guilty because I was the one who insisted we visit Mystical Feather."

"I thought that was Denny." Birdie looked confused.

"It doesn't matter." I wished I hadn't made a point of confusing her. "The hard truth is one person is dead, and you and Denver no longer have your Winnebago."

I didn't want to add that I suspected Paulina and her brother Mansoor might've had something to do with the murder. I still hadn't figured out how or why.

CHAPTER 14

Crusher's Harley was still parked in the driveway when I drove back home at ten. I pushed open the front door to find him sitting in the living room in one of the easy chairs and talking on the phone.

"Right. Keep digging. Okay, dude. I owe you one." He chuckled. "You're right. I owe you more like a hundred favors."

He ended the call and gestured for me to sit on the cream-colored sofa. "What happened this morning?"

I told him about my meeting with the Tollivers. "They kept the commune going, in spite of Royal's total mismanagement of the trust money."

"Did they have any idea about who might've killed him?"

"No. But June believes Royal not only killed Natasha, she also believes he killed his sister, Eugenie, and buried her body somewhere in the Ojai mountains."

"June could be right about Natasha, but she's way off base about Eugenie."

"Wait. What?"

He pulled up the image of a document on the screen of his smart phone. "My guy just sent me this." He handed me the phone so I could read more clearly.

My mouth fell open as I stared at the name Polinskaya. "Shut up! Are you sure it's the same one?" The 1976 marriage license was taken out in Princeton, New Jersey, by a man named Dr. Andre Polinskaya and his bride, Jean Saint. "That's her?"

"There's more. Scroll down." Three more documents appeared: birth certificates for Andre Jr., born in 1978, Paulina, born in 1981; and Michael (a.k.a. Mansoor the Magnificent), born in 1985.

"Holy crap, Yossi. This changes everything. Eugenie St. Germain changed her name to Jean Saint and married a year after her mother's death. Looks like she disappeared on purpose. Why? Did she suspect her brother Royal killed their mother? Was she afraid that if she challenged him for half the estate, he would kill her, too? If so, Paulina and Mansoor would have plenty of motive for killing their uncle." I looked at the screen again. "What do we know about the older brother, Andre Jr.?"

"Nothing yet. He seems to have disappeared, too. All records of him stop six months ago."

"Have you found any photos of him?"

"There's one." He swiped something on his screen

to pull up a three-year-old New Jersey driver's license photo of Andre Polinskaya. The unsmiling man had dark hair like his siblings, and his eyes smoldered like two lumps of coal.

"I can't swear to it, but I think I've seen this guy somewhere," I said.

"Well, he does look a lot like his siblings. Maybe that's what you see. . . ."

I shook my head. "No, that's not it." I poked my finger at the screen. "It's *this* man. I've seen *this* man before. Give me some time. I'll eventually figure out where."

After a lunch of grilled cheese on challah, Crusher went across the street to watch a football game with his friend Malo. Once he was gone, I called Lucy. "Are you alone? Can you talk?" I wasn't willing to cross her husband, Ray, until I knew he no longer blamed me for involving Lucy in another murder.

"Yeah, I'm alone. Our grandson Trey's in a soccer tournament this afternoon. I told Ray I didn't feel like going, which I don't. Those bleachers are *bow-coo* hard and cold on my rear. I've been waiting for your call. What happened at Birdie's this morning? Why are all those people from the commune in their house?"

I repeated everything I'd learned from the Tollivers and from Crusher.

"Dang! You're telling me Natasha St. Germain was Paulina and Mansoor's grandmother?"

"I know, right? When Mansoor said they come from a long line of psychics, he wasn't just blowing smoke."

Lucy said, "And that puts them right in the frame for murdering their uncle Royal. Are you going to tell the sheriff?"

"I probably won't have to. If they're doing background checks on everyone, they'll get to the same place soon enough."

"So, what are you going to do, girlfriend?"

"Not sure." I sighed. "Paulina and Mansoor have emerged as the prime suspects. But I still I find it hard to believe she could be a killer. I even find it hard to believe Mansoor could be a killer. He's too . . ."

Lucy chuckled. "I think *fastidious* is the word you're looking for."

"Right. Uh, I'm almost too afraid to ask. But until I know for sure, I'm going to be careful. Is Ray really mad at me for lugging you to another murder scene?"

"Oh, he'll get over it. He always does. And anyway, this time he's angrier at me than you because I fibbed about where we were going yesterday."

After I ended the call, I headed for my sewing room, where I did my best thinking. *How should I confront Paulina and Mansoor? Do they know what happened to their brother Andre Jr.?*

I had already cut each fabric shape for the Sunbonnet Sue blocks, along with its corresponding paper template. Now I prepared each shape for appliqué by ironing the paper template to the wrong side of the fabric. Freezer paper worked best, because the shiny side stuck to the fabric when heat was applied. The template shape was smaller than the fabric shape by a quarter inch, allowing me to fold the fabric edges toward the back and baste them in place, stitching right through the paper beneath.

This preparation was a tedious and slow process, but worth all the effort. When the time came to appliqué the shapes to the background square, the stitches would be hidden behind the beautiful folded edges. Once secured to the background, the basting stitches would be removed from each piece, and the paper template extracted through a small gap on the edge. Then the gap would be sewn shut. *Et voilà!*

Around four that afternoon, my phone rang. "Okay, Martha. I've been hearing you in my head all afternoon, and I know you want to talk to me."

There was no mistaking Paulina's voice. Lucy would've said Paulina was an amazing telepath, able to read my mind. I merely credited her call to a guilty conscience.

"And you'd be right. I have a lot of questions for you and your brother."

"Any chance we can take care of this over the phone?"

"Any chance the Kardashians secretly hate publicity?"

Paulina snorted in response. "How about tomorrow? My place at eleven. Mikey and I have some COW business to take care of tonight."

"I assume you're talking about Contacting

Other Worlds and not about shoveling patties in the barn."

This time her laughter boomed over the phone. "Sometimes there's not much difference."

She should know.

Monday morning at eleven I pulled into Paulina's driveway on Venice Boulevard in West LA. The cold air was filled with the delicious smell of beef and chilis cooking in a Mexican restaurant next door. At this point, I had no way of knowing whether Paulina and her brother killed their uncle. I could be walking into real danger. Just in case, I'd armed myself with a can of pepper spray and placed it within easy reach in my sweater pocket.

I lifted my hand but before I could knock, the door opened and Michael Polinskaya, aka Mikey, aka Mansoor the Magnificent, stood with a sheepish grin. He wore jeans and a long-sleeved black T-shirt. His long black hair was pulled back in a man bun. "Paulie tells me you want to talk?"

I edged past him and stood just inside the door, ready to escape if I had to. He plopped in a chair at the round table in the dining room Paulina always kept covered with a purple cloth.

Paulina appeared from the kitchen holding a tray with a pot of hot tea, three cups, and a half-empty plastic tray from a bag of Oreo cookies. She sat next to Mansoor and smiled at me. "I made a fresh pot just for you. I even added sugar, 'cause I know you like it that way."

Did she think I was crazy? Drinking something she could've poisoned? I sat at the table facing them. She poured three cups and placed the one with red roses in front of me. I ignored it. Mansoor drank from his cup almost immediately. Okay, the tea in the pot wasn't poisoned, but what if she'd placed poison in my cup before she poured the tea?

I crossed my arms and narrowed my eyes. "Not only was I shocked to learn the two of you are brother and sister, I also discovered Natasha St. Germain was your grandmother, her daughter, Eugenie, was your mother, and the dead man was your uncle. You didn't think those facts were important enough to share with me?"

"C'mon, Martha." Paulina held up her hand. "Don't get your panties in a twist. We didn't wanna tell you 'cause we couldn't be sure you and your friends would keep our secret."

I put my left hand in my sweater pocket and closed my fingers around the can of pepper spray. "Did you go to Mystical Feather to kill your uncle?"

Paulina gasped. "Of course not! Oh my God, I thought we were friends. How can you think such a thing?"

"Then tell me why you went."

The brother and sister glanced at each other.

Mansoor said, "About six months ago, Natasha's spirit came to me in a vision."

"You, too? She seems to be very fond of doing that."

He ignored my snarkasm. "Why wouldn't she? She said I was her favorite."

June Tolliver might disagree. "Go ahead, I'm listening."

"Natasha told me to ask Mama about the Mystical Feather Society. At first, I wondered how Mama would know about anything paranormal. She'd seemed barely interested in our careers. But since Natasha insisted, I went to Mama and asked her about the society."

"I was there," Paulina said. "Mama freaked when she heard Mikey say Natasha had talked to him. But when she calmed down, Mama told us who she really was. Up until that conversation, we had no idea she was Eugenie and that the famous Natasha St. Germain was our grandmother."

"Did she say why she kept that information from you, especially since you both turned out to be . . . what's it called?"

"Adept," Mansoor said. "People truly gifted with paranormal abilities are called Adepts. All three of us—me, Paulie, and Andre—turned out to be Adept. Natasha once confided in Mama that when she died, she planned to leave the society and the trust in Mama's hands, since the only gift Royal possessed was his personal charm. It wasn't until after Natasha died that Mama discovered her mother had left everything to her brother. Mama said she was hurt and confused."

"Why did Eugenie disappear? Why didn't she stay to contest the new will?"

Brother and sister looked at each other, sending some kind of silent signal.

Finally, Paulina addressed her brother. "Mikey,

she knows almost everything. We might as well tell her."

He nodded once and sighed. "Fine." He reached for an Oreo and nibbled around the edge in a circle.

Paulina clasped her hands in front of her on the table. "Mama told us that right after Natasha's death, her mother's spirit appeared in a vision."

Of course she did.

"Natasha told Mama there's a tree in southern India called *Cerbera odollam.*"

"We looked it up," Mansoor said. "It's known as the suicide tree."

"Natasha said she died because her tea had been spiked with the ground-up seed from that tree. After drinking the poison, Natasha slipped into a coma and died three hours later. It was the perfect murder because it looked like her heart just gave out." He made a poof sound. "Then she was cremated."

"Where would someone find *Cerbera odollam* leaves?"

"The thing is," Paulina leaned toward me and spoke in a confidential voice, "our uncle Royal had just come back from an ashram in southern India, where he had taken a group on a retreat. He must've brought the seeds back with him."

"Did Royal suspect your mother knew what he'd done?"

Mansoor shook his head. "Mama told her brother she was glad Natasha left him in charge. She said she'd always wanted to leave Mystical Feather and lead a normal life. And that's what she did. To stay safe and, after we were born, to keep us safe. That's why she changed her name and kept her past a secret."

Paulina noticed I hadn't touched the cup with roses on it. "Why aren't you drinking your tea?"

I fingered the can of pepper spray in my left pocket one last time. Then, using both hands, I reached across the table and switched our cups. "You first."

She rolled her eyes. "Really? You think I wanna poison you? Watch." She removed the cup with red roses from the matching saucer and swigged a large mouthful, put down the cup, and smiled. "See? No poison."

I looked at the cup I'd taken from in front of her. The loose leaves had settled to the bottom. I ventured a small sip of the sweetened black tea. Nothing happened. "So, back to Saturday. What was your plan once you got to Ojai? Were you going to ask Royal politely if he poisoned his own mother?"

"Oh no." Paulina flipped her wrist. "We already knew that much. We didn't have to ask. We were going to, ah, offer him sort of a deal. We wouldn't go to the authorities with what we knew if he'd make one small accommodation."

"And that was?"

"To take a golden parachute and hand over the Mystical Feather Society and Trust to us."

"A golden parachute? And what would that be, exactly?"

Mansoor eyed me across the table. "Our silence."

"So this visit was a shakedown. You two were essentially going to blackmail your uncle into giving you Mystical Feather."

Paulina examined her fingernails. "More like a hostile takeover. It's done all the time in business."

"Except the part about obstructing justice by concealing a murder. What did your mother, Eugenie, have to say about this plan of yours?"

"She has no idea we're doing this." Paulina said. "Her sixty-fifth birthday is coming up next month. We planned to give her the keys to Mystical Feather as a surprise present."

And a dead Royal today would ensure having those "keys" by next month.

CHAPTER 15

The pull of the chocolate cookies in the plastic tray distracted me. To be safe, I took a cookie from the middle of the stack. I pulled the two halves apart and raked the white filling with my lower teeth. It was the kind of Oreo with double the stuffing. "Is Natasha's spirit speaking to either of you right now?"

Paulina gave me the stink eye. "I know you're a skeptic, Martha, but we take these things very seriously."

"I know your mother changed her name from Eugenie St. Germain to Jean Saint and married a doctor. What kind of doctor is he?"

"Was," said Mansoor. "Our father died six years ago. He was a professor of political science at Princeton University."

"Did your father know your mother's real identity?"

Paulina shrugged. "Mama said he didn't. Our parents lived a very conventional life in the academic community."

"So, what did your conventional father think of your *gifts?*"

Paulina looked down with reddened cheeks. "We were an embarrassment to him, especially in his intellectual circle. That's why Mikey and I both moved to the West Coast. We figured it was easier that way."

"You said your father died six years ago. What did your mother do then?"

"She bought a fancy computer," Mansoor said. "She makes a nice living typing and editing academic papers."

After I had mined all the creamy white filling, I dunked the denuded chocolate cookie in my tea and changed course. "Tell me about your older brother, Andre Junior. Does he also have the gift?"

This time they glanced at each other without smiling. I'd hit a nerve.

Paulina said, "Why do you want to know about Andre?"

"Don't jerk me around, Paulina. Was he in on this plan of yours?"

She pressed her lips together and looked away.

"Where is he?"

Paulina shrugged, still avoiding my gaze. "Don't know."

"Look, you two. I know he dropped out of sight six months ago. What happened to him?"

"I told you, we honestly don't know." This time her eyes filled.

"When was the last time you saw him?"

"Six months ago. Just before he left for Ojai. He planned to infiltrate Mystical Feather. Andre said Royal wouldn't recognize him since our uncle never even knew we existed. Andre sent us an occasional text from inside the commune for about five months and then . . . nothing."

"So, you were hoping to find him on Saturday?"

"Yeah. Only we never saw him. I'm afraid Royal might've . . ." Her lips trembled.

She didn't have to finish the sentence. Paulina was afraid Andre could be dead and buried in the mountains, another victim of Royal St. Germain. Yet I had a gut feeling I'd seen Andre recently. His driver's license photo looked familiar.

Despite his germ phobia, Mansoor reached over and lightly touched the top of Paulina's hand with the tip of his fingers. Then he turned to me. "Are you going to grass on us?"

I shook my head. "I don't think I'll have to. If I can uncover your true identities, I'm sure the sheriff will eventually get there, too."

"Please, Martha." Paulina looked at me with pleading eyes. "I know it looks very bad for us, but we didn't kill Royal. We only wanted to get back Mystical Feather for our mother. Please. We need you to believe us. We need you to be on our side."

Mansoor swallowed hard and muttered, "And help us find our brother, Andre."

My gut told me Paulina and Mansoor were telling the truth. "Listen, I got involved in the first place because I was concerned for my friends Birdie and Denver. Right now, I feel kind of responsible for dragging you along." I frowned at them. "Even though you weren't truthful with me, I feel partly to blame for your predicament with the law." I stood to leave. "I'll do what I can."

"Thanks. I knew we could count on you." Paulina reached for my cup. "Sit back down and I'll read your tea leaves. A freebie for helping us."

Despite the fact I didn't believe in that stuff, I was curious about what she would say. I sat and waited while she turned the delicate china cup upside down and emptied the last of the liquid into the saucer. Then she peered inside at the leftover brown bits clinging to the side and bottom. "Hmm . . . I see a new person coming into your life." She looked up. "Big changes are ahead for you, Martha. Maybe not all of them will be pleasant. Do you want me to get out the tarot cards and do a reading? Again, no charge today."

Unpleasant big changes? I could see how someone vulnerable could be hooked by those vague warnings. Who wouldn't want to know more? Paulina was good at her craft. Very good. "No thanks. I'd rather be surprised." I pushed my chair back and rose. Big changes would be coming to their lives, too, no doubt in the form of a visit from the sheriff. "Thanks for the information. I hope you find your brother Andre."

On the drive back over the Sepulveda Pass to the Valley, I puzzled over the photo of Andre Polinskaya. Did he look familiar because he resembled his siblings? Or had I actually encountered him at some point? I wanted to show his photo to the Tollivers. Maybe they knew something. Of course, that would mean another trip to Ojai.

* * *

By the time I crested the Sepulveda Pass heading north on the 405, it was one in the afternoon and my stomach growled. A panoramic view of the San Fernando Valley spread below me, alive with thousands of vehicles scurrying around like ants in a nest. *Do I go home and forage in the refrigerator for the makings of a sandwich or do I choose any one of a dozen restaurants and treat myself to lunch?*

I chose the latter, eagerly anticipating a visit to my friend Rafi's restaurant on Ventura Boulevard in Encino. The thought of a hot falafel sandwich was too much to resist. Minutes later, I pulled into the little strip mall standing bravely between two towering glass office buildings. My little Honda Civic squeezed between a Jeep Wrangler and a new Mercedes SUV, the only space available in the tiny parking lot. I walked past the family-owned We Fix 'Em, a small appliance and sewing machine repair shop, and waved at the tall man standing inside.

The smell of cumin curled seductively around the door of Rafi's Middle Eastern restaurant. The bell over the door tinkled as I entered. Four men in casual clothes sat at a table in the back sipping from small cups that traditionally held Turkish coffee. I recognized a few of the Hebrew phrases they spoke. Two men in gray suits sat scarfing plates of shawarma and rice. One kept checking his big gold watch.

Rafi greeted me with a huge smile, wide arms, and a hearty "Shalom, Martha. *Ma nishma?*" How are you, or, literally, how is your soul?

I embraced the short but solid man. "*Tov, toda.*" Good, thanks.

He showed me to a table near the front window, where I could watch the passing traffic crawl along the busiest boulevard in the Valley. This part of Encino had become a major financial district, so spotting the occasional Maserati or Bentley wasn't that big a deal. Across the street, an Israeli bank building featured a clock on the outside with twelve Hebrew letters in place of numbers.

"The usual?" he asked.

"Yes, please. Falafel sandwich and a glass of iced tea."

The cook behind the counter had also seen me come in. With a smile and a nod, I watched him throw a round of fresh pita on the grill to heat while he scooped up balls of savory chickpea paste the size of walnuts and dumped them into a vat of bubbling oil. Then he cut the top off the hot pita and stuffed a bed of shredded cabbage, lettuce, and onions inside the pocket. When the balls of falafel were cooked through, he raised them out of the oil, briefly drained them, and then placed them in the bulging pita like eggs in a nest. Finally, he ladled a liberal amount of tahini sauce over everything, wrapped the sandwich in foil to keep it hot, and placed it on a plate to be served immediately.

Rafi knew what I liked. Along with the sandwich on the plate, he placed a tiny paper cup filled with a very hot green chili paste called *skhoug* and a bowl of pickled raw turnips. He set the plate and a glass of tea in front of me and sat in a chair on the opposite side of the table. While I tucked into my food, he said, "I haven't seen you in a while. *Ma hadash?*" What's new?

He ignored the fact that both my cheeks were stuffed with food. "Maybe you help with a little problem."

Tahini ran out of the side of my mouth and I erased it with a paper napkin. I made a motion in front of my mouth indicating I'd say something as soon as I swallowed. After some serious munching, I mumbled, "Sure, if I can."

"You remember Hilda?"

I certainly did remember Hilda. She was kind of a fixture in the temporary encampments along the Los Angeles River in Encino. She used to be a nurse before becoming homeless and felt a calling to help the sick as best she could. She made a little pocket money by recycling cans and bottles she gathered from the Dumpsters and garbage cans.

Hilda had helped me solve two murders. The first time she sold me an item she'd found in a Dumpster that provided an important clue. The second time she put me in touch with someone in the vagrant underground who had witnessed a murder. Hilda had formed a kind of bond with Rafi, and he agreed to let her sleep on the upholstered bench in his restaurant overnight in exchange for a little janitorial work.

"Sure, I remember," I said. "How is she?"

Rafi looked at the table and shook his head slowly. "She's good girl."

I smiled at his use of the word *girl* for the streetwise middle-aged woman with graying hair.

"Work hard. Honest. Don't ask for better from no one. But . . ." He looked up and I immediately read anxiety in his eyes. "I lose my lease in one month. They gonna tear down. Build condos. Offices. Too expensive for me."

"No! You're losing your restaurant? Please tell me you're going to reopen in another location."

There were dozens of Middle Eastern restaurants in the San Fernando Valley, but none were as good as Rafi's.

He shrugged. "I make good living in this country. Save money. Maybe I go back home to Afula. Open restaurant there."

Rafi gazed at me intently as I slowly decoded what he was really telling me. My friend Rafi was planning to return to Israel, which might have been a good thing for him. But he was also thinking about Hilda. Losing a safe place to sleep at night would be a huge setback for her. Where else would she find such an understanding "landlord" and friend?

"Ah," he nodded. "I see you finally understand problem. What to do, Martha?"

A glimmer of a solution began forming, but I'd need to do some research before I got anyone's hopes up. "There's a small chance I can help, but I need to talk to Hilda first. When does she check in every night?"

Rafi's smile lit up his dark eyes. "You help? *Mitzuyan*." Excellent. "I close at nine. Come back then. Wait here." He sprang up from the table and returned two minutes later with something inside a small paper bag. "Three baklavas." He winked. "One for you and two for Yossi. And no charge for lunch."

I thanked him for the food and promised to return later. I wasn't sure my plan would work, but it was worth a try, especially if I could save a soul in the process. I'd just add this task to the list of things I already had to do. Like finding out what happened to Andre Polinskaya and figuring out who killed Royal St. Germain.

CHAPTER 16

I woke up on Quilty Tuesday still thinking about my visit with Hilda the night before. I hoped my scheme would work out. I skipped my usual run to Bea's Bakery and Mort's Deli. Birdie had promised to bring my favorite applesauce cake made with plump raisins, and Giselle insisted on having lunch delivered from Spago in Beverly Hills.

I'd asked her, "Does Spago's deliver as far away as the San Fernando Valley?"

"They do for me," she'd answered.

Of course they did. When you were the sole owner of an oil company, maintained several houses scattered around the country, and traveled in your own private jet, people bent over backward to accommodate you.

Lucy arrived with Birdie and a young woman I recognized as one of the Mystical Feather refugees who'd been sitting in Birdie's house on Sunday.

The girl wore a white peasant blouse over a long cotton skirt reminiscent of the groovy sixties. Her red hair hung loose behind her back and her sad blue eyes revealed something was wrong.

I had to strain to hear her soft voice.

"Hi. I'm Ivy."

Birdie patted the girl's shoulder. "Ivy was fascinated with the quilts she saw in my house and asked if she could join us today."

I smiled a welcome, dragged a dining room chair to the living room, and invited her to sit. When she turned sideways, I noticed a big bulge under her blouse.

Birdie handed me a still-warm green glass jadeite baking dish covered in aluminum foil and smelling like cinnamon. She walked toward the middle of the sofa, fabric tote bag dangling from her arm. "Now that Denny and I are staying put, I'm glad I didn't give away all my fabric." She lowered herself gingerly onto the cushion, briefly rubbing her sore knees through the soft denim of her overalls. Then she reached in the bag and extracted a neat pile of multicolored fabric hearts already basted to freezer paper templates and ready to appliqué. "I'm going to make a quilt for Ivy's baby. I'll call it 'Mommy's Little Sweetheart.' "

I gaped at the large pile of three-inch hearts—representing hours of preparation. "Did you make all these since I saw you yesterday?"

Birdie waved her hand in front of her face and laughed. "Heavens no, dear. This is a UFO I've had lying around for years."

Quilters typically referred to abandoned projects as Unfinished Objects or UFOs. Serious quilters might have several tucked away in boxes or bags.

"Until I have the time to design another botanical appliqué, I want something to keep my fingers busy." She smiled at Ivy. "Making a baby quilt seemed like the perfect thing to do."

Lucy sat at her end of the sofa and crossed her long legs clad in skinny black trousers. A black turtleneck sweater and large gold hoop earrings completed the artsy urban look. She had brought her quilting supplies but no quilt. When she saw the confusion on my face she said, "I've decided to help your sister, Giselle, complete her Grandmother's Flower Garden quilt. At the rate she's going, it'll take her fifty years."

"Did I hear someone mention my name?" Giselle breezed through the front door, wearing a gray Eileen Fisher outfit of wide-legged pants and a long, loose jacket. Her green eyes, shiny auburn hair, and the red soles of her black stiletto heels were the only spots of color. In between, diamonds twinkled. She glanced at the newcomer. "Hello, I'm Martha's sister, Giselle. Who are you?"

"Ivy." The young woman flinched at my sister's forceful presence.

Birdie added, "She's staying with Denny and me."

Giselle sat in the easy chair and pulled out an orange "flower."

Lucy pointed to her. "See what I mean? It's the same one she was working on last week." She stretched her hand toward my sister. "Come on, girlfriend. You need help. Give me one of those."

"Gladly." Giselle handed Lucy a Ziploc sandwich bag with nineteen fabric hexagons inside: one yellow for the center of the flower mosaic, six dark blue for the first ring and twelve light blue for the outer ring.

My sister must've noticed the bulge under the newcomer's blouse. "My God, you're big. When is that baby due?"

Ivy placed a protective hand on the middle of her belly. "Three months."

Then Giselle did what she did best. "I don't see a ring on your finger. Who's the baby's daddy?"

At first the girl's eyes widened and then they filled with tears.

Fortunately, Jazz chose that moment to waltz into the house. He carried Zsa Zsa in his arms instead of inside her tote. Usually their outfits matched, but today Jazz wore a yellow knit sweater and the little Maltese wore a pink velvet dress. "Sorry we're late! We had to tinkle on the lawn."

"You or the dog?" Giselle asked.

"Very funny," Jazz said. "My poor baby managed to get her pinafore wet. So, we had to make an emergency wardrobe change in the car." He noticed Ivy and smiled. He took one of the dog's front paws and waved it back and forth. "Hello. My name is Zsa Zsa, and my daddy's name is Jazz. What's yours?"

Ivy's somber face split into the slightest smile, and the awkward moment passed.

Once everyone was settled with coffee and applesauce cake, Birdie tugged on the end of her braid and asked Ivy in a gentle voice, "How did you come to be at Mystical Feather, dear?"

"At first, I just wanted to find my spirit guide. Like, become enlightened, you know? I mean, I idolized Royal. He was so wise and kind. One day he told me privately that none other than his mother, Natasha St. Germain, came to him in a vision and said I was the one he was looking for his whole life." She smiled at the memory. "Me. Can you believe that?"

No.

"He was sweet. He got down on one knee and asked me if I could see myself with an older man."

Giselle rolled her eyes. "So, you let him get in your pants?"

"It wasn't like that!" Ivy scowled.

Giselle kept at her. "Really? What does he say now that you're pregnant?"

The girl looked up sharply, cheeks moistened by tears. "He's dead. I thought everyone knew that."

Giselle frowned at me. "Huh?"

I took a deep breath and told her and Jazz what happened on Saturday, leaving out the subsequent conversations I had with Paulina, Mansoor, and the Tollivers.

"What?" Giselle burst out. "You went to Ojai without me? I thought we were a team!"

"What about me?" Jazz asked in a hurt voice.

Birdie reached out and patted his hand. "It's just as well, Jazz dear. The sheriff might still think that one of us is the perp." Birdie loved cop speak. "You do have a rap sheet, you know." She referred to the time when Jazz was falsely suspected of murder. "But since you weren't actually there, you're in the clear."

Then she turned to Ivy. "I'll bet Royal was thrilled to know he was going to become a father."

Again.

"Not exactly. He told me a child would upset the harmonics of the mountain and he'd worked too hard to let that happen. He said the pregnancy was my fault and I needed to end it."

"But you didn't," Birdie urged gently.

"That's right. I thought if he could just see the baby, he'd change his mind." A shadow passed over her features. "Then last Thursday he told me I had to leave the mountain. Friday night I went to his house to try one last time. That's when I saw him with *her*. The new girl."

So here was someone else with plenty of reason to kill St. Germain. Would the parade of suspects ever stop? "I don't remember seeing you with the others on Saturday during the séance. Where were you?"

She turned to me with wide eyes. "I was there. With everyone else."

Lucy and I exchanged the briefest of glances, and I knew she was thinking the same thing I was. A pregnant girl would've stood out in that crowd and we would've noticed her.

"So, what will you do now?" Lucy asked.

"I'm going back to Indiana to have my baby. My aunt—she's the one who raised me—is sending me a plane ticket."

The lunch arrived from Spago Beverly Hills exactly at noon. Giselle tipped the driver two twenties and helped me unpack and serve the hot lunch. She'd ordered three salmon and truffle pizzas, Mediterranean salad with feta cheese, and a basket of warm parmesan garlic bread. "It's kind of off menu, but I told Wolfie to make it a dairy meal because you were kosher."

"*Wolfie?* You know Wolfgang Puck personally?"

She shrugged. "Who doesn't?"

Even with an extra guest, there was more than enough food to go around. At two, Lucy took Birdie and Ivy back home. Giselle and Jazz made no motion to leave, and I braced myself for what was coming.

"Okay, Sissy." Giselle leaned back and crossed her arms. "I know you. There's a lot more to the story you wouldn't tell us in front of Little Orphan Annie." She inclined her head toward the front door, which the pregnant Ivy had just closed on her way out.

Jazz jerked his thumb toward Giselle. "I'm with the rich girl. Dish."

I knew there was no escaping the inevitable. I began with my initial conversation with Paulina and Mansoor a week ago, finding the body of Royal on Saturday, the conversation with the Tollivers on Sunday, and ending with my second conversation with Paulina and Mansoor on Monday.

Jazz said, "*Bravo!* Now." His finger wagged. "Why did you deliberately exclude us from all the fun?"

"Fun? You call finding a corpse *fun*?"

"Oh, you know what he means," Giselle said. "We love a good mystery."

I sighed. What could I say to my sister? *You're too tactless to be trusted?* "The two of you would've brought our number up from six to eight strangers descending unannounced on the commune. That many people might've made Royal suspicious and defensive. We decided to keep things as simple as possible."

Giselle studied me through narrow eyes. I sensed neither she nor Jazz completely believed me.

I added, "What? I planned all along to tell you. But I waited until today when I could get you together. I didn't want to repeat the story twice."

Both their faces relaxed, and I knew they accepted my lie. Sometimes I scared myself with how dissembling came so easily to me.

Jazz put his sewing away and collected Zsa Zsa for their trip back to West Hollywood. He poised his hand over the front door handle. "You know how much Birdie means to me, right?" What he left unsaid was, *I better be included in anything that affects her life and her happiness.*

I rose from my seat to give him a hug. "Of course I do."

Jazz blew air kisses to the room and left.

I sat back down. "I want to run something by you, G." I told her about Hilda. "I know you haven't met her, but she's a warm-hearted person whom I trust. What do you think of my plan?"

"Well, I'd have to meet Mother Teresa first before I could pass judgment. But if she's as trustworthy as you say, I don't see a problem. What does she think about it?"

"She's still mulling it over. Until we know her

decision for sure, can we keep this just between the two of us? It's premature to tell anybody else."

"Of course, Sissy. I'll be the soul of discretion."

That will be a first.

Hilda's response came sooner than I expected. When she called at 7:15 that evening, I was in the middle of eating my solitary dinner of two Trader Joe's cheese tamales and watching *Jeopardy!*

"Okay, I'll do it. But only if everyone is happy with the arrangement. I'm reluctant to give up my work with the homeless, but my bones are getting too old for the rough life. If it hadn't been for Rafi's offer of a safe and relatively soft place to sleep at night, I might not've lasted this long."

"Perfect. As you may remember, every Friday night my family gets together to celebrate the Sabbath. Can you come this week? It will be the perfect time for everyone to meet everyone else."

"Sure. I remember that time a couple of years ago when I spent Friday night with you. Such a nice change from my normal routine."

I knew that living in the rough meant infrequent opportunities to attend to the basics like showers, personal grooming, and washing clothes. "I also remember you came early to shower and brought all of your laundry with you. Feel free to do that again."

"Thanks, Martha, but that won't be necessary. I've been working with the people who run the women's shelter in Van Nuys. They let me shower and do my laundry on a regular basis there."

We ended the call and I returned to *Jeopardy!* in time for the final answer. In the category of the Bible, the answer was "The name of King David's first wife." I shouted, "Michal! Who was Michal?" But nobody heard me.

I hoped that on Friday night, the ones who needed to listen would, indeed, hear me out.

CHAPTER 17

Before Crusher left for work Wednesday morning, I asked him to print out the photo from Andre Polinskaya's New Jersey driver's license. As soon as he was out the front door, I stuck the CD of Paul Simon's *Graceland* in my player and turned it up to maximum volume so I could hear it from every room. The African rhythms always got me moving on the days I had to do housework. I sang the chorus to "I Know What I Know" and bopped around the bedroom as I made the bed and gathered laundry. Later, in the kitchen, I took a break from unloading the dishwasher, closed my eyes, and undulated to the sweet harmonies of "Homeless." I thought about Hilda and how her life might take a more comfortable direction if everything worked out as I hoped it would.

Around eleven I received a call and turned off

the background music. "Ms. Rose, this is Director John Smith."

The FBI "mystery guest" Crusher had invited to Shabbat dinner last week.

"Oh? We're no longer on a first-name basis? What's the matter, John? Did my brisket give you heartburn?"

"I thought you were going to contact me with any information about St. Germain. You didn't think his being murdered in your friends' Winnebago constituted significant intel?"

Oh crap. I'd forgotten all about my promise to exchange information. "I'm truly sorry. It's not like I was deliberately scheming to hide anything. I was more interested in getting me and my friends off the mountain in one piece. And quite frankly, I just forgot about you."

"Ouch. That could hurt on so many levels. Only, it doesn't."

"So you found out about Royal's murder, anyway."

"The Mystical Feather Society and St. Germain in particular are both flagged. We were alerted the moment the Ventura County Sheriff responded to the nine-one-one. And wouldn't you know it? Your name popped right up in the middle of everything. Including the fact that the emergency call came from your phone. So, you may not've been thinking about me, but I certainly was thinking about you."

"Well, here's what I've discovered." I repeated the story already recorded in my formal statement to Detective Della Washington. Then I told him what I had learned from my conversations with the Tollivers, the pregnant girlfriend Ivy, and with the Polinskaya siblings Paulina and Mansoor. "They haven't heard from their brother Andre for a whole month. They're worried their uncle Royal may have killed him."

"The sheriff is quite capable of investigating that, along with the murder of St. Germain. So don't go poking around for new intel. You just might find trouble you can't handle. Remember, the killer's still at large. Be smart and gear down. Let law enforcement do their job."

Like I haven't heard that before.

Smith continued. "To change the subject, what will your friends the Watsons do?"

"I'm happy to report Birdie and Denver will not be moving to Ojai. They won't be losing everything to the Mystical Feather Society. In the end, the only thing they'll lose is their Winnebago, which is a small price, considering. By the way, did you know Mystical Feather was a clothing-optional retreat? We arrived during a naked séance."

Smith grunted. "That's a new one."

"So tell me, John. How much of what I told you did you already know?"

"I'm afraid that's classified."

"Oh come on. Really? That's all the feedback I get?"

"I can share the results of the autopsy. St. Germain was a sixty-five-year-old white male with a cirrhotic liver. He was six feet and one-half inch tall. He died from three gunshots to the heart. The first bullet was the kill shot, causing the victim to fall backward on the bed. The angle of upward penetration indicates the gun was positioned somewhat lower than the entrance wound. The second two bullets tell a more chilling story. The angle of entry indicates the shooter approached the fallen victim and shot from above. It was a cold and calculated execution."

I immediately pictured the diminutive Paulina aiming the gun up toward his heart. Could she be the killer after all? And then there was the pregnant girl, Ivy. Wasn't she also much shorter than Royal? On the other hand, the slope of the kill shot could indicate the shooter was sitting or crouching. Which meant anyone could've killed him. John Smith had given me no useful information. And he knew it.

I'd try to get information from Smith one last time. "The Polinskaya family is desperate to know if Andre is still alive, and I kind of promised I'd help. Can you give me something to take back to them?"

"No. You did a good job gathering intel. If you were younger, Ms. Rose, I'd encourage you to join the Bureau."

"*Jeez.* Was that supposed to be a compliment?"

"Yes. Unfortunately, at your present age, you'd be eligible for retirement, and that's what I strongly advise you to do now."

"Okay, okay, I get it. I'll contact you if I happen to hear anything new. Which is unlikely since I'm not investigating anything. So, don't be disappointed if you don't hear from me. Since I'm off the case."

He made a short huffing noise and ended the call.

I headed for my sewing room and looked at the photos of the missing man Crusher had printed out for me. I was sure I'd seen that face somewhere recently, but I couldn't pull it out of the back of my brain. Maybe it would come to me as many insights did—if I stopped obsessing. So I focused on my new project, the Sunbonnet Sue appliqué quilt I was making for my granddaughter. I needed to cut twenty twelve-and-a-half-inch squares from a background fabric for Daisy's quilt. Using the quilter's seam of one-quarter inch, each square would measure an even twelve inches once it was sewn in the quilt top.

I preferred to use a rotary cutter, a smaller, sharper version of a pizza cutter. The advent of that tool, coupled with acrylic rulers and cutting mats, enabled quilters to mass-produce precise geometric shapes. If our foremothers had sewing machines and rotary cutters, they would've used them gladly.

In preparation for accurate cutting, I ironed a three-yard piece of pink muslin, forty-two inches wide. Then I folded it in half lengthwise, lined up the selvedge edges, and ironed the fold. I repeated the process again to end up with a folded strip that measured ten and a half inches by one hundred and eight inches.

As I worked, I called my sister and told her about the call from Smith. "Even though he warned me to back off, I'm going back to Ojai tomorrow. I kind of promised Paulina and Mansoor I'd help them find their brother, Andre."

"I'm in, Sissy."

"I don't know, G. We'd be on our own. I can't take Paulina or Mansoor with me because they're still suspects, and it wouldn't look good if they returned to the scene of the crime. I don't dare ask Lucy if she wants to return, because I'm afraid Ray will ban our friendship forever."

"It doesn't matter, I'm . . ."

"The killer might still be up there, G. I wouldn't blame you if you decided to sit this one out."

"I've been trying to tell you, Sissy, that I want to go with you. I've got a meeting with a delegation from Taiwan tomorrow, but I'll just reschedule. They'll wait for me because they need a favor. So, I'm telling you, I'm in. When do you want to leave?"

"Early, maybe eightish." I pictured my sister yesterday in her Eileen Fisher outfit and Christian Louboutin stiletto heels. "Try to dress casual."

Giselle laughed. "Didn't you say this place was clothing optional?"

"Not *that* casual!"

"What about Jazz?"

"I'm calling him, too."

I ended the call with my sister and carried the long length of folded cloth over to the cutting table. I cut crosswise through the layers to get seven strips that measured twelve and a half inches by forty-two inches. I carefully unfolded and stacked the narrow strips one on top of another, matching the edges. The razor-sharp rotary cutter sliced across all seven layers of fabric every twelve and a half inches to make twelve-and-a-half-inch squares. Out of three yards of cotton fabric I ended up with twenty-one squares (twenty for the quilt and one extra) and lots of smaller, leftover pieces. The whole process took less than an hour, as opposed to the many hours it would've taken me if I'd used scissors to cut each square by hand.

Satisfied with the accuracy of my squares, I picked up my cell phone and called Jazz. "Are you interested?"

"*Mais oui!* Of course I am. Are we going in disguise like we did before?" He referred to the time almost a year ago when we posed as a cleaning crew to get inside a locked facility and interview a witness. "I still have the white boy 'fro wig somewhere in my closet."

"No, we're not going in disguise." While we talked, I used an ordinary pencil to mark the geographic middle of each background square for accurate placement of the appliqué. "But if you really want to blend in, you can remove all your clothes once we get there. . . ."

He gasped. "In front of Zsa Zsa? What kind of father do you think I am?"

I laughed and returned to finish my sewing project for the day. I counted out twenty plastic sandwich bags and placed one background square and all the appliqué pieces for it inside each bag, creating twenty little packets of sewing that were easily portable.

Later that afternoon I heard a cup of coffee calling my name. I stretched, glanced at the clock, and brewed one cup of decaf French roast. If I drank caffeine after two in the afternoon, I wouldn't be able to sleep at night. I carried my cup into the living room and sat on the sofa staring out of the front window, thinking about Ojai. Then it hit me. *Why wait until tomorrow to question the Mystical Feather people when a bunch of them are staying just five minutes away at Birdie's house?*

I finished my coffee, grabbed my purse, and drove to the Watsons'. Maybe I'd get some answers about the missing Andre. I knocked on Birdie's front door. Denver let me inside with a puzzled look. "Come on in. Was Twink expecting you?"

"No, and I'm sorry I didn't call first. But I had something important to ask your guests and thought this might be a good time to catch them before they go their separate ways."

He scratched his head and raised his eyebrows. "Everyone's here, all right. But some of 'em are meditating in the backyard. You might have to wait until they're through. They're sitting on the lawn buck nekked."

"I think I'll pass, thanks." The delicious aroma of spices and herbs came wafting out of the kitchen. "What's Birdie cooking? It sure smells good."

"Some kind of vegetarian thing for tonight. This crowd doesn't do barbeque. You'll find her in the kitchen with a couple other gals. I try to stay out of their way."

Birdie sat at the farm table in her kitchen drinking tea from a glazed pottery mug that had been thrown by hand, judging from the slight distortion in shape. "Martha. What a nice surprise. We've been cooking all day and I was just taking a break."

I spotted six loaves of home-baked bread sitting on the far end of the tile counter next to four pies cooling on wire racks

"You have to meet my new friends." She pointed toward two other women who were still working. "Everyone, this is my dear friend Martha."

The shorter woman looked like she belonged in a Dutch painting. She wore a long cotton skirt and peasant blouse, and a white bandana secured her long, chestnut brown hair. I guessed her age to be under thirty. She smiled at me with deeply dimpled cheeks and drawled with an accent somewhere east of Texas. "Pleased to make your acquaintance. I'm Anna from Savannah. I'm in charge of choppin' today." She reached into a huge bowl of raw vegetables, pulled out a large carrot that had already been peeled and cut it julienne style—on the diagonal. Each slice of the chef's knife knocked in a steady rhythm against the wooden cutting board.

I estimated the other woman to be in her fifties, judging by the silver threads in her long, dark braids and the thickening of her knuckles. She must've been one of the people who left the commune still clothed in a white robe because she now wore a white T-shirt and pair of old denim overalls I recognized as Birdie's. Many years before, my friend had skillfully embroidered a butterfly in rainbow colors on the bib. "I'm Hazel," the tall woman said in a somewhat less enthusiastic voice. Wielding a long-handled metal spoon, she stirred a huge pot of white beans seasoned with onions, garlic, and all those savory spices I smelled when I first arrived. "I'm in charge of the main dish tonight."

I took a deep, appreciative breath. "And it smells divine. I could tell the minute I walked into the house that something good was going on in here."

Hazel seemed to warm a little at the praise. She inclined her head toward Anna. "Beans are almost done. As soon as Pollyanna here is through cutting up those veggies, I'll add them to the pot just long enough to cook. Nothing worse than a pot full of mushy vegetables." She turned toward Anna. "Come on, girl. You finished with those yet?"

The shorter Anna handed over a large stainless-steel bowl full of chopped carrots, celery, potatoes, mushrooms, and shredded greens that looked like kale. She made a little curtsy. "Yes, your highness."

Hazel quickly added them to the boiling soup. "This dish was a favorite at Mystical Feather."

"I'm not surprised," I said. "How long did you live there?"

The taller woman screwed up her face and paused for five seconds. "Um, I think it was about seven years ago come summer."

"And how long have you been at Mystical Feather, Anna?"

She washed her hands in the sink. "Oh, I didn't live there, like Hazel and some of the others. I was just finishin' up a one-month retreat. I'm fixin' to go back home. Just waitin' for Meemaw to send me a plane ticket back to Georgia."

Birdie gestured for me to sit in one of the chairs. "Have a seat, dear. There's plenty of tea left." She hefted a white china pot and filled another hand-made mug with cinnamon-y smelling tea. Even with all her financial resources, Birdie wasn't the kind of person who would fuss over mismatched dishes. She pushed a pressed-glass plate of chocolate chip cookies across the table in my direction. "What brings you back so soon?"

I showed her a printed copy of Andre Polin-skaya's driver's license photo. "I'm trying to locate this man. His family is concerned because he was supposed to be living at Mystical Feather, but they haven't heard from him in a while. I'd like to ask the people from the commune who are still here if they recognize him and if they know what happened to him. His name is Andre."

Anna dried her hands and reached for the photo. "Like I said, I was only up there a month, but I'll take a look." She squinted her eyes at the photo. "Bless his heart. He looks familiar, but I'm not sure. . . . Does he have a beard now?"

I shrugged. "I don't know."

Anna walked over to the stove and showed the picture to Hazel. "What do y'all think, Hazel? Do you reckon this could be Freddy?"

"It would help if I could see." Hazel pulled a pair of glasses out of the overall bib and looked closely at the photo. "I don't know about any Andre. But this is definitely Freddy. He looked just like this when he showed up at Mystical Feather. He hadn't grown a beard yet."

Anna glanced at the photo again. "I think he looks better with a beard. I'm kinda partial to men with facial hair."

Hazel frowned. "You're *kinda* partial to any man with a pulse."

Freddy? I wasn't surprised Andre had changed his name. "When did he first come to Mystical Feather?"

Hazel looked up at the ceiling. "About six months ago I'd say. He was instantly popular with the younger women, being single and all."

Anna's jaw dropped. "*Younger* women? Don't deny it. You wanted him, too!"

Red spots dotted Hazel's cheeks and her hands flew to her hips. "A lot you know, missy."

Before they got into a full-blown argument, I asked, "Do you know what happened to him?"

The tall woman pushed her brows together, confused. "Happened? Nothing happened. He's one of the people who chose to stay behind at Mystical Feather."

"I was there last Saturday. I don't remember seeing him in the yurt," I said.

Hazel went back to tending the pot of the beans and veggies. "Oh, Freddy was there, all right. There's a bookstore just as you turn into the driveway to the retreat. Freddy's job is to run the bookstore and sign people up for classes. He's always working down there. That's probably where he was on Saturday when . . ." Her voice became sober and she said quietly, "when the trouble happened."

Of course! Now I remembered where I'd seen Andre before. He had come to the door of the bookstore and waved when the Winnebago first turned onto the driveway from Sulphur Mountain Road. I didn't connect him to his driver's license photo because the man in the bookstore had grown a beard. I didn't know what made me more excited—the fact that Andre Polinskaya was alive and well or the fact that my "little gray cells" had been working all along.

But the news about Andre raised more questions. Why did he stop communicating with his family? More important, where was he when St. Germain was killed? I could think of only one way to find out. Go to Ojai as planned and ask Andre/Freddy himself.

CHAPTER 18

Thursday morning I sat in the back seat of Giselle's midnight blue Jaguar so Jazz could have more legroom in the front passenger seat. The car had purred its way north on Highway 101 and transitioned smoothly onto Highway 126 east-bound. I told them what I'd discovered about Andre the day before.

"If we already know he's alive, why are we on our way to Ojai?" Jazz asked. "I had to find a babysitter for Zsa Zsa. She hates me when I do that. I also canceled a fitting this morning with Johnny Depp. I never cancel Johnny. He's my best client." Jazz was a busy men's fashion designer who created clothes for high-end clients, like Depp. He also had a secondary business creating clothing for their high-end pooches.

Giselle briefly twisted her head to look at Jazz.

"Big deal. I canceled a whole *country* to be here." She referred to the delegation from Taiwan waiting for her back in the corporate offices of her oil company. She paused, then glanced at me in the rearview mirror. "By the way, why *are* we going to Ojai?"

"Don't you want to find out what Andre has been up to? Maybe solve another murder while we're at it?" I asked.

Jazz gasped. "What if Andre's the killer? What if Paulina and Mansoor knew all along he was alive and schemed with him to kill their uncle?"

"Jazz is right, Sissy. We only have Paulina's word for it that Andre went missing one month ago."

They were correct. I knew only what Paulina and Mansoor had chosen to reveal. "You're right." I nodded in deference to the truth. "I have no proof there wasn't a grander scheme at play involving all three siblings. But," I pointed to my middle. "I have this gut feeling that Paulina and Mansoor didn't kill Royal. And I believe they really don't know of Andre's whereabouts."

"My Sissy's gut is good enough for me," Giselle lightly tapped the steering wheel for emphasis.

Jazz sniffed. "May I remind you, Giselle, that I have known our *petite* Martha for longer than you have. She hasn't always been right."

A good thirty years had passed since anyone could honestly call me "petite." I nevertheless enjoyed the moment.

"Okay, you have a point, Jazz." My sister changed lanes, preparing to exit the freeway. "Tell you what. I can turn this car around right now and take you back. Then you can toddle back to West Hollywood and do Johnny's fitting after all."

"Are you kidding?" Jazz gasped. "Don't you dare turn around. I'm only saying, Martha could be wrong. We need to be careful. Stick together. That's all I'm saying. . . ." His voice trailed off into silence.

Giselle laughed. "I thought so." She took the next exit, but it was to transition on Highway 150 going north to Ojai. "Tell me when we get close to Sulphur Mountain Road."

Twenty minutes later I told Giselle to slow down. "As soon as we get to that line of green Dumpsters, turn left."

She followed my directions and the Jag easily continued up the winding mountain road as if it were a midnight blue cat padding around in its native habitat. Five minutes later we reached the top.

"Look at that view." Giselle slowed the car to take in the grand vista of the narrow Ojai Valley spread below to our right. Oak trees and chaparral dotted the mountainside right down to the highway, which wound like a thin, gray snake past ranches and into town. Across the valley, the sun chased away the morning shadows on the pink Topatopa Mountains.

A metal mailbox sat on top of a wooden post at the beginning of a poorly paved driveway on our left. A wooden sign underneath announced MYSTICAL FEATHER SOCIETY. We turned into the driveway and almost immediately arrived at the adobe building with round Spanish tiles on the roof that housed the bookstore and teahouse.

"Park here." Before we left the Jag, I showed Giselle and Jazz Andre's driver's license photo. "This is him, although he has a beard now. Just pretend we're interested in signing up for a retreat. Don't say anything about Paulina and Mansoor or the murder. Let me do the talking for now. Okay?" I looked pointedly at my sister, who didn't know the meaning of tact or diplomacy.

"Of course, Sissy. Don't I always?"

I could write a book.

The three of us got out of the car. Giselle had dressed casually as I'd requested. She wore a pair of black tights, short black leather boots, and a sky-blue long-sleeved cotton tunic that ended just above her slender knees.

The last short skirt I wore was back in the '80s before my knees got too pudgy ever to appear in public again. In contrast to her elegant figure, I wore my usual white T-shirt, size sixteen stretch denim jeans, and navy blue Crocs.

Jazz also dressed in his version of Bohemian casual. He sported a yellow shirt with a mandarin collar that could have come from the early '70s. He'd rolled up the cuffs of his khaki chinos to show off his slender ankles and sockless feet in a pair of white espadrilles. I was pretty sure no one would suspect us of being amateur homicide investigators.

Opening the door to the bookstore triggered a tinkling sound from the bells over the door. The air smelled of sandalwood and patchouli. I guessed the red Mexican pavers on the floor served to keep the building cool in the hot Ojai summers. In the middle of the room, a glass counter held crystal jewelry, essential oils, incense, tarot card decks, and other small items for sale. A crystal ball about the size of a large grapefruit nestled on a small wooden bowl right in the middle. A cash register and credit card reader sat on top of the case.

Well-stocked bookshelves lined the three walls to our right, with the largest section devoted to the works of Madam Natasha St. Germain. Four chairs upholstered in purple velvet were pushed around a low table in the middle. To our left a small tea room with lace curtains over two windows held four square wooden tables, each with four chairs. A sign in the back read GENDERLESS RESTROOM.

A skittish young woman wearing an apron over her white robe stepped from a behind a door toward the back of the room. A wreath of delicate chamomile flowers sat on top of her long, blonde hair. "Hi. My name is Little Fawn. May I help you?" She smiled.

Giselle stifled a snort.

I promptly poked her hard in the small of her back.

"Ouch!" She frowned at me and stopped.

I put a weary-traveler smile on my face. "If you're serving tea, we'd love some. We've spent the last hour and a half driving up here from LA."

The young woman gestured toward the tables and chairs. "It's a little early for our afternoon tea. The pastries haven't arrived yet. We bake them fresh every day. But I can serve you some plain tea if you like."

I said, "That would be lovely. Do you have any literature on your retreats to look at while we wait?"

Jazz said in a voice that was a little too loud, "We're definitely interested!" One scowl from me and he sank back into silence.

"Yes, of course!" Little Fawn beamed, handed us three brochures, and disappeared through the door in the back.

"Looks like a smorgasbord of expensive *woo-woo* classes." Giselle chuckled. "Look at this one-day workshop: 'Reading Auras for Beginners,' taught by June Tolliver. Isn't she the one who's best friends with Natasha's spirit?"

"Allegedly," I said.

"Here's another," she continued. "A one-week class on 'Finding Your Spirit Guide,' and it's taught by Claytie Tolliver. It looks like the Tollivers have cornered the market on teaching around here."

Jazz made a low whistle. "Look at how much they charge for a month's stay at the retreat. It says, 'You will learn how to conduct your own séance' and it's also taught by Claytie Tolliver. Prerequisite is the class on finding your spirit guide. If you sign up for both courses, you get a package deal."

I was more interested in a pair of two-day workshops called "Introduction to Tarot Card Reading," and "Advanced Tarot." The instructor was listed as Freddy Pea. P for Polinskaya.

Minutes later, the young woman brought out three individual metal teapots full of hot water. I selected a bag of licorice tea from a wooden presentation box and dunked it in my pot. "I've been looking over the brochure, and I'm really excited about this intro to tarot workshop. When does the next class begin?"

"Freddy usually holds them over the weekend. I believe he's teaching one this Saturday and Sunday."

"Would it be possible to talk to him first? Is he available now?"

She sighed. "No, he's taking this week off to help with the funeral arrangements for someone."

"Do you mean Royal St. Germain?" Giselle asked.

Oh no. I sent her a mental message. *Don't go there, G.*

"You heard about him?" the girl asked in a small voice, eyes filling. "I've only been here three months, but he took me under his wing. He said the spirit of his mother, Natasha St. Germain, told him I was special." Her voice caught in her throat. "Royal was a great man. Gifted. Generous. Loving." She sniffed. "Now he's gone."

Giselle narrowed her eyes. "I heard he liked young girls. You weren't sleeping with the old geezer, were you?"

I kicked Giselle under the table, but she ignored me.

The color drained from the girl's face. "I don't know what you're talking about!"

From the way she marched through the door to the back room, I could tell Giselle had hit a nerve. Could this be the "new girl" Ivy talked about?

I scowled at my sister "Nice going, G. You just made it harder to talk to Andre—if not impossible."

CHAPTER 19

Little Fawn didn't return to the tea room while we drank our tea. When we finished, I walked to the glass counter in the middle of the room to pay and waited for two minutes, but the girl never reappeared.

"Stay where you are," I said to Giselle and Jazz. "I'll go find her." I walked to the closed door in the back of the bookstore and knocked. When nobody responded, I knocked again. "Hello? Is anyone there?"

Silence.

I pushed the door open wide enough to peek into the small room inside. An efficiency kitchen, big enough to make and serve tea, took up half the space. A laptop computer sat on a small desk in the other half of the room, along with a file cabinet and a small office chair with a swivel seat. The girl was still MIA. I spotted a door leading outside and carefully pulled it open. Three concrete steps led down to the dirt below. Beyond that was a thicket of oak trees and underbrush.

Little Fawn sat on the top step with her face in her hands, crying softly.

I cleared my throat to let her know she was no longer alone and sat on the step next to her. At first I said nothing until the storm of tears subsided. Then I touched her softly on the shoulder. "Are you all right?"

She shook her head, hiccupped, pulled a tissue from a pocket in her apron, and blew her nose. "No!"

"Please forgive my sister. She really didn't mean to hurt your feelings. Sometimes she says the worst things without thinking about how they'll affect other people."

When the girl didn't get up to leave, I dared to gently place my arm around her shoulders.

She leaned slightly toward me and accepted the comfort I offered.

"I can see how badly you miss Mr. St. Germain. He must've made you feel very special, like you were meant to be together."

She turned her head to look at me, her red-rimmed eyes wide with hope. "Do you really think so?"

I smiled. "I don't question your feelings for a moment, sweetie. But the fact is, Royal was paying child support to at least three other women who had been members of Mystical Feather, just like you. Plus, there's one young woman who is now carrying his baby. You might know her. Ivy?"

Little Fawn nodded. "Yes. She came to his house

last week while I was there and accused him of some awful things. After he sent her away, he told me she was disturbed and not to believe her. Are you saying she was right?"

I took a breath. "What I'm saying is Royal had a reputation for seducing young girls. You weren't the first. And if he had lived, the moment you became pregnant, he would have rejected you, just like Ivy and all the others before you."

Little Fawn stared at the distance, deep in thought. "I believed him. You know? He was so sweet."

We sat in silence a little longer, then she pulled away and rose. "I guess I'd better go back inside. I'm subbing for Freddy all week long."

"We need to pay for our tea," I also stood. "We'd like to sign up for Freddy's class this weekend. Do we do that here in the bookstore?"

"Yes. You'll have to buy a deck of tarot cards, unless you already have some?"

I shook my head.

"Okay. There's also a couple of books you'll need. I'll show you everything."

Giselle and Jazz sat waiting for us on the plush purple chairs in the bookstore area. Giselle jumped up when she saw us. She opened her mouth to speak and stopped when she saw me make the slightest negative movement of my head.

"Little Fawn is going to sign up each of us for the tarot workshop this weekend. We need to buy some items for the class."

"Oh, that's super terrific!" Giselle took out her credit card. "I can hardly wait to tell my own fortune."

Jazz finished filling out his enrollment form and handed it back to the girl. "Are pets allowed?"

We left Little Fawn in the bookstore and drove down the mountain in search of a restaurant in the town of Ojai. Fortunately, it was Thursday and we didn't have to contend with the usual weekend competition for parking spaces. We ended up at a tiny Mexican restaurant on Ojai Avenue. The waitress handed us menus that featured only vegetarian dishes.

Jazz ordered two cheese enchiladas with rice and beans, which he said were delicious. Giselle, ever mindful of her figure, ate a taco salad after she removed most of the sour cream, cheese, and guacamole. The only thing left was the lettuce. I ordered a taco with a wheat-based ground beef substitute on a bed of shredded baby kale in a blue corn tortilla. I should have ordered the bean and cheese burrito.

Instead of eating, Giselle mostly rearranged the lettuce with her fork. "So, what did Little Bambi have to say for herself?"

"Her name is *Little Fawn*," Jazz corrected her. Then he looked at me. "Yeah. What happened back there?"

I sighed and placed my mock taco back on my plate. "Poor thing was crying her eyes out." I gave Giselle the stink eye. "Honestly, G, don't you ever think before you open your mouth?"

Jazz's expression was sober. "You do have a

problem, Giselle. The first step is to acknowledge you're in trouble. The second is to ask for help."

My sister just rolled her eyes.

"Remember I told you what Ivy said about being exchanged for 'the new girl'? Well, I'm now sure that girl is Little Fawn."

"So I was right," she said. "Bambi *was* sleeping with the old geezer."

Who could argue?

After lunch we strolled down the street to visit the small Ojai Museum, which featured exhibits on the flora and fauna of the area and artifacts like stone tools from the Native American Chumash culture. We learned the name *Ojai* came from the Chumash word for "nest." A photographic exhibit documented the development of Ojai under the aegis of Edward Libby, the wealthy owner of the Libby Glass Company. Some exquisite examples of his best pieces were displayed in an enclosed glass case. Photos of remarkable local architecture were featured in another room. For a small museum, the exhibits were expertly designed and constructed by Roger Conrad, a local professional. By two in the afternoon, we headed home.

Giselle dropped me off at my house before four, in plenty of time for me to hop in my Honda Civic and buy almost all the groceries for Shabbat dinner the next day. The challah and dessert I'd get fresh from Bea's Bakery in the morning. I wanted the meal to put everyone in a good mood when I unveiled my plan to help Hilda.

* * *

By late afternoon on Friday, savory cooking smells began to fill the house. I put the finishing touches on the dining room table set for eight people: Quincy and Noah, Giselle and her fiancé, Harold, Uncle Isaac, Crusher, Hilda, and me. I was already pricing highchairs for when Daisy, my five-month-old granddaughter, would be big enough to join us at the table. I set the kiddush cup with kosher wine and plate of braided challah near Uncle Isaac's place at one end of the table. As the patriarch of our family, we always gave him the honor of reciting the blessings before the meal.

I covered the challah with a white linen cloth my bubbie had embroidered as a young bride. It bore an image of a plump bunch of grapes in purple, blue, and green threads and the words *L'kvod Shabbat v'Yom Tov.* In honor of the Sabbath and Holidays. I hoped my little granddaughter would one day use the same challah cover on her own Sabbath table and think loving thoughts about *her* bubbie. Me.

After a hurried shower, I towel-dried my shoulder-length gray curls and sprayed a liberal amount of my favorite rose perfume on my neck, shoulders, arms, and breasts. A glance at the clock told me I still had a half hour before people began to arrive at six. I slipped into my special outfit of long black skirt, pink silk blouse, and my grandmother's pearls. As I donned my strappy black heels, someone knocked on my front door. I hurried to the living room and stared at an unfamiliar middle-aged woman standing on my front porch.

She smiled. "Hello, Martha."

I frowned and desperately tried to remember where I'd met her before. Blonde streaks wove through her sandy-colored hair, which had been cut stylishly short around a weathered, tan face. A shade of light pink lipstick outlined her warm smile. She wore a cream-colored blouse under the slightly baggy jacket of a black pantsuit. Her only jewelry was a pair of wide gold hoops in her ears. Her smile broadened with amusement. "Aren't you going to invite me inside?" She gestured toward the living room with her hand.

The voice was familiar . . . as were those rough hands. The nails were cut short and the fingertips blunted by hard work. I looked back at the eyes twinkling in her face and my jaw hit the floor. "Hilda?"

She laughed and stepped inside. "The one and only."

"You look terrific."

"I figured I'd better make a good impression. This is a job interview, after all. My friend Brandy is the director of the women's shelter. I needed a second opinion and asked her to come shopping with me at the Goodwill store. We picked out the clothes and the earrings. Rafi insisted on paying for everything, including the new hairdo. I tried to talk him out of it, but he felt bad about closing the restaurant. He said it was the least he could do."

Hilda followed me into the kitchen. "Can I help you with anything?"

"Absolutely not. You're a guest tonight."

She leaned against the apricot-colored marble counter on the kitchen island and watched while I basted the three chickens roasting side by side in a large pan. I gathered some of the juice from the birds with the large plastic syringe and dribbled it over the chunks of rosemary potatoes roasting in their own pan.

"I haven't the first idea about how to cook kosher," she said.

I closed the oven door and straightened up. "Don't worry. You're smart. You'll learn."

We chatted amiably until Crusher came home. He hadn't seen Hilda for a couple of years, ever since he'd led a caravan of bikers into a homeless encampment to distribute quilts and personal hygiene supplies. He kissed me hello and grinned at our guest. "Nice to see you again."

"Happy Sabbath." She bit her lip. "Did I say it right?"

Crusher nodded. "Perfect. Happy Sabbath to you, too. If you ladies will excuse me, I've got to get ready." He didn't deposit his badge or shoulder holster on the table in the foyer as he usually did. Every Friday night, or whenever we had company, he wore them into the bedroom and stashed them out of sight.

Quincy, Noah, and the baby were the next to arrive.

Hilda's face softened as she gazed at my tiny granddaughter. "How sweet she is. I delivered a baby a few months ago who'd be about the same age."

Noah perked up and he smiled broadly. "Are you a doctor?"

"I used to be a nurse. Sometimes a midwife, when it's needed."

My son-in-law looked confused. "'Used to be? Sometimes?' Where do you practice?" The tone of his voice had gone from friendly to suspicious.

"Among the homeless." Hilda looked at him evenly, waiting for the next question in what was turning into an interrogation.

"What organization do you work with?"

"None. I work on my own."

"Without proper medical supervision? You'd better explain."

The happy optimism slid off Hilda's face and she looked at her hands. "Maybe this was a mistake. Maybe I should go. . . ."

I could've throttled my son-in-law, but my daughter beat me to it. "Noah!" She glared at him. "It's really none of your business, is it?" Then she reached out and squeezed Hilda's hand. "Please, please, please, don't let anything my husband says bother you. He can be a real idiot at times. I think the work you do is awesome."

Giselle and Harold arrived, helping my uncle walk slowly into the house. Uncle Isaac carefully measured each step all the way into the living room. Giselle helped lower him into one of the easy chairs.

"*Veh!*" he sighed. "It's no picnic getting older."

Hilda walked over to his chair and squatted down to be at eye level. "Do you remember me?" She smiled encouragement.

Uncle Isaac frowned and peered at her, searching for a clue. "I never forget a face. But maybe it's my age. I'm sorry. We've met before, maybe?"

Hilda smiled broadly. "Yes, we met a couple of

years ago. On a Sabbath just like tonight. I don't blame you for not recognizing me. I recently changed my appearance. My name is Hilda. I work with the homeless."

Uncle Isaac's face lit up with instant recognition and he beamed at the woman in front of him. "*Aber zicher!*" Of course. "You are that poor woman who was sent to prison."

"What?" Noah burst out. "You're a *felon*?"

"Shut it, Noah!" I glared at him. "Not another word. Do you understand?"

He opened his eyes wide with shock but kept his lips together as I had just commanded.

Hilda reached out and gently grasped Uncle Isaac's hand. "You have a very good memory, I see."

"Sit here." Uncle Isaac indicated she should take the easy chair near him. As soon as she sat, he said, "How have you been? Do you still help those poor homeless people, *Gott benschen zeh*?" God bless 'em.

Hilda drew a deep breath. "Well, that's one of the reasons Martha invited me here this evening. I'm afraid I'm getting older myself. Every day it gets harder and harder to live rough. That kind of work takes someone younger and stronger than me."

Uncle Isaac pinched his forehead, clearly distressed. "But where will you live? What will you do?"

"I'm a hard worker, but I need a real bed at night. I hope to find a job as a live-in helper with someone." Hilda glanced at me as if to say, *You take it from here.* She excused herself and asked for directions to the ladies' room.

As soon as she left the room, Giselle said in a quiet voice, "I like Hilda. You're right about her."

Encouraged by my sister's approval, I said, "I've got an idea. Uncle Isaac, what would you think about Hilda staying with you for a while? She needs someone to give her a break."

He looked at me with a sparkle in his eyes. "What? You think I'm a *shmegege*? I know exactly why you invited her tonight." He paused and looked at his hands shaking slightly with involuntary tremors. "*Nu?* I could use a little help."

My uncle might have been old, but, like he said, he was no fool. "So that's a yes? About Hilda?"

"*Shoyn. Fartik.*" Fine. Already done.

"You're such a *mensch,* Uncle. I knew I could count on you."

Now the next thing I had to worry about was getting to Ojai early in the morning and talking to Freddy/Andre.

CHAPTER 20

The Mystical Feather brochure said Freddy's beginning tarot class started at nine. Giselle, Jazz, and I left my house in Encino at seven on Saturday morning. At that hour the freeways and highways bore little traffic. My sister's midnight blue Jaguar pulled into the parking lot of the Mystical Feather bookstore in Ojai at 8:30 and parked next to a gray Prius.

"Before we go inside," I said, "I want to make sure we all agree on the game plan."

Giselle pulled down her sun visor and looked into the small mirror. "Go on." She applied red lipstick to go with her red-and-white-striped shirt. "I'm listening."

"We don't want Freddy to suspect we're there to spy on him. So, don't call him Andre, whatever you do. We go in there as students eager to learn about tarot."

"So, when are we going to tell him we know who he really is?" Giselle asked.

"We keep our mouths shut, *Giselle*," I looked pointedly at my sister, "and do *not* mention Royal's murder or anything about the Polinskaya family. As far as Freddy is concerned, we're just ordinary people."

"Fine." Giselle sniffed. "I can act ordinary."

That'll be the day. "If we get a chance to talk to him in private, I will be the one to ask questions. Agreed?"

Giselle nodded.

Jazz yawned and stretched. "I had a late night. I hope the guy is interesting. Otherwise, I might fall asleep in class. And I won't even talk about Zsa Zsa. She hardly spoke to me on Thursday when I picked her up from the dog sitter. You can imagine how incensed she was when I took her back there this morning. She looked straight at me, barked once, and peed on my shirt."

I looked at the front of his coral-colored polo shirt tucked into his tan trousers. "I don't see any stains."

"Of course you don't. I had to rush back home and change my outfit. I barely made it to your house on time." When we got out of the Jaguar, he inspected my clothes. "I don't think I've ever seen you in that blouse before. Is that from Guatemala?" He pointed to the parade of llamas cross-stitched in primary colors around the neck, puffy sleeves, and hem of the white shirt.

"Yes. It's hand embroidered. I thought I'd look more authentic as an aspiring fortune teller if I wore something ethnic and colorful." I tied a brightly flowered scarf around my gray curls and knotted it at the back of my neck. "What do you think?"

Jazz put one hand on his hip and the other on the side of his face and studied my clothes. "As a cultural artifact, I find the blouse understandable. As a piece of grown-up clothing, I find it almost unforgiveable. But I get what you were going for."

"You do, huh?"

"Yeah. Guatemalan Gypsy Casual."

I ignored his snarkasm and headed for the bookstore. "Let's go inside."

The furniture inside the tea room had been re-arranged to accommodate the class. All four tables were pushed together in a row, with four chairs on one side facing a flip chart on an easel. Judging from the new configuration, I guessed only four people had signed up for the class, and the other one was probably the driver of the Prius. She sat at the end of the row of tables, leaving the other three chairs together.

I sat next to the woman, Giselle sat next to me, and Jazz sat on the other end. The thirtyish woman wore exotic clothes made with a bright turquoise cotton printed with yellow leaf shapes. The colors looked cheerful against her coffee-colored skin.

I smiled. "Good morning. My name is Martha."

The woman graced me with a wide, warm smile and offered her hand. "Good morning. My name is Nkwa. It means the 'creator goddess' in Nigeria."

"Your outfit is beautiful. Is it also from Nigeria?"

"It's traditional dress, yes." She pointed to her

loose-fitting blouse over a long, wraparound skirt. "The blouse is called a *buba*, the skirt is *iro*."

I eyed a complicated red turban pleated around her hair and shaped like a fan in back. "That's a fascinating headpiece."

"I'm glad you like it. It's called *gele*. The shape is supposed to resemble a peacock flaring its tail."

"Thank you for sharing all that. What I don't know about Africa could fill a library of books."

Up to that point, Giselle had listened quietly to the conversation. She leaned in front of me to get closer to the woman. "I'm Martha's little sister, Giselle. You speak English very well. I just love the sound of African names, although they're impossible for normal people to pronounce. What's your last name?"

Nkwa leveled her gaze at my sister. "Applebaum."

"No!' Giselle hooted. "You're married to a Jew? My sister Martha's Jewish, but I'm not. I'm Catholic. Same father, different mothers. But my fiancé is Jewish. Harold Zimmerman. Can you imagine a name more Jewish than that?"

Nkwa's face remained parked in neutral throughout the rambling outburst. I suspected this wasn't the first time she'd had to deal with a reaction like Giselle's. "Applebaum is my father's name."

Giselle just wouldn't let it go. "I didn't know there were any Jews living in Africa. Was he there on business?"

I tried kicking her under the table, but my foot painfully connected with the table leg instead.

Nkwa regarded my sister with almost scientific curiosity, tightening her eyes as if observing Giselle under a microscope, waiting to see how she would react. "Actually, I was born and raised in Berkeley, California."

Giselle waved her hand. "Berkeley? Of course. That explains everything. Berkeley's always been a liberal stronghold. You look like you're around my age, forty-five. Am I right? Wasn't there a lot of racial mixing going on around the time we were born?"

I pushed Giselle back in her chair. "What is the matter with you?"

"What?" Her mouth hung open and her face registered a total lack of comprehension.

I turned back to the other woman. "Please forgive my sister. She means no harm or disrespect. She just lacks a filter sometimes."

Much to my relief, Nkwa relaxed back in her chair and gave me a rueful smile. "This is nothing new, Martha. I deal with that kind of ignorance all the time. If you are Jewish, you must know what I mean."

I screwed up my face and nodded. "Oh yeah. All the time."

A man in his late thirties with a dark beard and dark eyes entered the room from the door in the back. He wore leather sandals, jeans fashionably tattered, and a white shirt with a mandarin collar. Jazz had also worn the same kind of shirt the other day. Maybe that style was coming back.

The man stood in front of the flip chart and cleared his throat to get our attention. His voice was surprisingly deep for a man of average height. "Good morning. My name is Freddy Pea."

Aka Andre Polinskaya.

He wrote his pseudonym at the top of the flip chart with a black marker. "I'm going to take you on an amazing journey these next two days. But first, I'd like to get to know each of you. Let's start with the gentleman on the end. What is your name and what do you hope to get from this class?"

"Hi." Jazz raised his wrist and waved. "I'm Jazz Fletcher. I'm here because I'm curious."

Freddy smiled. "Curiosity is the beginning of wisdom." He wrote *Curiosity* on the flip chart and looked at my sister. "And you?"

I grabbed her upper arm and squeezed hard.

"My name is Giselle Cole, and I'm here because I can't wait to read my own fortune."

I heaved a sigh of relief when she closed her mouth.

Freddy wrote *Cartomancy (foretelling the future)* on the chart and pointed to me. "You?"

"I'm Martha Rose, and I'm also curious."

Freddy put a check mark after the word *Curiosity* and slid his final gaze to my neighbor. I noticed how his eyes matched the almond shape of his siblings Paulina and Mansoor. And above his dark beard I could make out the same high cheek bones.

"I'm Nkwa Applebaum, and I hope to learn more about the mysteries of the occult."

Freddy nodded and added *History, Enlightenment, Interpretation,* and *Application* to the list. "We can't possibly cover everything there is to know about tarot in just two short days, but I will give you an overview that'll point you in the right direction. Then if you study the books you purchased for the class, you'll be ready for the advanced course, where you'll learn how to apply all that you have learned. Are there any questions so far?"

Giselle raised her hand.

Oh, no . . .

"So I won't be able to tell my own fortune right away?"

Freddy said, "Afraid not. But if you keep studying, one day you'll use the tarot in the way it was intended. Madame Natasha St. Germain wrote an insightful chapter on using tarot in her book *Choosing the Enlightened Life.* I believe there are several copies for sale in the bookstore."

I could have kissed Nkwa for asking the question, "What about you, Freddy? How long did it take you to learn about tarot?"

He took a slight step backward, suggesting to me he wanted to distance himself from giving out personal information. "I've been interested in the paranormal ever since I was a boy on the East Coast."

Princeton, New Jersey, to be exact.

He pointed to the flip chart. "*Curiosity* motivated me to learn about various disciplines. The more I studied, the more I wanted to learn." He pointed to the words *History* and *Enlightenment*.

"Was it hard?" Jazz asked. "Becoming a tarot expert?"

"Fortunately, no. *Interpretation* and *Application* seemed to come naturally to me."

I dared to raise my hand. "Does paranormal ability run in families? Like, if I became adept at tarot, could my daughter and granddaughter also develop a talent in that direction?" I held my breath, wondering if he'd reveal his family connection to Madam Natasha St. Germain.

"The answer is yes and no. The potential for becoming adept may be passed down from generation to generation, but it doesn't always take."

"So, one sibling could have the gift but the other not?" *Like your mother, Eugenie, and your uncle Royal.*

He tilted his head and studied me for a moment. Did I say too much? Did he suspect I knew who he really was? "Correct." He put down the black marker on the shelf of the easel and picked up a fresh deck of tarot cards. "Now, let's take a look at your tarot cards." I removed my cards from the package. The deck seemed much thicker than an ordinary deck of playing cards.

Freddy continued. "Modern tarot decks have seventy-eight cards, consisting of four suits and twenty-two trump cards. The suits are named Cups, Swords, Pentacles, and Wands. Each suit has fourteen cards. The first ten are numbered one through ten. The other four are the King, the Queen, the Knight, and the Jack. Find those cards in your decks and arrange them according to suit in four piles, face up."

"I can clearly see the swords and the cups and maybe the wands. But what are pentacles, and what do they look like?" Giselle asked.

"A pentacle is an amulet. Think in terms of a coin or something round like a disc."

"Ahh." Nkwa's voice sang. "You mean like a pentagram?"

"That's a pentacle, yes."

Jazz gazed at his cards as he sorted them. "Ooh, these are beautiful." He held up a card marked Queen of Wands—a crowned woman holding a flowering staff in her hand and sitting on a throne. A lion and a black leopard rested at her feet. "They don't look anything like regular playing cards."

"That's right," Freddy said. "And each card has a meaning or characteristic associated with it." When we finished sorting, he said, "This group of fifty-six cards is called the Minor Arcana, or lesser secrets. In reading the tarot, these cards deal with day-to-day situations. Now check out the twenty-two cards left over. These do not come in suits. They're all different. They're called the Major Arcana, or greater secrets, and deal with more significant events."

"So are the Major Arcana the fortune-telling cards?" Giselle asked.

Freddy shook his head. "All the cards are not used just to tell us our fortunes and enlighten us about the choices we have in life. Tarot can't tell us what to do regarding the future. It can only show us possibilities."

He spent the rest of the morning talking about the history of tarot and how it started in Europe as a card game until the fifteenth century, when it became associated with the metaphysical. Some theologians went so far as to claim the tarot revealed ancient wisdom and divine inspiration. We learned that, over time, the tarot deck changed in composition and size (one version boasted ninety-seven cards and included astrological symbols and symbols of the four elements).

At noon, Freddy announced lunch was being provided in the Mystical Feather Society dining hall. "It's just a short walk up the driveway. You can leave your classroom materials here. They'll be quite safe with Little Fawn."

That was the first time I noticed the girl had slipped into the bookstore area and sat quietly watching us from one of the plush purple chairs. She gave me a slight smile and waved her hand in greeting, causing the long sleeve of her white robe to slide back toward her elbow. I noticed with some alarm what seemed like small vertical scars on her wrist.

Giselle headed toward the genderless restroom, and Jazz approached Nkwa. "I love your hat, and I'm dying to know how you make it stand up like that."

While they chatted, I walked over to Little Fawn. "How are you doing today, sweetie?"

She sighed. "I'm better, I guess. The sheriff finally took the yellow tape off of Royal's house. I went inside and got my things."

Five minutes later Jazz, Giselle, Nkwa, and I followed Freddy up the road, past the unlocked gate, and up the bumpy driveway. Giselle leaned toward me and whispered, "I didn't spill the beans, did I, Sissy. Sometimes you don't give me enough credit."

I was breathing too hard to respond. I just nodded. We finally reached the top of the driveway and walked on level ground. By the time we reached the long, low building that served as the kitchen and dining hall, I felt like I'd climbed Mt. Kilimanjaro.

Long tables with benches ran down the length of the green room. Someone had painted a mural featuring fruits and vegetables along the end wall. The piquant aroma of something delicious came from the kitchen and sharpened my appetite. Ten people, three of them nude, sat together eating and listening intently to Claytie Tolliver.

Darn! What if he recognized me? I retied the scarf under my chin babushka style and pulled it forward to hide my face. I turned my head away and prayed he didn't notice me.

Freddy beckoned us to sit with him at another table, thankfully located on the other side of the room. A basket of fresh hot rolls nestled in a red-and-white-checked napkin awaited in the middle of the table. I tore a steaming roll in half, spread pats of soft, yellow butter on both pieces, and watched it melt.

Almost immediately two white-robed women carried out trays of food. They placed generous bowls of hot vegetable and barley soup in front of us.

One of the women said, "Is that you, Martha? You never said you were taking Freddy's class."

Oh no. "Hello, June."

Freddy stopped eating, raised his eyebrows, and stared at us. "You know each other?"

"Oh yes," June said. "I met Martha at that safe house in Encino last Sunday. Turns out, Martha is one of the people who found Royal's body."

"What?" Freddy's smile evaporated.

"Yeah. Martha told me she feels guilty about getting those two psychics she brought with her in trouble. I'm guessing she's trying to find out who really killed Royal." She gave me a tight smile. "Right?"

Crap!

Freddy studied me for a moment. Then comprehension changed the expression on his face from curiosity to . . . what was it: panic, fear, anger? The edge of his voice sliced through the air like one of the swords on the tarot cards. "Is this true?"

I forced a smile. "Well, I did say I came because I was curious."

CHAPTER 21

Immediately after learning I was one of the people who found Royal's body, Freddy smiled woodenly and stood. "Excuse me, I just remembered I left something in my room." He hurried out of the dining hall.

June Tolliver's face wrinkled in confusion. "But your soup will get cold."

Giselle and Jazz looked at each other with wide eyes.

Nkwa said, "What just happened?"

"I'll find out." I got up from the table and hurried outside.

I found Freddy standing in front of the meditation yurt.

He waited for me to approach then looked around to make sure we were alone. "You're the one who brought my brother and sister up here? Who are you, anyway?"

"I'm a friend of your family, Freddy . . . or shall I call you by your real name, Andre?"

"Shh!" He looked around again. "Why did you come back here?"

"Paulina and Mansoor, or Michael, or whatever you call your brother, are worried sick about you. They asked me to find out if you are still alive. Why did you stop communicating a month ago?"

"You know about that?" He sighed and closed his eyes. "Things out here were much worse than I expected. Royal had this nasty habit of randomly showing up in people's rooms and going through their personal stuff."

I wasn't surprised. Birdie and Denver had said that when they returned from a hike in Sedona, they discovered Royal inside their Winnebago. "Go on."

He opened his eyes and frowned. "One day I caught him in my room going through my papers. Luckily, I had taken my cell phone with me. But I figured if he ever got hold of my phone and saw my text messages, I'd be thrown off the mountain. Or worse."

"Worse?"

"You know, Martha, they say people sometimes disappear from here forever. So, I deleted all my messages and my contact list. That way, if he ever did manage to steal my phone, he'd find nothing."

"Why didn't you warn your family what you were about to do?"

"I panicked. It wasn't until after I sanitized my phone I realized I should've told them." He blew out a breath. "Who else knows about me?"

"Giselle and Jazz know. My fiancé, who is a federal agent, knows. The FBI knows, and I think by now the Ventura County Sheriff knows."

"Jeez!" He hung his head. "You can't blow my cover with the people up here."

"Why not? Royal's dead. Why continue to pose as Freddy Pea?"

"Me and Paulie and Mikey want to give Mystical Feather back to our mother. Where it rightfully belongs. But we can't do that yet. There's other stuff going on up here."

"So, why didn't you contact your family after Royal was killed to let them know you were all right?"

"I know this is crazy, but, at first, I wasn't sure if Paulie or Mikey or both of them had gone off the deep end and shot Royal. I wouldn't blame them if they did. Our uncle deserved what he got."

"And now? Do you still think one of them could've done it?"

He shook his head. "No way. Natasha's spirit told me the killer is still on the mountain."

Again with Natasha's spirit? "Did you kill Royal?"

"Martha, if you could read my aura, you'd see pure blue." He tried to charm me with a crooked grin. "I'm just not capable of murder. I'm a professional intuitive. I help people."

"Where were you when your uncle was shot?"

"In the bookstore."

"Can you prove it?"

"I was alone."

"Did Natasha's spirit happen to mention who did kill him?"

"Not yet. She said, 'The killer will be revealed when the motive becomes clear.' "

"Why doesn't someone just ask Royal's spirit who his killer was?"

"Oh, Martha. You have so much to learn. Contacting the dead simply doesn't work that way. His spirit is still disoriented by his sudden death. He's not ready to communicate yet. I can tell you this, though. Royal used people. And when he used them up, he got rid of them. Any one of his victims could've shot him." He glanced at his watch. "Listen, we need to get back to the dining hall. I'm sure people are wondering what's going on."

"I've got more questions."

"Later. Right now we need to get back. I can't blow my cover yet."

"After class is over, then?"

He nodded. "Yeah. Okay. You will keep my secret, won't you?"

"For now."

"I'll call Paulie tonight to tell her I'm okay."

Freddy and I sauntered back into the dining hall with reassuring smiles pasted on our faces.

As soon as we sat in our places at the table, Nkwa looked at me. "What's going on here?"

"Nothing bad," I said.

Freddie cleared his throat. "I come from a long line of gifted psychics and mediums. Royal St. Germain was someone I looked up to." He picked up his spoon and swallowed some soup along with the lie. "He was a mentor. His death hit me hard. When I found out just now that Martha had actually seen his body, I sort of lost it. But I'm better. Thanks for asking."

I had to admire Freddy/Andre. He was as smooth a liar as I was. So, how much of what he'd told me was the truth? Had I just been conned by Royal's killer?

After lunch we returned to the teahouse at the bottom of the hill for the remainder of the day's lesson. Going down was easier than climbing up. Different leg muscles. Unanswered questions raced through my mind. Was Freddy really in the bookstore when Royal was shot? What was the "other stuff going on" he mentioned?

At one point his voice cut through my thoughts. "The querant, or seeker, cannot be a passive participant. Although she must approach the session with a specific question in mind, the tarot will not reveal her fortune but will address the essence of her inquiry."

I raised my hand. "I'm not sure I understand."

"I'll use my recent traumatic experience as an example." Freddy ran his fingers through his hair. "Suppose I was looking for a specific person. The wrong request would be, 'Who killed Royal St. Germain?' "

My whole body tensed, and I could feel Giselle shift in her chair beside me. I glanced at Nkwa, who seemed mildly curious but calm.

Freddy continued. "The tarot cannot provide such a specific answer. The proper question would be, 'What path of inquiry should I follow?' or, 'Am I on the right path to find those answers?' "

He looked straight at me. "Do you see the difference?"

I nodded. "I'm pretty sure I do."

"Good." He turned his wrist to look at his watch. "We have about an hour left. Time enough to do a reading for each of you."

Jazz beamed. "I've always wanted to do a tarot reading."

"Good. I was hoping you would." Nkwa did a little chair dance.

Freddy rubbed his hands together and picked up a deck of cards and shuffled them. "There are different patterns for laying the cards on the table when reading tarot. There's one design for True Love, which uses six cards; another for Success, which uses five cards; another for Spiritual Guidance, and so on. The more complicated spread is called the Celtic Cross, which requires ten cards. In the interest of time, I'll do the simplest spread of three cards for each of you. Even though it's simple, it can be the most powerful. So, think of a question. You first, Martha."

"I want to know if I'm looking in the right places for answers." *If he knows something more, something he hasn't told me, maybe he'll reveal it in this reading.*

"That's a good example of an open-ended question to ask the tarot." He handed me the deck of cards and I shuffled them four times as instructed. Then I cut the deck in half and he dealt three cards from the lower half.

The first card he uncovered was the Moon card

with a painting of a woman wearing a long white garment against a dark blue background scattered with white stars. Behind her head shone a large white moon emitting light rays of white and blue and yellow.

Freddy smiled. "The Moon card is one of the Major Arcana. It tells you that you have great sensitivity and imagination. It also tells you to trust your inner instincts. Don't let your rational mind interfere with what your body is learning from the universe."

Jazz nodded. "I can vouch for the fact Martha has great intuition." He turned to Giselle. "But she's not always right."

Giselle poked his arm. "Shh. Don't interrupt."

The next card Freddy uncovered was upside down. It showed the King of Swords, a man wearing a crown dressed in red and purple, sitting on a throne with purple snakes in the background. "This card is one of the Minor Arcana. It represents your rational, analytic mind. In the reverse position or upside down, it cautions you to be extra analytical. Thoroughly examine ideas and theories you may hear and don't rely on assumptions. Use your own judgment."

The third card, the Three of Cups, showed a woman and a man dressed in flowing blue and green robes. She held a golden chalice, while he hoisted an infant in the air. The details were outlined in black, suggesting segments in stained glass. "This card is also part of the Minor Arcana. It represents cooperation and teamwork. Don't rely on yourself alone as you follow your path. Remember to turn to your support network for help and encouragement."

"He's right, Sissy. Don't run off on your own like you sometimes do. That has gotten you into real trouble in the past."

My tarot reading was disappointing. It encouraged me to keep on going, but I didn't hear anything specifically helpful. On the other hand, what was I expecting? Like the daily horoscope in the newspaper, the advice Freddy gave was vague enough to apply to anyone. Still, a small part of me wondered if there was a hidden message in his remark about "teamwork." Was he hinting he wanted into my investigation? If so, why? And what else did he know?

As Freddy conducted three more readings, I admired the art nouveau illustrations on the cards he used. We learned in class that tarot decks weren't all the same. Literally hundreds of versions existed, many of which had themes like fairies, animals, fantastical creatures, or Egyptian gods. The artists' mediums also varied, including colorful woodblock prints, paintings, photographs, or even black-and-white etchings.

Sometimes, inspiration for quilts could come from unexpected places. For example, it occurred to me that tarot illustrations could translate beautifully into appliqué patterns. I visualized a quilt with twenty-two blocks, each showing one of the Major Arcana. The possibilities were limited only by the quilter's imagination.

When the class finally ended, I got up to stretch. Little Fawn signed with a furtive wave that she wanted to speak to me privately. I acknowledged her with a slight nod of my head and made my way slowly to the door in back. Once we were both inside the kitchen/office space, she closed the door and said in a low voice, "I'm not sure what this means, but I thought it might be important."

She pointed to the screen of the laptop sitting on the desk, displaying an Excel document labeled "Bookstore and Teahouse Accounts Payable." Running down the rows on the left side of the page were the names of publishers and vendors, presumably providing merchandise for the bookstore and teahouse. The twelve columns across the top represented months in the previous year.

At first, the document looked ordinary. But when I looked at the totals in the thirteenth column, I realized what Little Fawn was showing me. Some of the totals boasted five or six figures, far more money than needed to stock the small Mystical Feather Bookstore and Teahouse. Where was that money really going? And how did Little Fawn manage to come across this bombshell?

"Whose computer is this?"

"Freddy uses it. He runs the bookstore."

"Do you have regular access to this computer?"

She looked at the floor. "No, I'm just one of the helpers who works in the tea room."

"So, what made you look? And how did you manage to find this particular file?"

"As soon as Freddy saw me this morning, he closed the laptop real fast, like I wasn't supposed to see what he was doing. When he started the class out there, I got curious. So, I opened the laptop to see what was the big secret. The file popped up on the screen because he hadn't had time to close it out."

"Wasn't the laptop password protected?"

She smiled. "Yeah. But I'd seen him start it up a bunch of times. I knew where he kept the password." She pulled out the right-hand drawer on the desk, reached underneath, and showed me a yellow sticky note with a complicated alpha-numeric string. Then she replaced the paper and closed the drawer.

I had underestimated the girl and apparently, Freddy had as well. She might have been misguided in love, but that didn't mean she was stupid. "Well, what do you think this is, Little Fawn?"

She raised her chin. "I think Freddy was stealing money."

Embezzlement. Would that be a reason to kill Royal? "Have you told anyone else about this?"

She shook her head.

I closed the laptop. "Good. Let's keep this to ourselves for now. Don't let anyone—especially Freddy—know what you discovered. Can you do that?"

"Yeah."

We left the small room and rejoined the others in the bookstore. Just before class ended, Little Fawn had laid out tea and pastries. As everyone mingled and chatted near the plates of scones and cookies, I contemplated what I'd just seen.

Little Fawn was wrong about Freddy. The embezzlement had started long before he came to Mystical Feather. Was he protecting someone else or gathering information in an investigation of his own? Time to find out.

CHAPTER 22

I hung around in the bookstore with Jazz and Giselle until we were alone with Freddy. Once he saw he could no longer avoid us, he walked over to where we were sitting and plopped down in the empty purple chair. He surveyed our little group and sighed. "I hope I'm not going to regret talking to you." He reached for the leftover plate of sweets in the middle of the low table and took a thumbprint cookie filled with strawberry jam.

"Well, since you're psychic, what do our *auras* tell you about that?" Giselle's voice dripped with sarcasm.

Freddy stared at the area around her head and neck. "Interesting. You have a red aura. That means you say what you think, consequences be damned."

Is the Pope Catholic?

Freddy continued. "You also have a competitive nature and a great drive to succeed. You prefer to be the boss. It's hard for you to surrender your authority to another."

I had to admit Freddy was right. My sister was the CEO of a successful oil company. She was used to being numero uno. Consequently, she often had a hard time letting me take the lead.

Giselle shrugged. "Anyone who knows me could've said the same thing."

Freddy turned to Jazz with a charming, crooked smile. "You, on the other hand, have a green aura. You're highly creative, generous, and like to surround yourself with friends." His eyes flicked up and down for a nanosecond. "You also take good care of your body."

Jazz blushed.

Duh. Anyone looking at Jazz can see he's in great shape, especially for a man in his fifties.

"If you possess any flaw, it's that you tend to work too hard. Your saving grace is you also crave balance. Am I right in saying you're quite capable of relaxing and enjoying all the friends who tend to gravitate toward you?"

Jazz fluttered his eyes and grinned. "I do? Oh, how kind of you to say so. Really. You just made my day."

"Well," Freddy smiled, "it takes one to know one. I have a green aura, too. I totally get where you're coming from."

Jazz's shoulders did a slight shimmy. "Yes, I believe you do."

Was that some kind of gay code? "Wait, Freddy. Didn't you tell me earlier your aura is blue?"

He lowered his eyelids. "It changes."

Definitely gay code.

Freddy turned his attention to me. "Martha, your aura is a bright yellow. You're highly intellectual and intuitive. You can read people easily and are a good communicator."

Hmm. Maybe Freddy is psychic after all.

"You're drawn to the unorthodox. Your major fault is in your cynicism and tendency to be critical of others."

"As far as I'm concerned, those aren't faults. Those traits enable me to see past the bull. Like now. Let's get real, Freddy. Earlier today you mentioned there was 'other stuff' going on at Mystical Feather. What did you mean?"

"I'd rather not talk about it until I know for sure."

"As I see it, you have a choice." I crossed my arms. "Talk to me or talk to the police."

"Don't worry," Jazz crooned. "Her bark is worse than her bite."

Freddy glanced at Jazz and gave him a wry smile. "Okay. Okay." He took a deep breath and sat up straight. "When I first came to the mountain, I spent a lot of time floating from one job on the commune to another. One day, as I was straightening out the shelves where my grandmother Natasha's books were displayed, I sort of went into a trance and her spirit appeared before me."

Of course she did.

"How do you mean 'appeared'?" Giselle asked.

"A vision. Like in a black-and-white film. It only lasted for a few seconds. Long enough for her to tell me I should keep working in the bookstore and she would guide me to the answers I sought. Sure enough, after I'd been in the bookstore a month, Claytie Tolliver asked if I would help out by managing the place."

"How did Royal feel about that?" I asked.

"If someone else wanted to do the work, the lazy bastard was more than willing to step aside. I'd seen where Royal kept some accounting stuff in his house. I waited until he went on one of his tours that took him away from Ojai and slipped into his empty house late at night. The moment I got a look at those accounting books, I realized they were in a terrible mess. The bookstore records were often mixed up with the general accounts for the whole Mystical Feather Society. So, I decided to establish the bookstore and teahouse as a separate revenue center with its own set of ledgers. I made sure nobody saw me. I worked in his empty house almost every night for a week."

Giselle leaned forward, eyes narrowed. "How did you know how to do that? Are you an accountant?"

"Degree in finance from Princeton."

Where his father, Andre Polinskaya, Sr., taught political science. I reached for one of the cookies on the table. "Did Claytie know what you were doing?"

"Are you kidding? My whole purpose in coming here was to find out as much about Royal and Mystical Feather as I could without anyone knowing my true identity. I figured if I could find proof of a crime, it would help us take back Mystical Feather for our mother."

"Were you looking for any crime in particular?" Jazz prompted gently.

"I knew I had stumbled across financial crimes the moment I saw those books. So, I secretly began to tease out the data for the bookstore accounts and discovered major fraud going on. Money was being paid to vendors that didn't exist."

That explained the Excel document Little Fawn had just shown me. "On whose authority were these bills paid? Who wrote the checks?"

"That's what's so frustrating." He wrinkled his face. "They were automatically paid by direct transfer from the Mystical Feather general accounts. I was in the process of confirming Royal had authorized those transfers when he was killed. That kind of stopped everything."

"Couldn't you just sit in the lotus position somewhere and ask Natasha who was responsible?" Giselle scoffed. "Or did she only talk to you when you dusted her books?"

"She decides when and where to appear. I don't. The next time I heard from her was when I stood in the buffet line at the dining hall. We were making our own burritos and I got as far as the bowl with tofu ground meat substitute when she showed herself. She said my case would become even stronger if I kept digging. She said I was 'about to discover much more wrongdoing' if I continued my search incognito."

"How exciting." Jazz leaned forward, clearly hooked.

"How convenient." Giselle rolled her eyes. "What happened with the burrito?"

Freddy ignored my sister and blessed Jazz with that same charming smile. "From the first time I set foot on the mountain, I sensed there were a few wretched spirits hovering around the property."

Paulina and Mansoor had said the same thing when we first came to Mystical Feather. Not that I believed them . . .

"I thought the spirits might've been victims. I quietly asked around about previous members who'd gone missing. Nobody seemed to know much or, if they did, they wouldn't say anything. But I didn't give up. I figured if I could locate any graves and prove foul play, that would be the end of Royal."

"Didn't Natasha come to you in the shower to tell you where they were buried?" Giselle asked.

Freddy didn't respond to her constant digs. "Natasha's spirit did appear again. One evening when I was meditating inside the yurt. She instructed me to search the mountainside but not to tell anyone what I was really up to."

"Didn't people suspect something odd going on when you disappeared into the wilderness?" I asked.

"Not really. I told people I was going on a 'meditation hike' to get in touch with my spirit guides. One of the women, Anna, always asked to come with me, but I made excuses why I had to be alone."

He must mean Anna from Savannah. The Southern girl in Birdie's kitchen who said she was partial to men in beards. Clearly, she didn't decipher gay code.

"Each time I left, I explored another part of the mountain looking for possible grave sites. I thought I found one a week ago, but I haven't been able to go back and dig it up."

"Well, for God's sake, why didn't you go to the police?" Giselle wagged her head in disbelief. "They have all kinds of equipment to locate graves, like ground-penetrating radar and specially trained cadaver dogs."

"I didn't want to blow my cover before I had solid evidence. Think about it. Suppose I did call the police? And suppose they came and searched? What if nothing turned up? Royal would've thrown me off the mountain. Plus, once he knew my real identity, my whole family would be in danger."

"After all your hikes," I said, "you must really know your way around the mountain." *Just like Royal's killer, who used the scrub brush and trees to hide in.*

He nodded. "Probably more than most."

"So, where is this so-called grave site?" Giselle gestured vaguely to the great outdoors. "Why don't you show it to us now? There's still an hour of daylight left."

Freddy blinked rapidly. "All of you? I'm not sure that's a good idea. A group this size would be sure to attract attention."

"Is it in an area that is easily seen from the compound?" I asked.

"No, but . . ."

"So, we'll hike quietly. How long will it take for us to get there from here?"

Freddy glanced around uneasily and licked his lips. "If all of us go, about ten minutes." He surveyed our shoes. Giselle wore suede flats, Jazz wore leather loafers, and I wore sandals. "Martha, the ground is uneven and rocky in places. Plus, we might come across some poison oak or a rattlesnake. Do you really want to risk hiking in those sandals?"

"Rattlesnakes?" Heck no, I didn't want to take the risk. But what was the alterative? Staying in the bookstore and waiting for them to return? "I'll be fine. Let's get going while there's still daylight."

"I gotta lock up first. Meet me out back."

Giselle, Jazz, and I walked through the tiny kitchen/office and exited down the three concrete steps in back to the dirt below. I noticed a narrow trail leading downhill through the brush I hadn't seen before. Freddy soon joined us and grabbed a thick walking stick leaning against the back of the building near the door.

He headed toward the path. "Follow me. Step where I step." He held up the walking stick. "This is for beating the bushes to scare off any critters that may be lurking."

"Critters?" Giselle took one step backward and bumped into Jazz.

"Mountain lions are pretty shy and don't like people. But if we do encounter one on the trail, don't run, whatever you do. They'll think you're prey."

"That's *food* for thought," Giselle snarked.

"If we come across a snake, stop moving. I'll take care of it."

"Oh, yuck!" Jazz made a face.

"Likewise, if you see a tarantula or large trap-door spider, stay put. I'll use my stick."

I gasped. "Tarantulas?" Eww. Every molecule in my body wanted to race back to the safety of the Jaguar and wait for the others.

As we moved into the brush, I said a little prayer. *Dear God, please don't let there be any spiders. Especially not a big one. Amen.*

After two minutes of marching down the mountain single file, the only sounds we heard were the crunching of dry leaves under our feet and the swishing of vegetation as we made our way past low-growing coyote brush, purple sage, and native grasses. We used our arms and hands to fend off the dry branches of the tall scrub oak reaching out across the path. The only other sound was the squawking of dozens of crows gathering for happy hour in the tallest trees.

Freddy stopped abruptly and raised his arm. We all froze in place; Giselle stood behind Freddy and clutched his arm. Jazz stood behind Giselle, and I brought up the tail end. Freddy swiveled his head so we could see him place a finger on his lips. He mouthed the word *deer* and pointed toward the left at eleven o'clock. Grazing on the tender leaves of an elderberry bush twenty feet away was a female mule deer with a pregnant belly ready to pop.

Jazz whispered, "Ooh, isn't she cute?"

The deer's head snapped to attention, ears twitching. The black tip of her tail stood straight up as she sniffed the air. Then she turned and leapt away through the undergrowth.

Jazz made a face and whispered, "I'm sorry."

Freddy beckoned us onward. After another two minutes we made a sharp left turn off the trail. We continued crossways along the mountain through California live oak and buckbrush until we came to a small clearing, about three hundred yards below the Mystical Feather compound.

Freddy stopped and turned to face us. "It's safe to talk now if we keep our voices low. We don't want to take the chance of our voices carrying up to Mystical Feather." He pointed to the soft ground beneath our feet. "This is it."

Jazz looked down and stepped to the side. "The grave?"

Freddy nodded. "Notice how there's no old growth in this spot? And the dead leaves are not as thick here."

Only small plants poked through the thin layer of mulch covering the ground.

He cleared a spot and dug his fingers in the soil. "The dirt is not packed and hard here. I'm sure at one point it was disturbed."

"When?" Jazz gasped.

"Hard to say." He shrugged. "Maybe six months, maybe a year, according to one old guy who remembered something about it."

"Why didn't Natasha tell you in a dream?" Giselle jabbed him one last time. "That's the least she could do for her grandson."

Freddy growled at my sister. "If you're such a skeptic, ask yourself why you came here in the first place. Was it only to mock the paranormal or does a part of you believe what I'm saying?"

Giselle pulled her head back, as if dodging an imaginary blow. Then she took a swing of her own. "I think all this talk about dead spirits, auras, and tarot is a bunch of bull." Her voice took on volume as she spoke. "I think you're full of it."

"Easy . . ." Jazz hushed. He put a restraining hand on her arm.

"But if I'm right, what then?" asked Freddy. "How will you explain the fact I found the grave of one of the poor souls haunting the mountain?"

"Let's find out." I pulled my cell phone out of my pocket. "Let's call the sheriff and see who's right."

"No!" Freddy put a frantic hand over mine, dark eyes pleading. "Not yet. I already explained I don't want to blow my cover until I have solid proof. You're coming back tomorrow for the last day of class, right? I'll stash a couple of shovels by the back door and end the session early. Then we'll have plenty of daylight to come back here and dig up the body. Being the lazy slug he was, Royal probably didn't bother to go very deep."

CHAPTER 23

As we drove down Sulphur Mountain Road to the highway below, a gray Prius pulled out from a narrow driveway and followed us, keeping some distance back. Was that Nkwa's car, the one that had been parked next to the bookstore this morning? When we reached the bottom, we turned right, and the Prius turned left.

Get a grip, Martha. The world is full of gray Priuses. Besides, why would she be spying on us?

On the way back to the Valley, we talked about what we would do if we did find a body buried below the Mystical Feather Commune.

Jazz rubbed his stomach. "I'll probably throw up. You remember how queasy I got when we discovered poor Dolleen's body a year ago?"

"I'll take pictures of the body with my cell phone," said Giselle.

"I'll call Della Washington right away," I said.

"Who's she?" My sister briefly took her eyes off the road to look at me.

"The sheriff's detective who's investigating Royal's murder."

"How are you going to explain why we decided to look for a body in that exact spot?"

"Don't worry, G. We won't have to explain. Unfortunately, that will be Freddy's 'Come to Jesus' moment. He'll have to admit who he really is and why he's been poking around Mystical Feather."

I'd also have to call Director John Smith at the FBI if I was going to keep my word about exchanging information.

During our drive, the sun set over the ocean in a brilliant blaze of orange and pink, and we arrived at my house in Encino in the dark. My sister parked the Jag but didn't turn off the engine. "I'll be here at the same time tomorrow morning."

I opened the car door. "Wear clothes and shoes suitable for digging."

Jazz slid across the seat and opened the door on his side. "I'm not looking forward to getting Zsa Zsa from the dog sitter. She's going to have a hissy fit for being left alone." He walked to his blue Mercedes with the personalized license plate JAZZ FW. The FW stood for Fletcher-Watson, the combined last name he and the late Russell Watson secretly shared.

Crusher's Harley sat in the driveway and welcome home lights shone inside my house. I found him in the kitchen, chopping veggies for a salad.

"Babe. How was the class today? Can you tell my fortune yet?"

I laid my purse, tarot deck, and books on the hall table and joined him in the kitchen. He set the knife next to the wooden cutting board and turned to hug me. "I picked up some eggplant Parmesan from Tony's. I figured we both needed a break from cooking." A pan of the warm Italian delicacy sat in the middle of the stovetop.

"You know me well, Yossi."

He tossed the salad with our favorite Italian dressing and removed slices of a French baguette from under the broiler. The edges were lightly browned and melted butter with chunks of fresh minced garlic and grated Parmesan sizzled on top.

Once we sat at the table, I reached for a slice of bread. I bit through the crispy crust to the soft white inside, and my mouth filled with the savory melted garlic butter. While we ate, I told him about our day at Mystical Feather. "So, we're going back tomorrow. After class we'll return to the grave site and dig it up."

"*If* it's a grave." He paused with his fork halfway to his mouth. "What do you make of Freddy? Or shall I call him Andre?"

"Call him Freddy. He wants to stay undercover for now. He's very knowledgeable about the paranormal. And he has a real knack for reading people. I think that helps his claim to be a credible psychic. I also think he's gay. He flirted with Jazz."

"You know, if you do find a body out there,

you'll have to stop digging immediately and report it to the police. You don't want to disturb a crime scene."

"I know what to do. I'm not a rookie. I'm an experienced homicide investigator."

He closed his eyes and laughed.

The next morning Giselle and Jazz both converged at my house at seven. Giselle wore all white, even her tennis shoes. Jazz wore a long-sleeved blue cotton shirt and ankle boots made of fine Italian leather. I wore my uniform of jeans and Crocs.

Jazz carried a tote bag that looked suspiciously like a carrier for a small dog.

"What's in the bag?" I asked.

He sighed. "Zsa Zsa gave me the silent treatment all night. I couldn't leave her again today."

As if on cue, the little Maltese popped her head out of the top of the carrier and barked in greeting. She wore a tiny denim cargo jacket over a pink-and-blue plaid skirt. Jazz had loosely tied a miniature pink bandana around her neck.

"See?" Jazz stroked her head and cooed. "How could I leave my adorable little girl behind?" Zsa Zsa's tail wagged ecstatically.

Giselle announced she would drive again. We settled inside her Jaguar and left Encino just after seven. On the 101 freeway headed north, we got stuck behind an accident. We spent twenty extra minutes waiting to move past the collision and still managed to arrive at the Mystical Feather bookstore with five minutes to spare before class started.

We arranged ourselves in the same seats we'd occupied on the first day of class. Nkwa sat in the chair at the far end of the row of tables, I sat next to her, Giselle sat next to me, and Jazz took the chair at the other end of the row. Zsa Zsa settled down quietly in his lap.

Nkwa wore another colorful ensemble made with a print of yellow, black, and red diamond shapes. A white *gele* wrapped around her head. Her warm smile lit up her eyes as I took my place beside her. "Good morning, Martha. Did you do any of the reading last night?"

"Unfortunately, I was too tired. Did you?"

"Oh yes. I bought that book by Natasha St. Germain, *Choosing the Enlightened Life*. I read the chapter on tarot. According to her, she never began her day without spreading the cards for a personal reading. Her life was guided by the tarot. Once I know what I'm doing, I may try starting my day that way."

Freddy entered from the door in the back and took his place beside a fresh page on the flip chart. He scanned our faces. "Good morning, everyone. Today we're going to learn more about the meanings of each card. So, if you didn't bring something to write notes on, I've got plenty of paper here."

Zsa Zsa sat up and barked at the sound of his voice.

Jazz lowered his head and whispered, "Shh. We're all friends here." Then he looked apologetically at Freddy. "Don't worry. She's just excited to be in a new place. She'll settle down."

The rest of the morning we learned that each suit of cards in the Minor Arcana had a general meaning, each card within the suit had a more specific meaning, and in the upside-down position each card had an even stronger meaning. Memorizing all seventy-eight cards, including the twenty-two cards in the Major Arcana, was going to take a lot of studying.

Once again, we took a lunch break at twelve and hiked up the hill to the dining hall. Jazz stopped once to give Zsa Zsa a potty break. About five people sat at a table chatting and eating. Two of them were nude.

Giselle leaned over and whispered, "What happens if they spill hot soup?"

I chuckled. "That sounds like a question Lucy would ask."

June Tolliver and an elderly man with flabby arms carried trays of food to our table. The man wore a white chef's hat, a white apron, and nothing else. They served us chili and beans, freshly baked rolls, and iced green tea. When they turned to go, I averted my gaze. I was sure they were breaking all kinds of health laws.

An hour later we returned to the bookstore for the last half of class. I could hardly concentrate on Freddy's lesson. The thought of digging up a corpse weighed heavily. I'd added Detective Washington's phone number to my contact list on my cell phone last night. Just in case.

The lecture ended at two and Freddy spent the next hour giving each of us a tarot reading. Only, this time, he asked us to interpret the cards using what we had learned. Giselle did the best job. Her mind was quick, a gift that enabled her to be such an effective CEO. Nkwa was able to read the cards with little prompting. If this were real life, Jazz and I would've flunked out of school.

At three, Little Fawn brought out a pot of tea and a plate of chocolate chip cookies for after class.

Freddy said, "If you're serious about reading tarot, you should memorize the handbook on the meanings of each card. Use the three-card spread you learned here and consult the handbook for interpretation. You have a couple of weeks before I begin the advanced class. Thank you for coming. It's been a pleasure."

Nkwa hung around long enough to drink a cup of tea, then she left. I watched out the window as she got in her gray Prius and drove off. Little Fawn hiked back up the hill. We were finally alone at three thirty.

We trooped out the back door of the bookstore. Two shovels leaned against the wall of the building. Jazz put Zsa Zsa's carrier on the ground long enough to roll up the cuffs of his blue shirt. "I take it you and I will do the digging?"

Freddy shrugged into a camouflage backpack and handed one of the tools to Jazz. "Yeah. Follow me."

We trooped downhill through the trail. Ten minutes later we reached the same clearing where we'd been yesterday.

I patted the cell phone in my pocket, anticipating the call I might have to make. "If there is a body, you don't want to damage it with the shovel. Try not to shove the blade straight down."

"You sound like either a forensic expert or an archaeologist, Sissy."

"My undergrad degree was in anthropology," I said. "Does that count?"

Jazz nodded once at Freddy. "Let's do this."

Freddy scored a rectangle on the ground with the tip of his shovel roughly four feet by six feet. "We'll dig here."

Giselle and I retreated to the shade of the nearby live oak. Freddy scooped the dirt first by slipping the lip of the shovel into the soil and moving horizontally. He dumped the load in a mound over to the side. Jazz did the same, taking care to only remove the first two inches of soil. Zsa Zsa jumped out of her carrier and began digging enthusiastically with her front paws at the edge of the square.

Freddy was right. The ground was much softer here. They worked in silence for the next fifteen minutes, making fairly quick progress.

When they were twelve inches down, Jazz stopped, pulled a clean white cotton handkerchief from his pocket, and wiped the sweat from his brow and upper lip. "Did anyone remember to bring some water?"

Freddy dug into his canvas backpack, fished out four plastic bottles, and handed them around. "I also brought some energy bars if you need one."

Jazz opened the bottle, tilted his head, and drank half without stopping. His Adam's apple bobbed up and down with each gulp. When he stopped for air, he poured some water into his cupped hand and offered it to the little dog. Then he unbuttoned his shirt and handed it to me. Underneath he wore a ribbed cotton tank top that had become soaked with sweat on the chest and under the arms.

Freddy stared at the well-defined muscles in Jazz's bare shoulders. I thought for a moment they were going to have an "I'll show you mine if you show me yours" encounter, but the younger man kept his T-shirt on and resumed digging.

A slight breeze disturbed the leaves on the oak tree, causing my sister to shiver a little and rub her arms. "You know Sissy, I really like Ojai. It's very peaceful here."

"You mean as long as people aren't getting murdered?"

"You know what I mean. I've been thinking how nice it would be to build a house with a view way up on one of these mountains."

"They have insanely strict zoning laws here, G. You can't just buy a piece of land and build any old house. By the time you get through all the red tape, you might be too old to enjoy it. Plus, this area is prone to wildfires. You could find your brand-new house burnt to ashes one summer."

"Martha!" Jazz's voice cut into our conversation. "Come and take a look."

By now the hole was about eighteen inches deep and something peeked through the top layer of dirt. I dropped to my knees next to the hole to get a better look.

"Do you think that's the body of one of the missing Mystical Feather members?" Jazz bent over for a closer look. "Who could it be?"

Freddy shook his head. "Almost anybody. Royal was capable of anything."

"Darn! I wish I had thought about bringing gloves and a brush. If this is what I think it is, I don't want to touch it with my bare hands."

"I've had a long time to think about what I'd do if I came across a grave." Freddy dug in his backpack and handed me a new two-inch-wide paintbrush with soft bristles and a pair of bright yellow latex kitchen gloves.

The fingers of the size-large gloves extended an inch farther than my own fingers, making delicate movements impossible. I handed Giselle my cell phone. "We need to get a picture of this."

She knelt beside me. "What? That little white thing?"

I pointed to an area with something that looked like a white worm. "Exactly. Right there. Take a picture of that." When she finished, I began to carefully brush the dirt off the object. As the soil fell away, a carpal bone appeared.

I looked at Freddy. "You were right. I'm not an expert in anatomy, but I'm pretty sure that's a bone from a human hand. Take another picture now, G."

Giselle snapped a picture of what was clearly a bone and sprang to her feet, soft dirt clinging to her bare knees. "I've got to hand it to you, Freddy. I really doubted we'd find anything here, but, as my sister says, you were right all along."

Jazz gave me his hand as I awkwardly stood. I removed the latex gloves and gestured for my sister to hand me my phone. I scrolled down to the bottom of my contact list and sent the photos to Washington, Detective Della.

CHAPTER 24

Giselle, Jazz, and I sat under the oak tree while Freddy hiked back up the mountain to the bookstore parking lot to wait for the sheriff's deputies. Zsa Zsa slept quietly in Jazz's lap. Ten minutes after sending the photos to Detective Washington, we heard the keening of multiple sirens winding their way up Sulphur Mountain Road. After the noise stopped, car doors slammed shut and the sound of several excited voices cascaded rapidly down the mountain to where we sat.

Five minutes later, several sets of boots came crashing through the brush, Freddy leading the way. One of the deputies had strung bright yellow caution tape from the parking lot to our location. Not only would the tape secure the crime scene, it would provide a marked trail for the investigators to follow through the wilderness.

Detective Della Washington emerged into the

clearing right behind Freddy, wearing a deep frown and a black pant suit covered in dead leaves. Her young partner, Detective Oliver Heymann, appeared right behind her, followed by Sergeant Diaz and Deputy Willard. This was the same group I had met when we discovered Royal's body. Déjà vu all over again.

Washington glanced at the three of us. Then, without a word, squatted at the edge of the grave and peered inside. "Damn." She stood and turned to Deputy Willard. "Get forensics here. They'll probably be digging all night. Tell them to bring gear for a remote location."

Then she pointed her finger at me. "You're Martha Rose. The one who sent me the pictures just now." It was a statement, not a question. "And these other people are . . . ?"

Giselle tucked her straight red hair behind her right ear and took one step forward, being careful to avoid the hole. "I'm Giselle Cole. Martha's sister. And this is our friend Jazz Fletcher."

Jazz cuddled the little Maltese against his chest. "And this is my brave little girl, Zsa Zsa Galore." He held up one of her dirty front paws. Her red toenail polish barely showed through the soil still clinging to her white fur. "She helped us excavate."

Zsa Zsa wagged her tail and barked once, but Washington ignored her.

"Mrs. Rose, I made the mistake of assuming your business up here was finished once your friends the Watsons were persuaded not to join Mystical Feather. Yet, here you are again. And here's another dead body. How do you explain this?"

"We took Freddy's class on tarot this weekend." I glanced at him, sending a look that said, *Feel free to jump in any time.*

"How did you know about this grave?" Washington jerked her thumb toward the hole in the ground.

Freddy cleared his throat. "I was the one who told Martha and the others about it." He confessed he was really Andre Polinskaya and launched into an explanation of why he'd spent months posing as Freddy Pea and scouring the mountain looking for possible victims of foul play. "I'd heard rumors that some of the members had disappeared in the past. I thought if I could find proof, I could make a better case. You know, for the courts to restore what should've gone to my mother in the first place."

"And that's why you were using the false name of Freddy Pea?"

"Exactly," he said earnestly.

"Who else knew what you were up to?"

"Just my sister and brother, Paulie and Mikey."

Washington scrolled down the screen of her smart phone. "You mean Paulina and Michael Polinskaya?"

Andre nodded. "Yeah. Otherwise, nobody else knew. Not even my mother."

"Do you have any idea who this is?" Washington tilted her head toward the grave.

"I recently learned of at least two people it could be. An elderly man went missing a year ago, and a young woman disappeared a few years before that. I also heard rumors of other mysterious disappearances, but I wasn't able to get anyone to be more specific."

"I'm not through with my questions, Mr. Polinskaya. You're going to have to go to the substation in Ojai." She indicated Giselle, Jazz, and me with a sweep of her hand. "You can give statements to Sergeant Diaz, then you're free to go."

She turned to Willard. "What is the ETA for forensics?"

"They just sent a text." He consulted his phone. "They should be here in five, maybe ten minutes."

"Have someone escort Mr. Polinskaya down the hill. I'll be there after I've had a chance to talk to CSI."

We had no choice but to hike up to the parking lot. Two deputies escorted Andre to the back of a patrol car that disappeared down the driveway in a cloud of dust. Jazz, Giselle, and I gave Sergeant Diaz our separate statements and were finally released at seven that evening.

The tires of my sister's Jaguar crunched over the poorly paved driveway as we slowly made our way to Sulphur Mountain Road. We continued down the mountain, stopping at the highway junction and waiting for cross traffic to clear before making a right onto Route 150. The headlights of an oncoming vehicle momentarily blinded us before it turned onto the road leading to Mystical Feather. The older I got, the more difficulty I had recovering from glaring lights. Vision still blurry, I did a

double take as the car slid past us. Was that a reflection on the driver's window or was it a white
gele?

Once we transitioned to the 150, I remembered
my promise and called Director John Smith. "This
is Martha Rose."

"I know."

Right. Caller ID.

"It's late where I am," he said.

"Sorry. I didn't think you'd be asleep yet. It's
only a little after ten in Washington, D.C., right?"

"I'm not in that time zone."

"So, I'll be brief. You asked me to contact you if
anything new popped up. Well, this afternoon we
found a body buried on the mountain right below
Mystical Feather."

"I know."

"How . . ."

"Mystical Feather is flagged in the system. Remember?"

"We uncovered a finger bone before we called
the sheriff."

"That means the body's probably been there for
at least a year. That's how long it takes for soft tissue to decompose. How did you know where to
look?"

"Freddy, uh, Andre Polinskaya took us there."

"Explain."

I told him everything I knew about Andre and
his movements during the last six months. "If the
body's been there for a year, Andre can't be responsible. He only came to Mystical Feather six
months ago."

"I thought we agreed you wouldn't go looking for more trouble."

"It was just a tarot class, for heaven's sake. How was I supposed to know it would turn into another homicide investigation?"

"Let's see. After the tarot class you purposely went looking for a grave and you found one. What did you imagine such a discovery would turn into? A celebration?"

Smith had a point. "I wasn't thinking that far ahead. Anyway, we just finished giving our statements. We're on our way back to the Valley."

He didn't even try to hide a sigh of exasperation. "Who's handling this at the local level? Is it still Detective Washington?"

"And her partner, Detective Heymann."

"Okay. I'll take it from here." Smith ended the call without a "Thank you, Ms. Rose, for keeping me informed," or even a simple "Good job."

I pulled the phone away from my ear and glared at the black screen. "You're welcome," I said to the dead air.

We made it back to Encino at 9:30. Crusher's Harley was missing from the driveway and the house was dark. Even the porch light was off. I fumbled in my purse for my keys and turned to wave one last goodbye to my sister before going inside. I flipped the switch next to the front door and turned on the ceiling lights in the living room.

An envelope addressed to "Martha" was propped up against the brass dish on the hall table. The note inside said simply:

Babe,
New assignment out of town. Maybe two weeks.
Will call when I can.
Love you.

"Out of town" didn't necessarily mean a place outside of Los Angeles. That three-word expression was the code we used for his going undercover and being incommunicado. I sighed and resigned myself to enduring another of his indefinite absences.

The times when Crusher was deployed were the part of his job I really dreaded. Not only because he would be in danger, but Crusher, aka Yossi Levy, had filled the space in my heart that had remained vacant for years after my divorce. He was a big man with a big presence. The empty rooms in my house, which had once echoed with loneliness, finally felt full when he was around. It occurred to me that maybe the time had come to take his marriage proposals seriously.

I was too exhausted to eat (a very rare feeling). Even though I hadn't touched the bit of human bone with my bare hands, I still felt polluted. So, I took a long, hot shower. Afterward, I put on clean pink pajamas printed with smiling cat faces. Then I spent the next five minutes blowing hot air at my wet curls. I wanted in the worst way to tell Lucy and Birdie about our big discovery today. But the clock read ten thirty, too late to disturb anyone.

I made a cup of hot chocolate from a packet of Swiss Miss powder and boiling water. When I sat on the sofa, my orange cat, Bumper, jumped into my lap and settled into a purring fuzz ball. My thoughts turned once again to the mountainside as I sipped the sweet, hot drink with one hand and slicked down the cat's fur with the other. Despite the hot drink, I shivered a little. If St. Germain hadn't been shot to death, Birdie and Denver might've ended up in a grave just like the one we found today.

Who was buried there? When did Royal kill them? And why?

CHAPTER 25

Monday morning I woke up stiff and sore from climbing up and down the mountain over the weekend. I swallowed my fibromyalgia meds with my morning coffee and vowed to spend a quiet day recovering. I worked the crossword puzzle in the morning paper and waited until nine to call Lucy. I knew Ray would be gone and she'd be alone. I didn't want to risk a conversation with him until I knew for sure he was no longer angry I had involved his wife in St. Germain's murder investigation.

"Hey, hon. What's up?" Lucy asked.

"We dug up a body yesterday at Mystical Feather."

"What? Don't move. I'll be there in five minutes." She ended the call.

Sure enough, five minutes later Lucy knocked

shave-and-a-haircut on my front door and let herself in. "Are you serious, girlfriend? Another body?"

I handed her a cup of hot coffee and we settled on my cream-colored sofa. I told her about the Polinskaya family's connection to Madam St. Germain and how Andre had searched the mountainside for graves until he finally found one.

"Then the rumors about Royal killing members of Mystical Feather were true?" Lucy shivered. "I *told* you I had a bad feeling! I just knew the moment Birdie announced they were moving to Ojai that something very bad was up there on the mountain. It gives me the willies to think that Birdie and Denver could've become his next victims."

"Yeah. I think they dodged a bullet, all right."

"Now we're back to the question of who killed Royal, right?" Lucy gulped her coffee. "Personally, I think the three Polinskaya kids did it. I mean, they had motive, means, and opportunity. While we waited on the bench outside the yurt, Paulina and Mansoor could've lured their uncle to the Winnebago where Andre waited with a gun."

"I'm not sure, Lucy."

"Well, why not? We heard three shots, right? What if each one of them took a turn pulling the trigger? You know, like the twelve suspects did in *Murder on the Orient Express*. Andre could've gotten rid of the evidence somewhere on the mountainside before sneaking back to the bookstore. You said yourself he knew his way around that wilderness."

"It's possible. But what I'd like to know right

now is," I ticked off three fingers. "*Who* did we dig up, *how long* have they been there, and *how* did they die?"

Lucy drank the last of her coffee and turned down my offer for a refill. "For sure the police won't tell you. Can Yossi get a copy of the autopsy report?"

"It's actually the Ventura County Sheriff's office that's handling the investigation. And you're right, they don't give out that kind of information. Yossi can't help. He's out of town and unavailable. So, I've decided that just for today I'm going to stop worrying about the St. Germain family and Mystical Feather. I'm just going to work on Daisy's Sunbonnet Sue quilt. I haven't sewn in a while, and my fingers are itching to pick up a needle again."

"I know what you mean, girlfriend." Lucy sighed. "There's nothing as calming and satisfying as stitching by hand." She should know. She not only quilted by hand, she also pieced by hand, the way our foremothers did before the advent of the sewing machine.

Lucy rose from the sofa and placed her empty coffee cup in the kitchen sink. "I'd better run. Lots of errands today." She gave me a brief hug and walked out the door as quickly as she'd walked in. Her short orange curls bobbed in tune with the strides of her long legs.

I retreated to my sewing room and picked up the Sunbonnet Sue block I'd been working on before all the recent business with Mystical Feather. I used silk sewing thread for the appliqué, because silk fiber was finer than regular cotton sewing thread. And the tiny silk stitches were more likely to become invisible by sinking underneath the edge of the appliqué. I chose a spool of yellow thread to attach the dress, which featured little green watering cans on a yellow background, and a spool of pink thread to attach the solid pink bonnet.

Quilters use many different techniques for appliqué work. As an example, for a more rustic effect, the edges of the appliqué aren't turned under but sewn on raw. Any fraying of the edges only adds to the look. For a quick result, the quilter may use the zigzag stitch on the sewing machine to attach the edges of the appliqué.

Another example features a technique designed to emphasize rather than hide the stitching around the edges. Needle workers do this by securing the appliqué to the background with a blanket stitch using a contrasting embroidery thread, usually black.

Every quilt is a work of art. And, as with all pieces of art, there is no "right technique." Whatever the artist can imagine is correct. Whatever method she uses is the right method.

I was just finishing the appliqué on the green and yellow dress when the chiming of my cell phone jarred me.

"Martha? This is Paulina. Andre finally called me. He was detained last night for Royal's murder."

"Have they charged him yet?"

"Not yet. They're releasing him this afternoon. We really need your help."

Oh no. Despite Lucy's suspicions, my gut told me the sheriff was making a mistake. "What can I do?"

"He needs a lawyer. Can you recommend one?"

"Claytie Tolliver had mentioned he was going to consult a lawyer in Ojai who used to be a member of Mystical Feather. Do you want me to find out the name for you?"

"Yes! I'm on my way to Ventura to pick him up at the jailhouse. Call or text me whatever you find out. And thanks."

After we ended the call, I remembered exchanging phone numbers with the Tollivers. But when I searched for the piece of paper I wrote on, I couldn't find it. *Darn!* Maybe Detective Washington would help. I scrolled to the bottom of my list of contacts and called her.

"Della Washington here."

"This is Martha Rose."

"Don't tell me. You've discovered a third dead body?"

"Of course not. I understand you detained Andre overnight for the shooting of Royal St. Germain. Is that true?"

"No comment."

"On the basis of what evidence?"

"I'm afraid I can't discuss the details of an ongoing case. If you wish to know more, you should contact Mr. Polinskaya or his lawyer. I don't mean to be rude, but I'm waiting for an important call."

"Wait. Please don't hang up yet. Can you tell me anything about who we dug up yesterday? How and when did they die?"

"Too soon to tell. It's been less than twenty-four hours since the four of you discovered the remains. In a case like this, it takes several hours to carefully exhume the body. CSI is still excavating, as we speak."

I knew what she meant. The forensic people would treat the crime scene as an archaeological dig. In a slow and tedious process, they'd remove the dirt with trowels and brushes. Since the bones were in the ground for a long time, they'd be disarticulated, which would also slow things down even more.

"Well, when can I find out?"

"Probably when everyone else finds out. When the sheriff holds a press conference. Now, if there's nothing more, I'll take my leave."

"Do you realize that's an oxymoron? Take and leave? They're opposites."

"Goodbye, Mrs. Rose."

I fixed myself a tuna sandwich on challah and cracked open a can of Coke Zero. Then I called Birdie. I told her about finding Andre and unearthing a body on the mountain. "I remember Claytie saying he intended to speak to an attorney in Ojai, a former member of Mystical Feather."

"Oh yes, Martha dear. I do remember that."

"He referred to the lawyer as 'she.' Did he happen to mention her name?"

"Not that I recall. Why?"

"Andre is a suspect in Royal's murder. They're releasing him after detaining him overnight. But he needs a lawyer.'

"Heavens, that was quick work."

"Too quick, as far as I'm concerned. I need to find that attorney in Ojai."

Birdie sighed. "Good luck, dear."

So much for spending my day not thinking about Mystical Feather. I Googled *lawyers, Ojai, California* and found a million law firms in Ventura, Santa Barbara, and LA counties serving the Ojai area. I narrowed the crowded field to only eleven firms whose offices were located within the town of Ojai. I ruled out male solo practitioners and ended up with six possible law firms. A female attorney was listed in only two of them. One group specialized in divorce and family law. The other specialized in estates, wills, and trusts. *Bingo!*

Two names appeared on the web page—Albert Peabody and Jill Carstairs. She had to be the one I was looking for. If she was the lawyer Claytie talked about, who better to handle the Mystical Feather Trust than an estate attorney and a former member? As a graduate of Mystical Feather, would she agree to help the Polinskayas lay claim to the trust?

I called the number on the screen and a plummy female voice answered on the second ring. "Peabody/Carstairs. May I help you?"

"My name is Martha Rose, and I'd like to speak to Jill Carstairs, please."

"Are you a client of Ms. Carstairs?"

"Not yet."

"May I ask what this is regarding?"

If I told her I wanted a defense attorney, I might not get past this screening call. If I said it's about the Mystical Feather trust, the attorney could cite conflict of interest and refuse to see me. So, I did the only honest thing I could think of. I crossed my fingers behind my back before I lied.

"I want some legal advice regarding a trust." *Just not my own trust.* "I'm only in town for a short while." *Because I live close enough to commute.* "Is it possible to see her today?"

"One moment, please."

She put me on hold and, after one minute, came back. "Ms. Carstairs can fit you in today at four. Please be on time. She has another meeting at four twenty."

I glanced at the clock. It read one thirty, giving me plenty of time to make the one-and-a-half-hour trip to Ojai. "Thank you. Thank you. I'll be there."

Driving through downtown Ojai, one had the sensation of traveling back in time to Old California. The streets were lined with one-story stucco buildings topped with red-tiled roofs. The city fathers must've loved arches because they were everywhere. Quaint new age-y shops and restaurants stood ready to welcome visitors.

The office of Peabody/Carstairs was situated in a long one-story building fronted by a portico with, what else, arches. The law office sat between two other businesses. On one side, the window of Matilija Antiques featured green Depression glass plates stacked on top of a Georgian demi-lune table. Two doors away, blue-and-white gingham curtains covered the windows of the Topatopa Tea Shoppe.

I parked in the street at three fifteen, with plenty of time to spare. I moseyed into the tea shoppe and looked around. Delicious pastries inside a glass case beckoned: peanut butter cookies, chocolate éclairs, and carrot cupcakes with cream cheese frosting. My face was close enough to fog the glass with my breath.

"May I help you?" A man wearing a disposable paper shower cap and paper beard covering smiled. "If you have trouble making up your mind, I recommend the carrot cake. Fresh out of the oven with chopped pecans, jumbo yellow raisins, and pineapple chunks. It goes great with a pot of our organic cinnamon tea."

"Sold." I opened my wallet and handed him a ten-dollar bill. He gave me five cents in change. I lingered at the table long after I'd finished my tea. At five minutes before four, I traveled next door to the law firm of Peabody/Carstairs.

The reception room was decorated with a Mission-style sofa and chairs upholstered in red and yellow stripes. They stood in sharp contrast to the white plaster walls, where Navajo rugs hung. Woven reed polychrome baskets were displayed in a locked glass cabinet. The room evoked the sensation of walking onto a movie set of what a lawyer's office in Ojai should look like.

The receptionist sat behind a Mission-style desk and smiled. Her blonde hair was piled on top of her head in a studied heap. "Are you Mrs. Rose?"

"Yes." I walked up to the desk and smiled. "Right on time as you requested."

"Please have a seat. I'll let her know you're here."

I watched from one of the chairs as she spoke into her headset. She ended the call and said, "Ms. Carstairs will see you now. It's just down the hall to your right."

I made my way down a short hallway with a rest-room sign at the end. A nameplate on the door to my left read ALBERT PEABODY. The nameplate on the door to my right read JILL CARSTAIRS. *What if she refuses to talk to me? What if she refuses to help Andre?*

I took a deep breath, pushed the door open, and walked in.

CHAPTER 26

The middle-aged Jill Carstairs wasn't what I expected. She wore a bright red blouse that hid an ample bosom and stomach. Ribbons of orchid pink dye wove through her short, brown hair. One of her ears sported multiple haphazard piercings. The other ear had just one stud. Anyone who demanded symmetry in their attorney would feel acutely uncomfortable in her presence.

"How can I help you, Mrs. Rose?" A stack of metal bangles clinked on her arm as she rose from the desk and extended her hand. Her fingernails were cut short and her grip was firm.

"Thank you for seeing me on such short notice. I'm here about the Mystical Feather Society. I understand you used to be one of their members?"

Some of the friendliness of her greeting evaporated. "You told the receptionist you wanted to talk about your own trust. You never mentioned to her that you had a connection with Mystical Feather."

"Actually, I told the receptionist I wanted to see you about *a* trust. I didn't specify which one. Please forgive me if I caused any confusion. But you are the attorney for the Mystical Feather Society, right?"

She sank back into her tan leather desk chair and clasped her hands. "Yes, I'm the attorney of record. You seem to be a fairly sophisticated person, Mrs. Rose. Therefore, you must know I cannot and will not give you any information about a client."

"Of course. And I wouldn't ask you to."

She stared at the ceiling. "Rose. Martha Rose. Hmm. Your name is familiar. . . ." Understanding sharpened her face and she narrowed her eyes. "You were one of the people who discovered Royal's . . . my client's body."

"Actually, that's why I'm here. I'm pretty sure the sheriff detained the wrong person for his murder. I think he should look elsewhere. For example, now that Royal's dead, who will control the Mystical Feather Trust?"

"Ordinarily, I'd send you to the hall of records to hunt for that information. But, in this case, a search would be futile. The trust isn't a public document."

"I was afraid of that. Do you also handle Royal's will? Who will benefit from his death?"

"Look, I'm not unsympathetic to your cause." The colorful attorney opened a drawer, extracted a vaping pen, and began puffing the cool smoke. "But again, that information would be available only to the heirs or beneficiaries."

The odor of chocolate drifted my way, and I remembered the éclairs in the tea shoppe. "Do you have access to the society's financial records?"

Jill looked at me intently. "I'm not an accountant."

"Okay. To change the subject, did you hear we discovered another body buried on the mountain yesterday?"

Her jaw went slack. "What? You found Eugenie St. Germain?"

I shook my head. "It's not her. However, this discovery will substantiate the rumors about Royal dispatching people to an early grave. Maybe you could help identify the body. What years, exactly, did you live there?"

She was silent for a moment. "About ten years. From ninety-five to two thousand four. I joined right after I finished law school and passed the bar."

"During that time did you know of anyone who mysteriously disappeared?"

Jill gasped and covered her mouth with her hand. "Oh my God. About five years ago, I tried to contact my friend who still lived there. Royal said she 'just up and left without explanation.'" Her eyes grew misty. "I never believed him. Nina and I were very close. She wouldn't just disappear without contacting me. Do they have any idea who was buried there? Do you think it could be Nina?"

"According to Detective Washington, they're

probably still digging up the remains. She told me the sheriff will reveal the details in a press conference." I shifted in my chair. "If I may ask, why did you leave the mountain?"

"He didn't want to be a father."

"Let me guess. Royal?"

She nodded. "He could force me to leave the mountain, but he couldn't force me to have an abortion or leave Ojai. My friend Al Peabody gave me a job and helped me negotiate a settlement. Royal agreed to pay me child support in return for two things. One, I would do all Mystical Feather's legal matters for free, and two, I would never tell our child who his father was. Our son Stormy was born in February two thousand five. Royal's been sending me child support every month since then."

"How awkward was it to maintain a connection to the man who banished you from Mystical Feather?"

"Actually, it wasn't that bad. Royal was never really nasty or abusive. He was just self-centered. I knew what I was getting myself into, right from the beginning of our affair. He never hid the fact he didn't want complications, like children, in his life. So, as long as he kept sending money for Stormy, I was okay with our arrangement."

"I know it's none of my business, but what do you tell Stormy about his father?"

"You know sulky teenagers. He's angry because he thinks his father abandoned him. However, now that Royal's dead, I have no reason not to let him know who his father was. I just need to pick the right time."

"Do you know of any other children he fathered?"

Jill shrugged. "I knew there were more before me and after me, but I didn't want to get involved. For Stormy's sake."

I conjured a picture in my mind of the spreadsheet Little Fawn showed me. *Of course!* A piece of the puzzle finally became clear. Andre was tracking bogus payments; like the monthly checks going to Carstairs Consulting. Royal wouldn't have been able to legally use trust money to pay child support. To get around that, he created phony accounts. I wondered how many of those "vendors" were actually former lovers and their children.

What if Royal had stopped making payments? What if one of his former girlfriends got pissed off enough to kill him? What if Jill killed him? Her son was one of his heirs and would have a legitimate claim to his estate. As a lawyer, she'd make sure of that. And what about Stormy? Did he somehow discover who his father was? Just how angry was he? Could he have killed his own father?

I said, "The person who's the prime suspect for Royal's murder needs an attorney. Can you represent him?"

"I don't do criminal law. Why is your friend a suspect?"

"Eugenie St. Germain didn't die on that mountain, Jill." I told her how Eugenie fled for her life, changed her name, and had three children. "All three of those siblings had a strong motive for killing their uncle. But I don't believe they did it."

Jill put away the vaping pen and pursed her lips. "I'm tempted to help Andre with his legal problem. He's Stormy's cousin, after all. But that would pose a severe conflict of interest. However, there's someone here in Ojai who's really good." She wrote a name and number on a piece of paper. "I'll contact him and tell him to expect your call."

I took the paper and recognized the name as one I'd seen on my internet search. "Thanks again for your time."

"Not at all."

We rose and shook hands.

I retraced my steps to the tea shoppe and bought two chocolate éclairs to go.

Before I started the car for the long drive back to the Valley, I called Paulina.

"Were you able to find that lawyer in Ojai?" she asked.

"I did better than that. I just walked out of her office. Her name is Jill Carstairs. Because Mystical Feather is her client, she can't help Andre. But she gave me the name of someone up here who can." I read the information to her. "How is Andre?"

"He's meditating right now. Trying to get his center back."

"Does he plan to return to the mountain?"

She paused. "Yeah, I think so."

"Well, tell him to be careful. Royal's killer may still be around. What about you and Michael? Going to the jailhouse to fetch your brother must've been a yucky experience."

"I'm fine. Mikey's taking his third shower. Listen, Martha, thanks for the help."

"You're welcome. Ask Andre to call me when he finds his center." I ended the call.

I kept thinking about those chocolate éclairs all the way back to Encino. At six thirty I finally pulled into my driveway, exhausted and in need of a quick sugar fix. I lifted an éclair out of the bag and took a bite before I ever reached the kitchen. I ate the other one while watching *Jeopardy!*

I never did hear from Andre.

CHAPTER 27

Tuesday morning I woke up feeling almost pain free. I quickly dressed in jeans and straightened up the house for the Tuesday morning quilters. I brewed a fresh pot of Italian roast five minutes before everyone arrived.

Lucy showed up with Birdie, a plateful of oatmeal cookies, and the pregnant young Ivy. The girl could've been mistaken for Lucy's granddaughter—they both had flaming red hair, only Lucy's looked more orange and came from a bottle. Birdie had also added new color to her white hair since I last saw her, streaks of purple in addition to the turquoise.

Giselle walked in and stopped short when she saw Birdie. "My God. You look just like *My Little Pony*. How long do you have to go around like that before the color washes out?"

Ivy stifled a giggle.

Jazz was the last to arrive, carrying Zsa Zsa in a blue denim tote with little mesh windows for the dog to look out of. "Good morning, everyone." He took Zsa Zsa out of the carrier. She ran straight to my cat Bumper's bowl on the kitchen floor and loudly lapped up water.

"I'm off sugar," Jazz announced. "I brought a healthy alternative for a change." He opened a grocery sack and removed a round plastic tray from the supermarket with cut veggies arranged in little communities of color. He placed the tray on the glass coffee table, along with a half-pint container of baba ganouj and one of hummus. "Just a reminder, no double dipping allowed. It's unsanitary."

"I'm surprised you care," Giselle waved her hand, "since you let your dog drink out of the same bowl as Martha's cat."

He lowered his eyelids halfway. "I do worry my baby might catch something awful from the cat. No offense, Martha."

When everyone was settled and sewing, Birdie said, "Lucy told me how you found a body on the mountain. And to think Denny and I were ready to join that group. . . ."

Tears slid down Ivy's cheeks. "I'm having a killer's baby."

"I'm surprised to see you again," Giselle addressed Ivy. "I thought your aunt was going to send you a plane ticket back to Ohio. Or was it Idaho?"

Ivy's hand flew to her belly in a protective gesture. "Indiana. My aunt lives in Indiana. When I told her I was pregnant, she changed her mind about me coming home. She said she put in the effort to raise me even though I wasn't her child. And now she expects me to do the same for my baby."

Birdie reached over and patted her arm. "Don't worry, dear. You can stay with Denny and me as long as you need to."

Lucy and I glanced at each other. *That's our Birdie,* her expression said.

I told them about my visit to Jill Carstairs, the lawyer in Ojai, and how the disbursements to "Carstairs Consulting" were really child support payments in disguise. "I wouldn't be surprised if those other inflated vendor accounts in the Mystical Feather Foundation were the same." I turned to Ivy. "Did Royal ever mention helping you and the baby financially once you left the mountain?"

She slowly wagged her head and avoided my eyes. "He just told me since I insisted on keeping the baby, I had to leave."

Didn't Jill Carstairs tell me Royal made it clear from the beginning he didn't want children? "I'm curious, Ivy. Did the two of you ever discuss what would happen if you got pregnant?"

"He said he didn't want children. But I thought he was just afraid. I thought he'd change his mind once he saw our baby, you know? But when I found him with the *new girl,*" her timid voice became hard around the edges, "I knew we would never be a family."

She looked up and something about the glint in her eyes made me wonder. Could this young woman have killed St. Germain, the father her baby would never know? Was Birdie unwittingly giving shelter to a killer?

We sewed in silence for a few minutes.

Even Ivy was stitching. Since our last visit, Birdie had tutored her in the fine art of appliqué. This morning the young newbie sat patiently laying invisible stitches around the outside of a pink heart shape on a cream-colored background. "I'm glad Birdie's teaching me how to appliqué. I think this is going to be the most beautiful quilt in the whole world. I'll keep my baby wrapped in it all the time."

Birdie's smile lit up her face. If she wondered about the girl's innocence, she didn't show it. Had Ivy touched a spot in the childless Birdie's heart much like a daughter or granddaughter would have done? I hoped for my friend's sake I was wrong to suspect Ivy killed St. Germain.

Suddenly Ivy winced. "Ow! I stuck my finger with the needle. And . . . oh no! I got some blood on the fabric."

"Don't worry about a little bit of blood," said Lucy. "You're not the first person who's bled on their quilt. There's an easy quilter's remedy for that. Just spit on the blood and watch it dissolve."

Ivy wrinkled her face. "Huh?"

"Just do it," Lucy pointed to the fabric in Ivy's hands. "A person's saliva is the perfect solvent for their own blood."

Ivy spit delicately on the fabric. "Wow! It really works."

As I reached for an oatmeal cookie, Jazz picked up a celery stick and loaded it with baba ganouj, a puree of roasted eggplant. He thrust it toward me. "You should try this instead, Martha. It's much healthier. From the way you were huffing and puffing up that mountain on Sunday, don't you think a little self-discipline in the food department would be helpful?"

Even though he criticized my wardrobe every chance he got, Jazz had never made a crack about my weight. He must've seen my surprise because he hastily added, "You know I love you like a sister, right?" He didn't wait for an answer. "I had a dream last night that you were the one lying in that grave. When I woke up, the message was clear: *Tell Martha to stay away from sugar.*"

I rolled my eyes. "Thanks for the warning, *Bro.*" I bit into the cookie.

Later that afternoon, when I was alone again, Andre finally called. "I wanted to thank you for finding that lawyer. He said he'd take my case." His deep voice was strong and betrayed little concern. "I'm feeling much more confident now."

"That's a relief. Listen, Andre, I saw your spreadsheet in the computer at the bookstore."

"How . . . ?"

"Little Fawn. She's smarter than she looks. Anyway, I think I discovered what those inflated vendor accounts were all about." I told him about Jill Carstairs and her son, Stormy. "So actually, you have at least two cousins we know of: Stormy Carstairs and Ivy's baby. There are probably more of them floating around. I have to warn you they may come forward to claim Royal's estate."

"I don't care about his personal things. Let

them have it. But control of the Mystical Feather Trust and the society belongs to my mother."

"What will you do if they challenge your claim?"

"Fight for what's right. I read my tarot this morning. The Six of Cups came up reversed. So did the Tower. But the High Priestess was upright."

"Sorry, Andre. I tried to be a good student, but the significance escapes me now. What does it mean?"

"Big changes coming. Upheaval. Crisis. Uncovering secrets. Letting go of the past. I was really encouraged by the cards. Our success rests on our willingness to move forward, and I'm ready. Even my brush with the sheriff fits into the picture the cards drew for me. It forced me to finally reveal my true self."

"As Eugenie's son? As Natasha's grandson?"

"Of course. I tried to tell them it was Natasha's spirit who directed me to explore the mountainside for graves. Of course, they didn't believe me."

"Has Natasha spoken to you recently?"

"That's why I'm calling you. She came to me in my meditation yesterday and told me what to do. I'm going back to the mountain tomorrow to find a killer. And you're coming with me."

CHAPTER 28

Wednesday morning I rolled out of bed after a restless night alone. As I waited for the coffee to brew, I turned on news radio and learned that two federal agents were injured in a sting operation the night before in San Pedro. The agents had seized a large cache of assault weapons destined for Mexico. If guns were involved, so was the ATF.

I shivered. Crusher still hadn't called. His undercover assignments with the ATF were the most exciting for him and the most difficult for me. I knew my fiancé well enough to be confident he could take care of himself in a violent situation. But that didn't stop me from worrying.

Andre Polinskaya showed up at my house at ten on the dot. He had shaved off his beard and once again looked like his New Jersey driver's license photo. His clean-shaven face bore a strong resemblance to Paulina and Mansoor: black hair, high cheekbones, and dark, almond-shaped eyes. He gave me a hopeful smile. "Are you ready?"

I nodded and looked around for the car he came in, but nothing was parked in my driveway or on the empty street. "How did you get here?"

"Paulie dropped me off. She and Mikey wanted to come with us, but I told them to stay away. If something goes horribly wrong and you and I don't make it back, there will be two people who'll know where we went and why."

Somehow his explanation was less than comforting. "Aren't you being a little over pessimistic? The killer can't possibly think nobody would investigate if we went missing, too."

He shrugged. "People have died up there, Martha. We have to be very careful."

He had a point. We got in my Honda, backed out of the driveway, and headed for the 101 freeway going north.

"So, why did Natasha's spirit tell you to take me—of all people—back to the mountain? I'm not an Adept. I can't read people's auras, nor can I tell what someone's thinking."

Andre chuckled. "You're closer to being Adept than you think. Your intuition is sharper than most people's and you're really smart. You see patterns other people may overlook. You're compelled to solve puzzles. And you have a strong sense of justice. Natasha said you'd be my perfect counterpart."

I took my gaze off the road long enough to scowl at him. "Are you serious? I never even heard of Madam Natasha St. Germain until a couple of weeks ago. How can Natasha know about me in such a short a time?"

"There are no physical barriers in the spiritual world. Time and space don't exist either. The spirits can see everything and go everywhere. You really should read Natasha's books."

Like that will ever happen. "If Natasha's spirit is really all-knowing, why didn't you just ask her who killed Royal?"

"She doesn't work that way. She suggests or she points me in a certain direction. I think she means for me to discover the facts on my own."

"There are other spirits where Natasha came from. None of them would tell you who the shooter was?"

"Think about it. If I made claims and accused people on the basis of what I learned from the spirit world, who would believe me? No, we need to find something even the skeptics in law enforcement can understand."

I nodded. "Yeah. We need evidence or a confession."

We drove in silence for the next five minutes. I thought about all the people who held a grievance against St. Germain. The three Polinskaya siblings topped the list. They had the most to gain from his death—control over the Mystical Feather Society and the trust money. However, my gut told me to look elsewhere. Was this feeling of mine what Andre called "sharp intuition"? Or was I merely being blinded by my fondness for Paulina?

In addition to the siblings, on the list of victims

were the various women Royal had seduced and then discarded. We still had to identify who all of them were. Using the spreadsheet Andre had put together, we could track who he was paying off. Any one of them could've snapped. And what about Jill Carstairs's troubled teenage son, Stormy? Was the kid angry enough to shoot the father who rejected him? Finally, there were the families of members who had disappeared. In the past, the FBI had failed to locate any bodies. Did some relative decide to carry out a little vigilante justice?

When we passed the town of Westlake Village, the freeway narrowed, and traffic slowed a bit. Andre cleared his throat. "Uh, is your friend Jazz married?"

"No, he lost the love of his life a couple of years ago. Why? Are you interested?"

"Yeah. Is he involved with anyone?"

"He used to have someone, but I think they've broken up. Isn't he a little bit old for you?"

"I prefer someone more mature."

Who was I to judge? There was a similar age difference between Jazz and his late partner, and their May-December relationship lasted for twenty-five years until the older man's death.

Andre continued. "Would you give me his number?"

"I don't feel comfortable with that. Jazz has been through a lot lately. How about I give him your number? If he's interested, he'll call you. Will that work for you?"

Andre smiled. "Sure. Thanks."

We arrived at Sulphur Mountain Road at 11:30.

Five minutes later we turned left onto the driveway marked by the Mystical Feather Society sign. Andre asked me to park next to the bookstore and tea shoppe. Three other cars were also parked there. A red Hyundai, a sheriff's black-and-white, and the CSI van sat in a neat row.

"Looks like forensics is still processing the grave," I said.

"I wonder why they're taking this long. We found the body three days ago." The door to the bookstore was unlocked. He held it open and, in a gesture of chivalry, indicated I should enter first.

The shop was empty except for Little Fawn sitting to our right in the bookstore side of the shop. Her white robe contrasted sharply with the purple velvet upholstery. She looked up when the bell over the door tinkled, and a wave of relief washed over her face once she realized who we were. "Is that you, Freddy? I was worried bad when you were arrested. Did the police make you shave your beard? Are you back for good?"

"First of all, I wasn't arrested or charged with anything yet. They only detained me for questioning. Second of all, the beard was part of a disguise. I shaved it off because I no longer need to hide behind it."

"Disguise? What disguise?"

Andre and I walked over to the chairs and sat with the girl. "You're the first person at Mystical Feather to find out my real identity. My name isn't Freddy Pea."

Little Fawn's eyes widened, and her mouth formed an O.

Andre continued. "My real name is Andre Polinskaya. My mother is Eugenie St. Germain, and she's very much alive. My grandmother is Madam Natasha St. Germain."

The girl gasped. "For real? Then that would make you Royal's what? Cousin?"

"Nephew."

"Everybody thinks the body you uncovered is Eugenie. But if you say your mother is still alive, then who's buried in that grave down the hill?"

"We don't know yet." He briefly scanned the room. "I'm glad to see you're still working here."

"Claytie Tolliver asked me to keep this place open while you were gone. Poor guy. He's trying to run things now that Royal's gone."

"How's he doing?" I asked.

She shrugged. "All's I know is he asked me to look after the bookstore."

Andre excused himself and went through the door in the back leading to his office. Two minutes later, he strode through the door and over to where we sat. "Little Fawn, the laptop that was on my desk is gone. Who took it?"

"It's gone? I never noticed. Ever since Claytie asked me to keep working here, nobody's bothered to come down from the commune."

"So you've been alone in the bookshop every day?" I asked.

"Yeah. We don't get as many visitors during the week."

"When was the last time you saw the computer?" Andre scowled.

Little Fawn wrung her hands. "I'm sorry. I didn't

know I was supposed to do anything with it." She looked from me to Andre and back again. "Was I supposed to?"

"It's important we find the computer." Andre's voice carried an edge. "Think back."

"Okay." She sank back into the plush purple upholstery and closed her eyes. "Sunday afternoon I left the bookstore before you did and went back up the hill."

"Right. It was still here when I locked up on Sunday afternoon. What happened after I left?"

Little Fawn opened her eyes and looked at us. "When we heard the police sirens, Claytie told us to stay together in the dining hall while he went down to find out what was going on. Some of the deputies escorted him back to the dining hall and took statements from each of us."

"Did you hear anyone say who the victim could be?"

"Like I said, everyone thought it was Eugenie."

"Go on," I urged. "When did Claytie ask you to work in the bookstore?"

"The next morning. Claytie looked like he hadn't gotten any sleep. He asked if I would manage the bookstore and teahouse for him until all the legal stuff was settled." She smiled. "Not everyone thinks I'm just a dumb little kid. Anyways, he handed me the key and told me, 'Carry on as usual.' And that's what I've been doing."

"Think," Andre urged gently. "Did you see the laptop when you opened the bookstore Monday morning?"

Little Fawn sat silently for a minute. "It must've

still been there because everything else was the same as we left it the day before."

"Are you sure? Try to picture yourself in the back room Monday morning. Do you see the computer?

"I want to help, I really do. But to tell you the truth, I just didn't notice. The computer was your thing, not mine, so I never thought about it."

Andre frowned. "That's not entirely true, is it? You thought enough about the computer to use my password and show Martha a file."

The girl's cheeks reddened, and her voice was defiant. "So what if I did? I'm not dumb, you know. I think that file shows you were stealing money from Mystical Feather."

I interrupted their discussion before it escalated. "Yes and no, Little Fawn. You were very clever to notice that someone was using funds inappropriately, but it couldn't have been Andre. He's only been here six months, and that file goes back a year."

"Oh." She spoke softly.

"Did you mention the file to anyone else besides me?" I asked.

"I may have said something in the dining hall before the deputies came to interview us."

"This is important, Little Fawn." Andre leaned forward and pinned her to her seat with a severe stare. "Who, exactly, heard you mention the file?"

She swallowed. "Do you think the same person who killed Royal also took the laptop?"

"Yeah. It's possible." Andre kept staring at her

with the same intensity. "So, who heard you talking?"

Tears gathered in Little Fawn's eyes. "Everyone heard me talk about that file." She looked at me and her chin trembled. "I know you asked me to keep the information to myself, but when we heard they arrested Freddy—er, Andre—I thought it would be okay to tell the others."

"Well, obviously it wasn't," Andre snapped at the girl.

"I'm sorry. I really am." Something about the tone of her voice rang false. I suspected that underneath her tears, the girl had been proud to be the bearer of juicy gossip.

The mystery deepened with each new revelation: St. Germain's murder, the body on the hill, and the financial crimes. What was the relationship between them? I wondered if Little Fawn realized that by admitting she read the file, she might've put herself in danger. "Listen, sweetie. I'm concerned for your safety being all alone down here. Do you have a friend in Mystical Feather? One who can hang around with you in the bookstore?"

She reached for a tissue in the pocket of her apron and dabbed at her eyes. "Yeah. I could ask White Raven to keep me company."

"Excellent choice." Andre must've seen the confusion on my face. "White Raven is the oldest member here. He's eighty."

"I think I know who you mean." I had seen only one person here who might fit the description.

"Isn't he the one who works in the kitchen and walks around nude? How much help could he be in case someone comes after Little Fawn?"

The corner of Andre's mouth curled in a half-smile. "He practices yoga every day. He's also got a black belt in karate."

Oh no! I tried in vain to wipe away the picture in my head of a naked eighty-year-old man extending his leg in a martial arts kick.

It was clear Little Fawn couldn't give us any more information. Andre stood to leave. "We're going up the hill. I'll find White Raven and ask him to get dressed and join you."

I stood, too, and shouldered my purse. "By the way, I'm surprised to see the forensic people still working. I thought they'd be finished by now. It's been three days."

Little Fawn pushed herself up out of the comfortable purple chair. "Didn't you hear? They found another body down there."

CHAPTER 29

My stomach plunged when Little Fawn dropped the bombshell of a second body found on the hill.

Andre grimaced. "When?"

"Yesterday morning."

He wagged his head. "Damn. That must mean the rumors about Royal getting rid of people were true."

Now that I knew Little Fawn couldn't keep a secret, I got up and headed for the door of the bookshop. "Let's go outside and talk."

Andre glanced briefly at the girl and followed me to the parking lot. We got in my Honda while I pulled out my cell phone. Detective Della Washington answered on the second ring.

"This is Martha Rose. I'm at Mystical Feather with Andre Polinskaya. We heard you discovered a second body."

"Hah! I just won twenty bucks from my partner."

"Sorry?"

"I bet twenty bucks you'd call again, wanting information about our activities up on Sulphur Mountain. The question was never *if* you'd call, it was *when* you'd call. My guess was between eleven and noon today."

My watch read 11:55. "Congratulations. I guess that means you owe me one."

"One what?"

"One honest conversation." I ignored her grumbling at the other end. "What have you found out about our body? The one we discovered on Sunday. Gender? Age? Manner of death? How long they've been there?"

"You know I can't answer your questions, Mrs. Rose. Even if I wanted to, which I definitely do not. Why do you keep asking?"

"Because I think you should extend some professional courtesy to me."

Washington's laugh was rich and mellow. "Professional?"

"Exactly. I may not be a sworn officer of the law, but I'm not without valuable experience and knowledge. I've solved several murders."

"I'd say that only proves you were lucky."

I wasn't going to let her dismiss me so easily. "Well what about this? My fiancé is a federal agent. And my son-in-law is a homicide detective with the LAPD."

"With all due respect to your exalted status as

girlfriend and mother-in-law, I refer you to the public information officer at our HQ in Ventura. Goodbye, Mrs. Rose. It's been real." She ended the call before I could speak.

"Anything?" Andre had listened without comment to my side of the conversation with the detective.

"No." I shook my head. "But I have another idea." I scrolled up my contact list from W to S and called Smith, Director John, at the FBI.

His voice croaked. "Yeah?"

"Hello, John. I'm calling from Mystical Feather in Ojai. In the spirit of mutual cooperation, I want to share something I just learned."

"It's the middle of the night."

"Sorry. It's noon here. You said you wanted me to call you with important information. But if you need to sleep, I always call you back with my *shocking* news."

I heard him grunt, as if he were turning over in bed. "Go on."

"Ventura County CSI discovered another body on Sulphur Mountain."

"When?" He sounded more awake.

"Tuesday morning."

"Yeah," Smith yawned loudly. "I knew about that one. I thought you were calling about additional graves."

"You knew about the second grave and didn't contact me? What about our understanding? What about mutual cooperation?"

"Mutual? That means you share information with me, and other people share information with me. Mutual as in: Intel gathering is a *mutual* effort."

I couldn't help but smile. "That was a very deft evasion for the middle of the night."

"Why are you back at Mystical Feather?"

I told him what Andre's forensic accounting uncovered. "I have a gut feeling the phony vendor accounts are linked to Royal's murder. Plus, we just discovered Andre's computer and the file have gone missing, which suggests that the shooter either lives on the mountain or is someone who has easy access."

"All the more reason for you to leave," he said.

"I hear you. So, what can you tell me about the body we found Sunday afternoon?"

"Male. Elderly. Died at least a year ago. Cause of death undetermined."

"What about the new body? Where was it found?"

"Next to the first one. It appears that particular clearing became a serial killer's dumping ground."

"For Royal St. Germain."

"Apparently so. And before you ask, I know nothing yet about the second body. The remains are still in the process of being removed. Now, here's my advice. Leave Ojai, go home, and wait. The wheels of justice may be slow, but they grind exceedingly fine."

How often had I heard that quotation? "Believe me, I don't intend to stay on the mountain. But

Andre does. He has a huge personal stake in solving Royal's murder."

Smith grunted again. "Detective Washington isn't happy you keep insinuating yourself in the investigation."

"The two of you talked about me? I'm flattered."

"You wouldn't be if you knew what she said. As we speak, the Bureau is preparing to conduct a wider search for more bodies. I should be back in the country soon. We'll talk again then."

We ended the call and I repeated to Andre what I'd learned from Director Smith. "What did you tell me before about a man going missing around a year ago?"

"Yeah. His name was Max. Older guy."

"Who told you about him?"

"White Raven," he said. "He told me one day Max disappeared without a word. Do you think that's the body we found?"

"I wouldn't rule it out. Let's drive up the hill to the commune. We need to talk to White Raven anyway about keeping Little Fawn safe."

The tires of my Honda Civic crunched over the gravel as we slowly headed up the driveway. When we got to the gate, Andre got out of the car and swung it open. Then he jumped back in the car. "I guess nobody bothered to get a new lock after the sheriff used bolt cutters on the old one."

We weren't surprised to discover Birdie's Winnebago was gone from the parking area bordered by shrubbery, presumably towed away to some facility where it would be taken apart by forensic experts. I parked the Honda at the end of a row of vehicles: two white vans, the red Mercedes, and a gray Prius.

We left the car and walked toward the glass yurt. I huffed and puffed as we trudged the fifty yards uphill. I could barely find my voice. "Where do you think White Raven is?"

Andre glanced at his watch. "It's noon. He'll be in the kitchen."

The ground leveled off once we reached the yurt, and my desperate breathing returned to normal. Out of curiosity, I glanced inside the yurt and saw four people sitting inside in a tight circle.

We made our way to the dining hall, and all conversation stopped as we entered. Five people in white robes sat together at a table near the fruit and vegetable mural and stared at us as we made our way to the door at the other end of the room.

A nude White Raven didn't hear us enter the kitchen. He stood with his back to the door at a large stainless-steel sink in the middle of a long stainless-steel countertop. He wore a starched white chef's hat and a white chef's apron that tied in the back. Although I didn't want to, I could see the clear definition of sinewy muscle beneath the sagging skin of old age.

Andre cleared his throat to get White Raven's attention.

The old man turned around and a grin split his face. "Freddy! We didn't know what happened to you after the sheriff took you away. Glad to see you're back. Since several people left Mystical Feather, we're shorthanded. A lot of the chores aren't getting done. We could sure use your help."

"There's something I want you to know. My name isn't Freddy Pea." Andre told the old man the truth about his identity and why he came to Mystical Feather.

"So, what you're saying is you're the true heir to Madam St. Germain?"

Andre nodded. "One of them. I'm about to tell the others."

The old man squinted at Andre's face. "My spirit guide told me you needed my help. Now I know why." Then he smiled at me. "And who do we have here?"

Andre jumped in. "Oh, sorry. This is Martha Rose. She took my class last weekend."

"Yes, I recognize you." He gazed at my face. "You have a lovely yellow aura. Have you decided to join us?"

"I'm not sure." I was grateful for the apron that covered his front.

"Listen, I'm really worried." Andre proceeded to tell the older man about the missing laptop and spreadsheet.

"Yes. Little Fawn told us all about the file."

Andre sighed. "Little Fawn is the only one who saw what was in it besides Martha and me. I'm afraid whoever didn't want that information to see the light of day might feel desperate enough to get rid of any witnesses. She needs someone to stay with her and keep her safe. Can you do it?"

"Of course! I'll go to the bookstore right now."
White Raven removed his hat, revealing a full head
of thick, white hair.

"Good," Andre said. "I'm going to call everyone
to the yurt. Can you escort Little Fawn back up
here?"

"I'm on it."

When White Raven began removing his apron, I
turned my face away. "Maybe you should put on
some clothes first. She's a young girl."

He giggled. "Of course. Clothing options apply
only on this side of the gate. Everyone must be
dressed if they want to go past the gate and down
the driveway. I'll just throw on a robe and fetch
her." He walked fast toward the exit.

I blew out my breath. "What next?"

Andre chewed on his bottom lip. "After everyone gathers in the yurt, I'll tell them the whole
story. While I'm talking, you can watch people for
any suspicious reactions."

We left the kitchen and as we walked through
the dining hall, a woman waved at us. "Hey,
Freddy! You look great without a beard. Wanna
tell us what's going on?"

He stopped walking long enough to say, "I'm on
my way to the yurt to do just that. Can you go and
round everybody up? It's important."

"Sure!" the woman said.

The group of five stood and followed us out of
the dining hall. Once outside, they split up in
search of the others.

The circle of four people inside the yurt turned

to look at us as we entered. I instantly recognized two women: June Tolliver and a woman wearing a blue-and-white fabric headpiece pleated in back to resemble a peacock spreading its tail. Nkwa.

June smiled brightly. "Are you joining our class on reading auras? You're a bit late, but you're always welcome."

Andre pressed his palms together. "I'm very sorry, June, but I have an important announcement that every member of Mystical Feather needs to hear, and I don't think it will wait."

June nodded and looked back at her three students. "I apologize, but we're operating under extraordinary circumstances at Mystical Feather. You may have to wait a bit while we handle some necessary business. Oh! I know what you can do. . . ." She reached into a black fabric tote bag and pulled out three boxes of crayons and some white paper. "While we have our meeting, you can practice drawing pictures of peoples' auras and color them in."

Everyone looked from June to Andre and back again, but none of her students made a move to leave.

I stepped closer to Nkwa and bent down to whisper. "I didn't know you'd signed up for more classes. How's this one?"

Nkwa rose off the floor in one fluid motion, especially nimble for someone dressed in a long wraparound skirt. She stood next to me and spoke in a low voice. "I have to say I prefer Freddy as a teacher. All June has managed to do is tell stories about how she and Madam Natasha were such good friends and confidants. She's given us very little instruction regarding auras. By the way, what are you doing here?"

"Long story," I sighed.

"Is it true Freddy discovered a grave on Sunday?"

Nkwa was a nice enough woman, but I didn't want to give the outsider any more details. "Yes, but I don't know anything else."

Through the glass walls of the yurt, I saw people heading toward us from all directions. Claytie Tolliver was one of the last to show up. Little Fawn had described him as tired and worried, but I thought his distress went deeper. His eyes seemed to have sunk inside dark circles of skin and darted unceasingly from person to person. The fingers of his left hand tapped against his left thigh, as if broadcasting a secret code through his body. He reminded me of a feral cat trapped in a cage.

June left her circle of students and joined Claytie nearby, standing on his left side. She grabbed his peripatetic hand. "Steady, Papa. Remember your blood pressure."

Claytie's hand stopped tapping. "Did Freddy mention what he wanted to tell everyone?"

"Whatever he wants to share with us, it can't be bad, Claytie." She smiled at him and stroked his arm. "If it's *that* important, my dear Natasha would've told me."

After a quarter of an hour, the remaining members of the commune, including Little Fawn and

White Raven, gathered around Andre in the yurt—
twenty people, including the nonmembers from
June's class and me.

Andre asked Claytie, "Is this everyone, then?"

Claytie nodded. "All that's left."

Andre cleared his throat. "I have a confession to
make. I joined Mystical Feather under false pre-
tenses."

A sea of confusion washed over the faces of the
crowd.

"You've all heard rumors Royal's sister, Eugenie,
disappeared soon after Madam Natasha St. Germain's death. Some of you have even come to wonder if the body we found on Sunday was hers. But
I'm here to tell you Eugenie isn't dead."

The listeners gasped, murmured comments,
and became silent when Andre continued speaking.

"After Madam Natasha died, Eugenie ran away
to the East Coast and changed her name to Jean
Saint. She married a professor, Andre Polinskaya,
and had three children."

June gasped. "Are you sure? Natasha's spirit
never breathed a word about that."

"My name isn't Freddy Pea. It's Andre Polinskaya. Junior. I am the son of Eugenie St. Germain
and the grandson of Natasha St. Germain."

Claytie's face turned a whiter shade of gray.
Everyone spoke at once.

Andre once again held up his hand for silence
and got it. He spoke about how his mother was
supposed to inherit the Mystical Feather Society

and Trust but was cheated out of it by her brother. "I'm here to restore Mystical Feather into my mother's hands, where it should have been all along."

I scanned the room as Andre spoke. The faces registered both shock and relief.

A woman with thick eyeglasses said, "Oh yes, I can see a family resemblance now."

A young man pulled his long hair to the back of his neck and secured it with some kind of stretchy thing. "Oh man. Did Royal know who you were?" When Andre shook his head no, the man asked, "Why didn't you tell him?"

"I needed to gather evidence on how he'd mismanaged the Mystical Feather Trust. Turns out, he was committing financial crimes."

"Oh my gosh. Did you kill your uncle?" I couldn't tell who had asked the question.

"No," Andre said. "But the person who did may very well be in this room."

Another wave of shock rolled through the voices. "No."

"Impossible."

June muttered sadly, "I think you're wrong, Andre. Nobody in this room could've killed that man. We all loved Royal."

Andre frowned at her. "He used people and committed fraud. He was a liar. I uncovered evidence to prove it. Only my laptop, along with my research, have gone missing." He glanced at me. "We think the person who killed him also stole that evidence."

I could no longer keep silent. "Among other despicable traits, Royal was a serial killer. The bodies on this mountain will prove it. I believe it's only a matter of time before they find more graves of people who suddenly disappeared over the years."

White Raven's voice was thin and wispy. "Maybe they'll find my friend Max. . . ."

"Maybe we already did," Andre said gently.

I felt slightly queasy. Something about this discussion sent alarms ringing in my head. What was it?

CHAPTER 30

Little Fawn raised her hand as if she were still in school. "Will we be able to stay here on the mountain?"

Several voices murmured, "Yeah. What'll happen to us?"

Andre said, "You're okay until my mother decides what she wants to do with Mystical Feather. I suspect she'll decide to keep everything going if there's enough money left in the trust. Anyway, I wanted to give everyone a heads-up on what's likely to happen."

"Are you in charge now, Andre?" The question came from White Raven.

"Yes." His gaze swept across the group. "I'll be staying in our family's home. The white house where Royal lived for the last few decades was built by my grandmother, Natasha."

Something odd flitted across the expression on Claytie's face. What was it? Surprise? Anger?

June squeezed her husband's hand and gave him a reassuring smile. "Well, this does change everything, doesn't it, Papa?" Then she turned to Andre with the same smile. "I apologize, but Claytie and I have been staying in the big house. We didn't expect anyone from the family to show up." She chuckled. "We didn't know our beloved Royal had any family left. How could we? We'll just go back there with you and remove our things."

The group began to break up and drift out of the yurt. Claytie and June left with Andre and me and walked the short distance to the white house with the lemon tree in front.

"Do you have a key?" Andre asked.

Claytie turned the knob on the door. "If there is one, we've never found it. Royal maintained an open-door policy. The only thing he allowed to be locked was the bookstore and the gate across the driveway."

What had Andre said? *Royal had a bad habit of going through people's things.* No wonder he didn't allow locks. He could hardly snoop if everyone had a bolt on their door.

The inside of the house was cooler than the outside, thanks to thick adobe walls, high ceilings, and tile floors. I stood next to Andre, just inside the door, and tried to absorb the peculiar ambiance of the living room. The walls and ceiling were painted lavender and the windows were dressed with purple velvet drapes. A dozen large floor cushions in jewel colors formed a ring around a predominantly red Asian carpet. In the middle of the carpet stood a tall brass hookah with a hose long enough to reach the cushions. Expensive TV and audio equipment sat pushed against the longest wall.

"It looks like a Moroccan whore house," I whispered to Andre.

He laughed softly. "And just how do you know what that looks like?"

June headed for the stairs. "I'll just go and grab our things from the bedroom. We probably brought more than we needed, but we didn't know how long we'd be staying here."

Andre inclined his head toward the stairs and gave me a look that said, *Better go with her.*

I knew what he meant. No telling if June might decide to remove something valuable from the house. "I'll help you." I followed her upstairs.

The lavender master bedroom was large enough for a purple sofa, purple drapes, another large wall-mounted TV, and a small refrigerator. One door led to a spacious bathroom with a heart-shaped jacuzzi. Another led to a walk-in closet. The unmade bed was king-sized and mounted on the ceiling above it was a giant mirror. I spotted a tiny red electronic light that indicated a camera might be hidden somewhere up there.

Did Royal film all his trysts? What did he do with the videos, and where were they? Did he watch them for pleasure or something more sinister, like blackmail?

June began emptying drawers and piling clothes in a couple of expensive-looking brown leather suitcases. "We don't own much," she sighed. "This won't take long."

I helped fold a couple of long robes. When I placed them in the suitcase, I noticed the gold initials RSG engraved on a metal plate under the handle. "Um, June, doesn't this luggage belong to Royal? It has his initials right here. See?"

"Well," she huffed, "I didn't see any harm in taking it. Goodness knows he doesn't need it anymore."

"Until the estate is settled, I'm afraid you can't take anything that belonged to him. It'll be up to his heirs to decide how to dispose of his possessions." I ignored her frown. "Let's find something else to pack your stuff in. What did you use to bring all your items over here?"

June's mouth turned down in a pout and she pointed to two empty cardboard boxes and a half-dozen grocery bags in the corner of the room.

"Let's use those." I began removing her things from the suitcase.

Without speaking or acknowledging me, she retrieved the boxes and bags and began jamming clothes in them with furious thrusts. When she finished with the clothes, she went into the large en suite bathroom and collected various toiletries and placed them in the plastic grocery sacks. "I don't know why you got involved in all this." She swept her arm in a wide arc meant to convey all of Sulphur Mountain. "Do you have something going with Andre?" She gave me a quick once-over. "I hardly think he'd be seriously interested in someone as old as you."

Whoa. Where was that smiling, helpful woman of an hour ago? The person who now stood before me was the steely June I'd met in Birdie's kitchen. Then I remembered what had been bothering me since our conversation in the yurt today. In Birdie's kitchen, June said Royal deserved what he got. Yet today she claimed everyone loved him. So, what was the truth?

"You're only half right about Andre. I hardly think he'd be serious about any woman, young or old." I closed the empty suitcases. "Where did you find these? I'll just put them back."

"Closet." She spat out the word.

Claytie walked into the bedroom. "I just came upstairs to find out what was taking you so long."

June looked at her husband and pressed her lips together in a hard line. She shook her head once as if to say, *Don't ask.*

I picked up one empty suitcase and opened the door to the roomy closet. Through the darkness, I could just make out a row of shoes on the floor underneath a rack of shirts on hangers. I reached along the wall for a switch. Before I could flip the light on, something hit my head from behind and the darkness suddenly got darker. And silent.

CHAPTER 31

The first thing I noticed was the pounding headache. I felt like a tiny construction worker inside my skull was trying to escape by hammering open my cranium. The second thing I noticed was the hard floor beneath me. Every bone, muscle, and nerve in my body throbbed with fire and pain.

Where am I? What happened?

I tried to lick my lips, but something sticky sealed my mouth shut. Duct tape? I opened my eyes slowly and carefully to the near darkness of a small room. Only a sliver of light showed between the bottom of the door and the floor. My shoulders ached, and my left arm and hand were numb from lying on that side for . . . *how long have I been here?* Only when I tried to move my arms did I realize my wrists were bound together behind my back by duct tape.

Oh my God.

I tried moving my legs and discovered my feet were also bound together at the ankles. The strong smell of copper pennies nauseated me. Something sour rose from my stomach to my throat. My heart rate doubled.

I've got to get out of here.

"Mmmf!" I tried to scream as I inched my way to sitting. I fought against the panic rising in my chest. My head continued to pound and the skin on the back of my scalp stung.

Think, Martha. What's the last thing I remember?

I'd been helping June pack her things and—oh, yes—I walked to Royal's closet with his leather suitcase. Claytie and June were behind me. Had Andre also walked into the room? Who knocked me out? Were all three in it together? After all, Andre was the one who suggested I go upstairs with June.

Is that where I am? Royal St. Germain's closet?

I tried once again to lick my lips and managed to push the tip of my tongue between them to the tape over my mouth. The moisture of my saliva seemed to slightly weaken the adhesive. I kept producing small amounts of spit to paint on the tape with my tongue.

My hair was glued to my left cheek by something sticky.

Oh my God. The copper penny smell. My head must be bleeding. Gotta get my cell phone. Where's my purse?

I heard voices coming into the other room. I continued to frantically wiggle my wrists out of the binding. I made fists and pushed my wrists away from each other to stretch and weaken the tape.

"It's finally dark enough to move her body. We

have to do it tonight because the police will be back in the morning."

She's talking about me!

Claytie's voice sounded worried. "That Nigerian woman came looking for Martha a couple of hours ago."

"I know, Claytie. You've already told me ten times."

"I can't help it, Junie. Did I do right? I said Martha had decided to take a nap in the guest room and I didn't want to disturb her. The woman said she'd come back later. We can't keep getting rid of people this way."

"Keep getting rid of people?" Did June and Claytie help Royal put those bodies on the mountain?

"Don't lose your nerve now, Claytie. We've come this far. If we keep our heads down, we'll come through this, just like all the others before. Here, take Martha's purse. Keys and cell phone are inside."

Oh no. Not the phone.

"This is what we do. You'll dump her car in the Vons parking lot downtown. Leave the keys in the ignition and the purse on the front seat. I'll be right behind you in one of the vans. I'll bring you back. If anyone asks, we'll say they left Mystical Feather. And when they find the car with her purse, keys, and phone, they'll think the two of them disappeared from the parking lot, not from here."

If I do manage to get free, please, God, how will I phone for help?

The couple's voices faded as they walked out of the bedroom and down the hallway.

"Don't forget to wear gloves, Claytie. The first thing the police will do is look for fingerprints."

"You're so smart, Junie. Like always."

Like always? How many times have they done this before? June said "they" left Mystical Feather, and "the two of them." I think they mean to kill Andre, too. How long before they come back?

After another few minutes of struggle, my right hand broke free. I brought my arms to the front and removed the tape from the other hand, rubbing my wrists. I slowly peeled the tape from my mouth. One end stuck to the hair on the left side of my face. Instead of wasting time trying to untangle it, I let the tape hang.

I needed light to see my ankles. I half scooted on my butt, half dragged myself to the door, pulled the lever handle downward, and swung it open a crack. By the light from a lamp in Royal's purple bedroom, I could see well enough to unwind the tape on my ankles.

Free!

I got on my hands and knees, turned my toes forward, and, with one huge and painful effort from my thighs, I hoisted my butt into the downward-facing dog yoga position. Then I slowly inched my upper body upward until I was vertical. My head spun and I slouched against the closet doorframe until the lightheadedness passed. Slowly creaking the open door wider, I made sure the coast was clear.

I looked around for my shoes, but they were

gone. I was sure the Tollivers were going to use them, along with the other items, to stage an abduction scene from the Vons parking lot. Royal's closet held several pairs of shoes. I selected a pair of brown leather cowboy boots several sizes too large. Even though I swam in them, they'd be good protection if I had to duck into the wilderness and hide.

I headed into the bathroom and gasped at my reflection. I was right about the dried blood sticking to my cheek. I leaned down, splashed water on my face to clean off the worst of it, and removed the end of the duct tape. Then I scooped my hand into a cup and drank water straight from the tap.

The clock on the nightstand next to the bed read 8:14. I reasoned it would take Claytie and June about a half hour to drive into town and back. I clomped downstairs to the kitchen with the boots slapping against the floor. A wooden block holding knives sat on the black granite countertop. The one with the longest blade had a serrated edge and could extend my reach by another sixteen inches. I wasn't about to let either one of the Tollivers get close to me again.

Maybe I'd find an old-fashioned landline in Royal's office. The boots slapped loudly against the tile floor as I half-walked, half-shuffled to the office. A low moan came from the floor. I flipped on the light switch. Andre's wrists and ankles were bound together like mine had been, and duct tape covered his mouth.

"Andre! It's Martha. I'm going to get us out of here."

He lay quietly on the floor, eyelids fluttering. Had he been drugged? I pulled the tape from his mouth and used the knife to saw through the duct tape around his wrists and ankles. Once freed, both his arms and legs remained limp. I laid the knife on the floor next to him and shook him by the shoulders. "Andre! You've got to wake up!"

"Aaangg," he moaned with a slack jaw.

I rushed back to the kitchen, throwing open cupboards until I found the one with drinking glasses. I filled the tallest one with water and hurried back to throw it on Andre's face. "Wake up now!"

"Achh," he coughed and briefly opened his lids to reveal eyes rolled back.

I slapped both his cheeks until he bent a desultory right arm over his face to fend me off. "Mmabaa."

"That's right, it's Martha. You've been drugged. You've got to fight to wake up. If you don't, we're both dead, 'cause I'm not leaving you."

Whatever drug they had given him was more powerful than the will to stay awake. Despite another glass of water in his face, he slipped into unconsciousness.

Royal St. Germain didn't have a landline. The clock on the wall read 8:39. At the most, we had five more minutes before June and Claytie returned. I debated whether to risk leaving Andre to find someone on the mountain with a cell phone when I heard the front door open.

Too late! Please, God, give me the strength to protect myself and Andre.

Adrenaline coursed through my body as I grabbed the bread knife and prepared to fight for my life. I had the initial advantage, because neither Claytie nor June knew I was free. However, once they saw me, the odds would be in their favor. Two against one.

I clutched the knife handle with both hands, raised my arms over my head like a samurai, and took a deep breath.

Here goes nothing.

I charged out of the office, screaming at the top of my lungs, "Don't come any closer! The police are on their way!"

I couldn't believe who stood before me with a gun in one hand and a wallet with a badge and photo ID in the other. My jaw dropped open.

"Special Agent Nkwa Applebaum, FBI."

I began to cry.

CHAPTER 32

The following Tuesday, my fibromyalgia was still causing me pain from my ordeal in Ojai. But I was determined to host our Tuesday group as usual. I dressed in a comfortable blue caftan with embroidery around the neck and sleeves. Then I brewed a large pot of coffee. Our little quilting group would grow in size today and include a very special guest.

Jazz was the first to arrive, wearing a lavender shirt and beige linen capri-length slacks. Judging from the smoothness of the skin on his ankles and lower limbs, I guessed he must've recently waxed his legs. From what he'd told us about manscaping, I was sure that wasn't all that had been waxed.

Zsa Zsa wore a matching lavender dress with a red bow in her curly topknot, and as soon as

Jazz placed her on the ground, she trotted off, little painted toenails clicking on the hardwood floor.

"Are you positive he's coming?" Jazz fluttered with anticipation and glanced repeatedly out the front window.

"Beyond a reasonable doubt." I took the platter of raw cut veggies from his grip. "Did you bring something to go with these?"

Without a word, Jazz reached in the tote bag recently vacated by his little white Maltese and pulled out a Rubbermaid plastic container of homemade tzatziki, a delicious blend of Greek yogurt, lemon juice, garlic, and shredded cucumbers. "You know, Martha, I've come to love you like the sister I never had. If anything had happened to you up on that mountain, I would've never forgiven you for not taking me along. You seem to forget I'm an expert in jujitsu."

He was probably right. It would've been harder for June and Claytie to capture three of us. "I'm sorry, Jazz. It really was a spur-of-the-moment decision to go alone with Andre back to Ojai. There wasn't time to call everyone."

He put both arms around me and started to sniffle. "Are you sure you're okay? I've heard of people suddenly dropping dead from the effects of a concussion weeks after the event."

I hugged him back. "The scalp wound on the back of my head is still raw and sore, but the headaches have stopped, and the head scans have been clear."

He pushed me back at arm's length and gave me the once-over. "You know, this blue item you're wearing today really works. It's very forgiving of a curvy figure." He hastily added, "But of course you know I design for all body types and I love your curves."

"Of course."

"So, Martha, dish. Who killed Royal St. Germain?"

"We'll know for sure when my special guest arrives. Until then, we'll just have to live with our curiosity."

Next to arrive were Lucy, Birdie, and the pregnant girl Ivy. Lucy wore her green sweater and green slacks. She handed me a plate of oatmeal cookies with raisins and chocolate chips. "How're you feeling today, hon?"

"Good. I only wish Yossi was back."

"Isn't there some kind of hotline you can call at the ATF if you need to speak to your loved one who's undercover?"

"No."

"Well, it's a dang good thing you're a hard-headed woman! Anyone else could've died." Her eyes misted over. "I'd really miss you, if you had."

Birdie twisted the end of her long white braid. "Oh, Martha dear, Denny and I feel responsible for what happened to you. We're so sorry. Just think of it. If you hadn't come with us in the Winnebago that day, we would've given everything we had to the trust and be stuck on that mountain."

She handed me a white cotton kitchen towel wrapped around a warm loaf of freshly baked white bread and a jar of homemade raspberry jam. "I brought you some more comfort food."

My friends had been bringing me comfort food every day since I returned from the mountain. The refrigerator was crammed full of chicken soup, mac and cheese, baked lasagna, and a pot of white bean and chicken chili. Brownies, applesauce cake, almond cookies, and homemade bread stood in a tempting row on the apricot-colored marble kitchen counter. This was the second loaf from Birdie in the last six days. I took her offering and added it to the others lined up. "How thoughtful, Birdie. You really shouldn't have."

Ivy presented me with a hand-quilted nine-inch square potholder made from a Log Cabin quilt block on one side and an Ohio Star quilt block on the other side. "I sewed this for you. Birdie's teaching me how to hand quilt."

"Thank you, Ivy. What a lovely gift, and useful, too." I tried to gauge the size of her belly under her gauzy pink blouse. "Is it my imagination, or are you bigger since I saw you last week?"

The girl giggled. "Yeah. It happened suddenly. Zohar is very active."

"Zohar?" I was surprised Ivy had lifted a name straight out of Jewish mysticism. The Zohar was the primary text in Jewish Kabbalah. The Hebrew word *Kabbalah* meant to receive, and *Zohar* meant light or brilliance. It was hoped the student of mysticism would achieve enlightenment regarding the true nature of God and God's relationship with man from studying the book.

"So, you're having a boy?"

"I don't know. I want the sex to be a surprise. I chose the name because it could go with either a boy or a girl. And also because Zohar was the name of Madam Natasha's first teacher." Ivy was right. Although an unusual choice for a name, Zohar could either be feminine or masculine.

Next to arrive was my half-sister, Giselle, who breezed through the doorway wearing a creamy silk shirt and black trousers. She handed me a huge pink bakery box tied with white string. "Miniature éclairs from Benesch. I know how you love them."

I hefted the large box. "How many did you get, for God's sake?"

"Four dozen. They're small. You said we were having more people than usual. I didn't want to run short."

I chuckled to myself. Running out of toilet paper or food was the worst fear of the Jewish homemaker. Maybe Catholics weren't all that different.

She walked into the living room and sat in an easy chair. "So, are you ready to tell us who killed Royal and who was buried on that mountain?"

"That information is coming with our special guest, who's on the way as we speak. Right now, I don't know any more than you do."

Soft knocking came from my front door. The three Polinskayas stood before me.

Paulina, short, round, and becaped in purple velvet, stepped forward and gave me a hug. "Thank you, Martha. You saved Mystical Feather. You saved Andre. Our family owes you a lot. You'll get free tarot readings every day for life. Here." She handed me an unopened bag of double-stuffed Oreo cookies.

I stepped aside to let them in. "We were lucky, that's for sure."

"Madam Natasha was right about you." Andre gave a timid smile.

"Have you recovered from the drugs?"

"Yeah. I had a two-day hangover, but I'm fine. Is . . . ?" He craned his neck to search among the people already seated in the living room. When his gaze landed on Jazz, a smile lit up his face. Color crept up Jazz's cheeks.

Michael Polinskaya, aka Mansoor the Magnificent, was the last to enter the living room. He approached one of the dining room chairs I'd placed there for extra guests, removed a handkerchief from his pocket, and spread it on the seat. He folded his hands in his lap and sat without letting his back touch the chair. Looking at the floor, he pulled an envelope out of his pocket and handed it to me. "This is the fee you paid me when we first met at Paulie's house. I wanted to give your money back."

Finally, my special guest arrived wearing an orange and black geometric print. The large and pleated white *gele* covering her head made her resemble a nun.

"Welcome," I gushed at the woman who'd saved my life. "Everyone is here and they're excited to meet you."

"I hope you've recovered from your ordeal." FBI Agent Nkwa Applebaum smiled as she entered the house.

I guided her to the living room and spoke to my friends. "Most of you have only heard about Agent Applebaum. She saved my life. Andre's life."

Giselle stood and began to clap her hands. To my astonishment, everyone else did the same. Nkwa showed no signs of embarrassment at the attention. She smiled confidently and sat in an empty chair. After I handed her a cup of coffee, she placed five miniature éclairs on a plate. "I love these things."

Giselle was the first to speak. "I bought those. Now tell us, who killed Royal?"

Nkwa scanned the faces in the room while she chewed. "According to Claytie Tolliver, his wife, June, shot Royal St. Germain."

"How can that be?" Birdie creased her brow. "It's my understanding that if anybody leaves the circle in a seance, it breaks the connection to the spirit world. June Tolliver was part of that circle, wasn't she? Wouldn't everyone notice if she left?"

"I think I've figured that one out," I said. One glance at Nkwa's cryptic smile told me she knew as well. "Correct me if I'm wrong, but if everyone is holding hands, all a person has to do to leave the circle is to take the hands of the person on the left and the person on the right, pull them toward each other and have them grab hands. Once they've connected, the one who wants to leave can let go without disrupting the circle."

"Exactly. That's how they take breaks."

Birdie frowned. "Wouldn't the people on either side of June remember that happening?"

Nkwa reached for one last éclair. "Andre, maybe you can answer that question?"

"Sure," he said. "The people holding hands in the circle can be so far into a trance, they never notice or remember someone left the circle. It's happened to me."

The FBI agent smiled at him. "Thanks. Anyway, once we arrested the Tollivers, Claytie opened up. He was quite relieved to get things off his chest; he couldn't stop talking. He blamed everything on his wife."

"Do you believe him?" I asked.

"I'm inclined to, yes. June, on the other hand, wanted us to believe her husband was responsible. But, of course, he couldn't be the one who shot St. Germain because he was leading the séance. Some of you were even witnesses to that fact and could corroborate his story if called upon to do so. Correct?"

Ivy bit into an oatmeal cookie, dropping several crumbs and a raisin on the front of her belly. She put the raisin in her mouth and brushed away the crumbs. "I never liked them, June and Claytie. They acted like they were the bosses, not Royal."

"So, who locked the gate?" Andre asked.

"June had been on her way to see St. Germain when you pulled into the parking lot. Using the brush for cover, she slipped down to the gate, locked it, and then returned for St. Germain. She forced him at gunpoint back through the brush and into the Winnebago. The rest you know. He died instantly."

Andre added, "Why did she kill him and what was the point of doing it in the RV?"

"As for *why*, the Tollivers had been siphoning off money every month into a false vendor account. St. Germain found out and threatened to call the police if they didn't return all of it."

"Yeah," said Andre. "I uncovered several other accounts where money was being siphoned off. But the computer with the file was stolen."

"Not stolen," said Nkwa. "The day you discovered the grave, the sheriff searched the bookstore and seized it. Your hard work was important. The file will be very useful in their investigation."

Giselle gestured toward Andre. "He was right, before. Why kill Royal in the RV?"

"According to Claytie, June wasn't only ambitious, she was clever. Killing St. Germain in the RV was just her way of misdirecting the sheriff in their murder inquiry."

Andre made eye contact with Jazz and whispered, "Did you make this tzatziki?"

Jazz nodded.

Andre dunked a raw broccoli floret into the dip. "It's amazing."

"What about the body on the hill we dug up?" Giselle asked. "And how many more have you found?"

Nkwa swallowed before speaking. "The body you uncovered belonged to an elderly man named Max. He'd been there for about a year."

White Raven had been worried about Max. At least now White Raven could properly mourn his old friend.

Nkwa continued. "You asked how many bodies are up there. We've only begun our search. As you know, a second body was found buried next to Max. According to the information Tolliver has given us so far, my guess is more than four, less than ten."

"And our uncle Royal killed them all?" Paulina tugged her cape a little tighter around her arms. "Maybe that's what was interfering with his connection to the spirit world."

"According to Claytie Tolliver," Nkwa said, "it was his wife June Tolliver who poisoned those people. Tolliver had to bury the bodies to conceal her crimes. He swore St. Germain never knew the truth about those killings. Like everyone else, St. Germain thought the missing people left without a goodbye."

Something rang a bell at the mention of poison. "What did June use to poison people?"

Nkwa shook her head. "Tolliver said it was the seed from some exotic tree."

Now the bells were clanging away in my head. "Did June ever go to India?"

"Tolliver maintains June had an affair with St. Germain. In nineteen seventy-five they visited an ashram in Kerala, India. When the two of them returned to Mystical Feather, Madam Natasha told June to leave her son alone and leave the commune. Two days later, Natasha was dead. Apparently, that was only the beginning of June's vow to get even."

My mouth hung open at what Nkwa suggested. "Wait. Are you saying Royal didn't kill his mother, after all?"

"There's a strong possibility June Tolliver was behind *all* the killings, including Madam Natasha."

"So, my Royal was innocent?" Ivy's hand went to her belly. "I knew it!" She looked at the mound under her blouse. "Zohar, your daddy wasn't a killer after all. Isn't that great?"

Birdie wrung her hands gently, being careful not to hurt her arthritic fingers. "Oh, those poor people. Why did she kill all of them?"

Nkwa shrugged. "Our investigation is just beginning, Mrs. Watson. Sometimes the motive is as simple as jealousy or greed. In Max's case, his medical bills threatened to drain the trust, so June got rid of the problem."

I cleared my throat. "I have one last question."

"Go ahead."

"How did you end up at Mystical Feather in Andre's class?"

"I was wondering when you'd get around to that."
Nkwa smiled. "You seem to have friends in high
places, Martha. My boss, a certain director in the
FBI, sent me to watch over you."

"John Smith?"

Nkwa answered me with a wry smile.

"And how did you know Andre and I needed to
be rescued?"

"I became suspicious when Claytie told me you
were taking a nap. I walked around the outside of
the house, trying to find a place to look inside. But
every window was covered, and every door locked.
I also tried calling your cell phone several times."

"Did you try to call me?" Andre asked.

Nkwa nodded. "Of course. When neither of you
answered, I knew something had gone sideways.
That's when I found you inside the house."

"You really saved our lives," Andre said. "I think
June and Claytie were prepared to bury Martha
and me alive."

Nkwa's dark eyes grew intense as she spoke.
"I'm sorry I didn't follow my earlier instinct to
check the inside of the house, but I had a choice
to make. The evidence against the Tollivers was
mounting, and if we hoped for a conviction, I had
to play the investigation by the book. I couldn't
enter the house to check on you without first ob-
taining a warrant. So, while I waited for the warrant, I watched the house. When I saw Claytie
drive your car off the mountain, followed by June
driving the van, I knew I had to do something. *Exi-
gent circumstances* allowed me to enter the building

without a warrant if I knew someone was in danger. I have to say, though, I admire your courage and determination to survive. You would've made a formidable agent, Martha."

"John Smith told me the same thing." *Only he said I was too old.*

CHAPTER 33

Friday afternoon at five thirty, I'd finished my preparations for Shabbat dinner. The scalloped potatoes were baking in the oven, tender asparagus stood in the steamer, and two large slabs of salmon were seasoned with butter and wrapped in foil ready to poach. A dessert platter piled with sweets from Bea's Bakery waited on the sideboard.

Two unlit candles in silver holders claimed a place of honor in the middle of the table. I'd arranged a loaf of raisin challah and a cup of kosher wine near the chair where Uncle Isaac would sit. I still had a half hour to shower and dress before my family would begin to arrive: Quincy's little clan, Giselle with Harold, and Uncle Isaac with Hilda. I still hadn't heard from Crusher, who'd been working an assignment for the last two weeks, and I missed him terribly.

Much as I tried to fight it, a little seed of fear

took root in my head. What if he'd been hurt somewhere and couldn't call for help? I shivered as I remembered how I woke up bound and gagged in Royal St. Germain's dark closet. *Dear God, please protect Yossi.*

My prayer was answered sooner than I expected. I'd just finished buttoning my pink silk blouse when I heard the front door open. Size fourteen boots clumped down the hallway toward the bedroom. My heart did a little flip when Crusher appeared with a huge grin. "Oh Yossi, thank goodness you're home."

He gathered me in a bear hug and lifted me off the ground. "Babe. I've missed you, too." His kiss, warm and urgent, held the promise of a loving reunion later that night.

Thank you, God, for keeping him safe and bringing him back.

"How are you feeling?" He examined the back of my head. "Director Smith was at our debrief. He filled me in on your misadventures and I came home as soon as I could."

"What was the FBI doing at an ATF debriefing?"

"We were concluding another joint op." He cupped my chin in his hand. "I don't know what I'd do if anything happened to you."

"I'm fine now, Yossi. Really."

He kissed me again and inclined his head toward the living room. "Let me take a quick shower, then I'll join you out there." I put on my strappy black heels and hummed all the way to the kitchen. I tied on a white apron to protect my Sabbath clothes and went to work. The potatoes came out of the oven and the salmon went in. I turned on the flame under the steamer of asparagus. The time was six, and our family would be arriving soon.

Ever since my ordeal at Mystical Feather, I'd been thinking a lot about how fragile life could be. One minute you were fine and the next you were shot to death. Or poisoned to death. Or, in the case of my own near miss, bludgeoned to death.

Getting hit on the head knocked me into a different perspective on life. I could no longer justify postponing certain things until "the right time." When would it ever be the right time? Putting something off—especially the thing I really wanted—no longer sounded like prudent behavior, but more like laziness or fear.

I made up my mind to make some big changes in my life, no matter how uneasy I felt. Hadn't Paulina foreseen those changes when she read my tea leaves? "Not all the changes will be pleasant," she'd said. Sure enough, I had a scalp wound to prove that fact. Paulina also said a new person would come into my life. Well, I could think of several new persons: both good guys like Special Agent Nkwa Applebaum and the Polinskaya brothers and bad guys like June and Claytie Tolliver.

My thoughts were cut short when Quincy and Noah arrived. I rushed to gather my infant granddaughter Daisy in my arms. She giggled with pleasure as I kissed her face and tummy. She was already showing signs of genius. "Bubbie loves you," I said, using the Yiddish word for grandma.

"Baba!" she grinned.

"Did you hear that?" I stared at my daughter and son-in-law. She's brilliant. She can speak already. And she obviously knows my name."

Quincy rolled her eyes. "She calls everything by that name, Mom. Baba is her one go-to word."

I danced around in whirls and twirls with my granddaughter in my arms. "Say Bubbie again, Daisy."

"Baba!"

I gave her a big kiss on her plump little cheek. "They don't believe you can talk, but I understand you perfectly."

Daisy smacked her lips and held out her hands to her mother. "Mmmaamm." A minute later, Quincy sat on the sofa breastfeeding discreetly under a receiving blanket thrown over her shoulder.

I bent to kiss the top of my daughter's head. "This picture couldn't be any sweeter."

Giselle and Harold had picked up Uncle Isaac and Hilda and driven them to Encino. Hilda helped my uncle over the threshold and into the house. Thanks to the bump on my head, my new perspective on life allowed me to see my aging uncle in a more realistic light. In his eighties and suffering from Parkinson's, he looked fragile and tired. My heart sank when I faced the fact he wouldn't be around forever. I knew he wanted to see one big change in my life, and I vowed to make that happen while he was still around.

"Good Shabbos, *faigela*."

I loved it when he used my Yiddish pet name, little bird.

"Shabbat shalom, Uncle. How are you doing?" What I didn't want to ask in front of Hilda was how things were working out between them.

He must have understood the subtext of my question and a huge grin stretched across his face. "*Oy va voy!* Life is sure easier now that Hilda's moved in." He looked at her and his face softened. "This *maideleh* is real *balabusta*. She's a kosher cook, already. And boy can she cook!"

Hilda smiled fondly at him. "You're a good teacher, Isaac. And interesting. I could listen to you talk all day long."

"Can you believe it? After Hilda gets her driver's license, I'm going to buy a car. A blue one." He looked at Crusher, who had just walked into the room wearing a Sabbath outfit almost identical to his own; white shirt and black trousers. "*Nu?* Maybe you can tell me the right car to get when the time comes."

Quincy, Daisy, Giselle, and Hilda joined me to begin our weekly celebration. I covered my head with a scarf to show respect in the presence of the Divine. I lit the candles, watching the flames dance. Then I circled them three times with my hands, covered my eyes, and recited the blessing over the Sabbath candles—first in Hebrew and then in English. *Blessed art Thou, oh Lord our God, King of the universe, who sanctifies us by Thy commandments and commands us to kindle the Sabbath lights.*

Hilda's voice joined ours as we all said, *Omeyn.*

I added a silent little *thank you, God,* for bringing her into Uncle Isaac's life.

Uncle Isaac presided at the head of the table

and recited the *kiddush*, the traditional prayer blessing the Sabbath wine. Then he blessed the loaf of challah and passed around pieces to everyone. That was my signal to bring the rest of the meal to the table.

Using the side of my dinner fork, I concentrated on cutting neat little squares in the potato kugel on my plate. *Should I say something now, or wait until everyone leaves?*

My stomach fluttered with anxiety as I thought about my options. *As much as everyone at the table will be surprised to hear what I've decided, shouldn't Crusher be the first person to know? He's been so patient. . . .*

I'd managed to reduce the kugel to nine bite-sized pieces when my daughter Quincy's voice dragged my attention back to the Sabbath table. "Earth to Mom. Come in, please." All conversation stopped as seven pairs of curious eyes focused on me.

Embarrassment warmed my cheeks. "Sorry."

Quincy continued to probe. "Is everything okay? You've hardly touched your food. Are you ill?"

I gave my daughter a tight little smile. "No, I'm fine."

My sister Giselle lowered her fork and pinned me down with laser eyes. "Then if you're not having a stroke, give it up, Sissy. What's going on with you?"

I sighed with resignation. Clearly, I wasn't going to be able to discuss this first with my fiancé, Yossi Levy, aka Crusher. I reached for his hand. He encouraged me with a slight nod of the head. "Go on, babe. Whatever it is, I've got your back."

I cleared my throat, found my voice, and gazed into his impossibly blue eyes, into the face of the man who had waited patiently for me to get past my fear of failure. "No more waiting, Yossi. I—I'm ready to get married."

The table erupted into a chorus of "Mazel tov,"

Yossi lifted my hand to his lips and kissed it tenderly. "It's about time."

Please turn the page for a quilting tip from Mary Marks!

I think some of the most beautiful quilts are made for highly personal reasons: grief and loss. Everyone who has experienced the loss of someone close knows that pain. Each person copes in their own way; there are no rules.

One way of coping with bereavement is to make a memory quilt using items from the lost person you can't bear to part with. Do you still have the shirts or neckties he wore? Do you have her dresses or blouses? Did they have a collection of T-shirts with logos that were meaningful?

Each of those fabric items can be used to make quilt blocks in any pattern. For example, neckties can be used to make the Dresden Plate pattern or Grandmother's Fan. If you Google "memory quilts images" you see a huge array of designs using those fabrics. The possibilities are endless. Are there photos of them in your family albums? Letters they've written? A child's drawing? You can also scan these items and print them out on fabric.

Memory quilts aren't new. People have been making them since long before the age of photos and scanning. The coffin quilt, or graveyard quilt, was made by incorporating coffin-shaped pieces of fabric in the design. One famous coffin quilt was sewn in the nineteenth century by a grieving mother over the death of her sons. Perhaps the most famous memory quilt dealing with the death of a loved one is the AIDS quilt, which contains 44,000 blocks—each one uniquely designed in memory of a loved one who died of the disease.

The reason for sewing a memory quilt doesn't have to be about death. For example, if a family was moving out of the area, their friends and relatives might each pen a farewell message on a block to be included in a quilt. I wrote about such a quilt in *Gone but Knot Forgotten*. Although the "Declaration Quilt" was purely fictional, it could easily have happened in the real world.

Is your child going off to college? How about making a T-shirt quilt. Is your child or someone special having a baby shower? How about providing each guest with a square of fabric to write their name and a message? Is someone you know retiring? How about scanning photos of that person documenting their life from childhood to retirement.

A memory quilt can be a record sewn in fabric of a person's life or of the community they are leaving. And the best news of all is the quilt doesn't have to be bed-sized. It can be smaller for throwing over the lap, smaller still for hanging on the wall, or even for covering a throw pillow. The possibilities are limited only by your imagination.

Blessings!

Connect with U(s)

Visit us online at
KensingtonBooks.com
to read more from your favorite authors, see books
by series, view reading group guides, and more.

for sneak peeks, chances to win books and prize packs,
and to share your thoughts with other readers.

facebook.com/kensingtonpublishing
twitter.com/kensingtonbooks

Tell us what you think!

To share your thoughts, submit a review,
or sign up for our eNewsletters, please visit:
KensingtonBooks.com/TellUs.

Nail-Biting Romantic Suspense from Your Favorite Authors

Grab These Cozy Mysteries
from
Kensington Books

Forget Me Knot Mary Marks	978-0-7582-9205-6	$7.99US/$8.99CAN
Death of a Chocoholic Lee Hollis	978-0-7582-9449-4	$7.99US/$8.99CAN
Green Living Can Be Deadly Staci McLaughlin	978-0-7582-7502-8	$7.99US/$8.99CAN
Death of an Irish Diva Mollie Cox Bryan	978-0-7582-6633-0	$7.99US/$8.99CAN
Board Stiff Annelise Ryan	978-0-7582-7276-8	$7.99US/$8.99CAN
A Biscuit, A Casket Liz Mugavero	978-0-7582-8480-8	$7.99US/$8.99CAN
Boiled Over Barbara Ross	978-0-7582-8687-1	$7.99US/$8.99CAN
Scene of the Climb Kate Dyer-Seeley	978-0-7582-9531-6	$7.99US/$8.99CAN
Deadly Decor Karen Rose Smith	978-0-7582-8486-0	$7.99US/$8.99CAN
To Kill a Matzo Ball Delia Rosen	978-0-7582-8201-9	$7.99US/$8.99CAN

Available Wherever Books Are Sold!

All available as e-books, too!

Visit our website at **www.kensingtonbooks.com**

Romantic Suspense from
Lisa Jackson